# FORGOTTEN

## THE SAVIORS OF SOULS BOOK 3

## SHIRLEY O'NEIL

**World Castle Publishing, LLC**
Pensacola, Florida
Copyright © Shirley O'Neil 2020
Paperback ISBN: 9781951642938
eBook ISBN: 9781951642945
First Edition World Castle Publishing, LLC, July 20, 2020
http://www.worldcastlepublishing.com
**Licensing Notes**
Cover: Karen Fuller
Editor: Maxine Bringenberg

# CHAPTER 1

As Hayley Johnson sat at Mr. G's restaurant with her fiancé, Lee Franklin, she gazed out the twelve-pane window at Sutterville's streets four floors below, allowing her gift of clairvoyance to foresee the future.

Her second sight pulled her away from the lights reflecting off the wet, dark asphalt on Creek Mill Road, taking her to a clearing enfolded by forest. She looked up at a semi-clear day, the sunlight beaming down between the clouds. A sense of familiarity came over her as she scanned the surroundings. Then Hayley recognized the area. Her memories took her back to her childhood when she had attended elementary school. Her grandfather had taken her on adventures each summer vacation, locating caves and abandoned mines in the Appalachians. Trees over a hundred years old surrounded this grassy field. Across this meadow, she remembered her and her grandfather visiting several times.

While exercising her gift of clairvoyance, Hayley's acute psychic awareness made her feel as if she physically stood at the edge of the meadow in the midst of mighty oaks, pines, and hemlocks. In the distance, she watched a cloaked figure weaving in and out of the shadows, coming toward her. Fear compelled Hayley to run. Before she could react, an icy unseen force hurled her back to the present, her attention returning to the town's lights and the November drizzle.

Hayley shuddered. *It's coming. But what and when?* "Lee, we're in danger."

"Is the threat immediate?"

"It's in the future, but I don't know when." She sat back in her chair, took a moment to relax, shut her eyes, and replayed the foresight in her mind. After setting her fears aside, Hayley analyzed what she'd seen. She opened her eyes and spoke in a low tone, keeping their conversation between them. "You know I'm always detached from my visions — a bystander, never physically in the vision myself. But this time, I was attacked by someone evil. It was chilling. I felt like an intruder."

"Maybe you were," Lee said, the creases in his forehead deepening. "Do you still feel threatened?"

She closed her eyes, cleared her mind, tested the energy around her, and opened her eyes again. "No."

His concerned expression softened. "Good. Relax." He reached across the dining table and took her hands in his. "It's your birthday. I want you all to myself."

She remembered when she'd first met Lee, and how she'd fought to keep him from knowing her feelings for him. But thoughts of him tormented her day and night. She knew from past experience how men reacted to her oddness — hearing voices no one else could hear, seeing people no one could see but her, and reacting to visions of death which played in her mind, making her appear mental. Hayley believed only anguish could come from letting Lee know her as more than just an employee. *How* could I have thought otherwise? Plus, the dangers in flirting with the boss weighed on her. *I wanted to keep my job.* For years she had read the newspaper stories covering the Paranormal Search and Analysis investigations and wanted nothing more than to be part of the team. *How could I have just thrown my dream away by letting my fantasies of Lee ruin everything? Nothing I tried stopped me from thinking of him. Once I found he had similar feelings for me, my world turned right side up.*

Lee had been her first—first kiss, first lover, the first man she'd given her heart and soul to. When fate stepped in to reveal the reason for their overwhelming attraction for one another, she'd found Lee had been her love throughout time, lifetime after lifetime—her true soul mate.

*He's right. I should stay in the moment. The day's been perfect so far.* Hayley sipped her Cabernet Sauvignon while she thought about her birthday's early morning hours spent in Lee's comfy king-sized bed, how his touch had melted her, how their heated passion flamed until dawn, and how she planned to entice him again later tonight. *The best birthday ever. Now, dinner with him by candlelight at this elegant restaurant.*

She glanced around, absorbing the room's ambiance. A few round intimate tables draped with white linen tablecloths, in this reserved area off the main dining room, were each accompanied by two round-backed chairs upholstered in pale celery and gold diamond-patterned satin. The dim light emanating from a small number of crystal sconces along the light golden walls allowed candles on each table to set the tone for a romantic dinner. The stone fireplace sheltered a blazing fire, warming the cool evening air. *Why ruin the moment?*

She'd worked all of her life to learn to control her gifts to see the past, present, future, and, scariest of all, the dead. *No more intrusions. Easy enough.* With her eyes closed, she pictured herself turning off a beacon and saying goodnight to her abilities. "Done. I'm all yours."

His smile embraced her. "While we're waiting on dessert...." From the inside pocket of his charcoal gray sharkskin suit, Lee extracted a blue velvet box and placed it in front of her. "Happy twenty-ninth birthday, my love."

Filled with curiosity, Hayley set her wine glass to the side, lifted the box, and peeked inside. Her eyes widened as she removed a gold bracelet with charms glistening in the candle's glow. "So beautiful."

While the candlelight flickered and its shadows danced on the white linen tablecloth, Lee rose, moved his chair next to hers, and sat. He held out his hand. "Let me tell you what each charm symbolizes."

His gift dangled in the shimmering light as she passed it to him.

Tenderly he placed it on her wrist, brought her hand to his lips, and kissed her palm. Starting at the clasp, he touched the first charm, a ghost made from mother-of-pearl. "This represents the day you joined our company and became a ghost hunter."

Hayley thought about when she'd taken the job, and how she'd worried if her coworkers would view her as a freak of nature, like everyone else she'd encountered—her peers, her neighbors, and even her parents. But her trepidations melted away once she realized her coworkers embraced her with unconditional friendship. They were no longer just friends but family. Now she couldn't imagine her life without them in it.

"Next, a globe. Your first case that took us halfway around the world to the island in Micronesia. The oceans are inlaid lapis and the continents diamond chips."

*The globe, the beginning of our trip and the start of our romance.* She remembered their first night's layover at the Hotel del Coronado, where she shared a room with Kathy, the team's historian and research assistant. *If Kathy hadn't told me that Lee was crazy about me, I would've never guessed.* She brushed her fingers across her heart necklace, its point resting in her pronounced cleavage and tastefully, but tantalizingly, dipping into her gown's deep neckline. *This dress she selected for me when we shopped in Coronado still makes Lee stammer.*

Lee went to the next charm, a wine bottle clustered with rubies. A warm smile crossed his face. "Our first date, wine and the sunset on the beach at the Del."

*My cold ocean-drenched body leaning back against his wet bare chest, his arms around me while we sipped our wine and watched the sunset. Heaven.*

One by one, he went through the other charms, four more holding memories of her first case and three remembrances of the haunting under his mansion. He came to the next. "An engagement ring. When you said yes, it was the happiest moment of my life."

Hayley gazed at her left hand, remembering the look of love on his face when he placed the ring on her finger, and how the joy she felt could have filled the universe.

She held the last charm close to the candlelight. "What's this?"

A boyish grin crossed his face, a playful twinkle danced in his mahogany brown eyes. "A gift within a gift. A passport to future memories. A trip to anywhere in the world. Your choice."

Memories of her childhood littered her mind. All through her youth, she had looked through travel magazines while trying to keep her mind off her so-called talent. Daydreaming about being somewhere else in the world helped her ignore the frightening voices and the visions in her head until she learned to master her abilities.

Because she'd always been unable to see her own future, she couldn't have foreseen she'd be traveling with her future husband. She admired her engagement ring. *I never would've guessed.* "Maybe the Hawaiian Islands again. Our trip there was only a layover. But I need time to think about it."

His smile broadened. "Yes, it was too short, like our layover in Coronado. I can still picture you at the Del's beach wearing the bathing suit Kathy talked you into buying. My libido did summersaults."

Her cheeks flushed at the thought. She'd never worn anything so skimpy in her life. But the distraction of Lee's hard naked torso when he had removed his shirt on the shore had pushed her shyness aside. "You were wicked hot yourself."

He chuckled. "You, the beach, wine, and the sunset.... Let me know when you decide, and I'll book the flight."

She leaned toward him, her lips a breath away from his and whispered, "Thank you." Her hands caressed the nape of his neck, and her mouth met his, her deep kiss lingering before their lips parted.

"You're welcome," Lee replied, his arms reluctant to release her.

He waited until she settled back into her seat, then returned his chair across from hers, sat, and watched her admire her gift.

*And I'll have a surprise for you when we get home,* she thought.

***

Once home, the wrought-iron security gates swung open, allowing Lee's Aston Martin to enter the estate. The nearly naked trees along both sides of the entrance awaited the coming cold months. Their colorful leaves littering the pavement swirled in a wisp of wind as Lee drove in.

When the driveway curved, his home came into view. They followed a long drive lined with Norway spruce leading to the front door of his home.

Hayley recalled the first time she'd seen the three-story, red-brick mansion with its two wings extending forward, lengthened by three-story round towers protruding from each wing. "It's a smaller version of an English estate," he had told her. Not until much later in the day did he mention the home belonged to him. *I would've known if I was allowed to foresee my own future. I couldn't have been more surprised.*

Lee pulled up to the mansion's entrance and parked. His butler, Lewis, wearing black dress pants, a white shirt, black tie, and gray vest, assisted them as they left the vehicle and hurried ahead to pull open the home's carved wood doors.

"I hope you've had a wonderful birthday, Miss Johnson," Lewis said, taking her double knit cardigan.

"Thank you, Lewis."

"Anything I can get you, sir?" he asked while helping Lee off with his overcoat.

"No thanks, Lewis. We intend to have a quiet evening and turn in early."

"Very well, sir."

Lee took Hayley's hand as they walked beneath a double-tiered empire chandelier hanging from the vaulted ceiling in the center of the foyer. But instead of climbing the grand staircase, they walked down the hallway and took the elevator to the third floor. When the doors slid aside, Lee accompanied her to his chambers to relax for the evening, or so she had led him to believe.

She entered Lee's bedroom as he held the door for her. Mahogany paneling gave the room a cozy feel. Embossed bronzed tin tiles covered the high ceiling. Pale blue drapes dressed the twelve-pane windows. The vastness of the room dwarfed his huge bed, covered with a blue, brown, and bronze-colored chenille bedspread, pulled back to reveal brown Egyptian cotton sheets.

"I'll shower first if you don't mind," Hayley told him.

"Go right ahead," he replied.

She went to Lee's walk-in closet, undressed, threw on a robe, and walked through a door to the bathroom.

The bathroom, twice as big as her bedroom at home, had three vanities with Brasilian-gold marble countertops, their cabinets resembling fine rose-wood furniture, two as she entered from the bedroom and one by the door leading to the sitting room. In the center of the bathroom, the glass-enclosed shower could hold, possibly, nine or ten people.

Once in the shower, the warmth of the water refreshed her, giving her the boost of energy she needed to accomplish her calculated plan. As the tepid water ran down her body, she focused on the details of the upcoming ploy she'd create to entice Lee to hunt for her. She instinctively ran the washcloth over her body, going through the motions without a thought, her mind taking her step by step through the halls and into the bedrooms of Lee's mansion. *I have to move quickly.*

After finishing her shower, she hurried to dry off, anticipation spurring her on.

Wearing her thick white terrycloth robe, she strolled out of Lee's bathroom, entering his bedroom. "Shower's all yours."

"I'll only be a few minutes," he said.

"I'm not going anywhere. Take your time."

After hearing him step into the shower, she grabbed the pile of intimate clothing she'd taken from her share of his closet and had hidden behind a chair next to the fireplace. She hurried to the bedroom door, knowing she had only a few minutes, pulled her robe's tie taut, and sneaked out of the room into the hallway. *Game on.*

Hayley ran barefoot to the corridor leading to the south wing, remembering this floor contained seven bedrooms. And Lee's chambers took up the entire north wing; his bedroom— *Large enough to fit my entire house in;* the bath—*Who has a Jacuzzi and a sauna in their bathroom?;* closet—*Once you think you've seen it all, you haven't;* his office—*I haven't seen that room yet,* and the sitting room in the north tower overlooking a sea of grass and the spruce-lined drive.

She continued to trot. *He'll start looking for me in the closest bedroom, then work his way toward the south tower.*

Her heart pounded, her footsteps silent on the carpeted floor. She passed the first door. If he found her inside, their hide-and-seek would end too soon. She peeked into the next room. *Twin beds. Not convenient for a romantic encounter.* She jogged on.

With labored breath, Hayley reached the south hallway, turned left, and entered the next room. The lights came on— *motion detectors.* The cold November air nipping at her face and legs didn't surprise her. She knew these seldom-used rooms were infrequently heated.

She rubbed her arms and glanced around. The chandelier cascaded from the pale yellow ceiling. Above the black walnut headboard carved with grapes, vines, and leaves, the green walls displayed a fresco depicting an Italian vineyard.

After placing her extra clothing on a chair near the door, Hayley hurried to the bed and snatched up the throw lying at its foot. Quickly she pulled back the green silk bedspread, stuffed the throw and a pillow under the covers, forming the silhouette of a sleeping person, and pulled the covers up. Aware of the fleeting time, she sprinted to the chair, grabbed a bra and panties, and dropped them in a conspicuous place on the carpet.

Hayley surveyed the room. Knowing that Lee had recently programmed the voice-activated computer butler to respond to her voice as well as his, Jim's, and those of other prominent personnel in the home, she said, "Dim the lights, Max."

"Yes, miss," Max replied through a speaker somewhere in the room.

The lights dimmed.

*Perfect.* She pulled her robe taut again and hurried into the hallway, quietly closing the door behind her.

Hayley moved on to the next bedroom. *This is one of my favorites, with its walls a light golden hue.* Pale blue velvet drapes covered the tall windows. A chandelier hung from a high fresco ceiling depicting blue sky and puffy white clouds. She rushed to the four-poster bed, untied the powder blue canopy sashes, padded the bed with pillows, and pulled the canopy's curtains closed. She crossed the room, picked up the remainder of the clothing she earlier had set on a nearby table, took a couple of intimate items from the pile, and placed them strategically by the bed.

Standing back, Hayley scrutinized her work. *Looks good.* "Max, dim the lights."

"Yes, miss."

The lights dimmed.

"Perfect." She turned, dashed out of the door, and gently closed it.

She staged the next room as she had the others and moved

to the final room. There, adjacent to the south tower, on the far golden wall, dark brown velvet drapes hung beside the elongated vertical windows. Even though they were three floors up, without neighbors, Hayley closed them, turned, and dashed to the bed. Its fruitwood frame had four marble bedposts twisting their way to the carved canopy rails draped with golden satin.

Hurriedly Hayley untied each sash, let the canopy curtains close, and slid her robe from her shoulders, letting it drop to the floor. She giggled with anticipation while ducking inside the curtains, lifting the bedcovers, and crawling between the cold sheets.

A crystal chandelier hung from the cream-colored ceiling above her head. She said, "Dim the lights, Max. Give Lee this message: 'Tag, you're it.'" Hayley shivered. "Oh, and heat the room to the same temperature as Lee's bedroom."

"Yes, miss," the computer voice replied.

The lights dimmed.

Lying in bed, she eagerly awaited Lee's arrival. Ten minutes dragged on, but she knew he had to check each bedroom before finding her. Then she heard him open and close the door and toss his robe onto the chair. When he spread aside the curtains and slid under the covers, desire filled her.

He ran his hands across her curves and kissed her bare shoulder. "I'm so glad you're not a pillow." His soft lips met hers. His heated kisses fanned the flames within her.

Slowly, he ran the tip of his tongue across her jawline, brushed his finger down her temple, and tucked her hair back. When he nibbled her ear, his warm breath further fueled her passion.

Hayley tilted her head in offering. His moist lips caressed her throat. She moaned when his kisses feathered across the curve of her breast. Her hand slid down to his thigh.

His breath caught.

"Sir, Jim would like to speak with you," Max said.

Lee's lips barely lifted from her breast. "No, not now." Hayley noticed his desire didn't wane while his kisses continued to explore her skin.

"He says it is urgent, sir," Max replied.

When Lee raised his head, Hayley felt the heated moment slip away. She lifted her hand from his thigh and placed it on his chest. Disappointment flooded her.

Through pursed lips, he groaned. "Is the house on fire, Max? If it isn't, tell him I said no."

"No, sir, the house is secure. He said he will not leave. He awaits you in the corridor outside your door."

Lee rolled away from Hayley. "Damn it. This better be an emergency."

They climbed out of bed, threw on their robes, and crossed the room. Lee yanked open the door. Hayley followed him into the corridor.

Jim Newton paced the hallway. He wore bunny slippers, plaid pull-tie pajama bottoms, and a white T-shirt with the slogan "Who Ya Gonna Call?" and a *Ghostbusters* insignia.

Hayley stared at the bunnies. If the timing weren't so bad, she would've laughed.

"This had better be good, Jim," Lee said.

Jim ran his hand across the nape of his neck.

*He looks like a madman,* Hayley thought, *with his wide eyes, disheveled hair, and shaking hands.*

"There's a witch in my bedroom," Jim said.

"You should've known that before you brought her home," Lee said. "This doesn't come close to being a good reason to—"

"No, damn it. She's a real witch, materialized out of thin air like a damn ghost."

# CHAPTER 2

In the corridor, while Jim explained, Hayley glimpsed a shadow out of the corner of her eye. Glancing over her shoulder, she saw a slate-gray bird flying toward them. She gave a startled gasp. *What the...?* It had a wingspan of nearly four feet, she estimated, a white brow line, and white bands peppered with black and gray on its belly-and-breast feathers. She repeatedly touched Lee's shoulder. "Lee, look! Look!"

He turned when the bird perched a few feet away on the chandelier. "What the hell's that bird doing in my house? Is this what you're calling a witch, Jim?"

Jim's face paled. "It's the witch, I swear."

"It's a goshawk. I've been seeing one around lately. It got in somehow. I'll call Lewis." He patted the pocket of his robe. "Okay, no phone. I'll have Max —"

"No. I'm tellin' ya, this is important!"

Lee glared at Jim. "This is not a good time to be a lunatic."

"You've still got sex on your mind," Jim said. "Look at me, damn it. Don't I look as scared as a bee-stung jackass?"

The bird spread its wings, opened its sharp curved beak, and screeched.

Jim pointed a shaky finger at it. "Damn thing's gonna attack if ya don't do what she wants."

*Is Jim right?* Hayley walked closer and stared at the bird. "Who are you?"

The bird glared at her, its eyes turning crimson.

In her mind's eye, Hayley saw an Indian woman standing at the foot of her bed, watching her sleep. The hairs on the back of Hayley's neck stood on end. *That feather I found on my bedroom floor the other morning belonged to her.*

Alarmed, she hurried back to Lee, grabbed his hand, and led him to the elevator. "We need to get to Jim's room fast."

Lee stopped and looked over his shoulder. "What about the bird?"

Jim darted into the elevator with Hayley. "You can stay here if ya want. The witch wants Hayley. She said nothin' 'bout you."

"So you understand bird language?" Lee asked.

"She wasn't a bird when she spoke to me, but she is now. She's a witch, remember? And we'd better do what she says."

Lee joined them. "Exactly what *did* she say?" He pressed the second-floor button, and the elevator door closed.

"Her exact words were, 'Beckon her, Sweet William. Bring to me the seeress, my love.'"

*The seeress? She knows I have psychic visions?* Hayley felt violated and stunned that her abilities didn't warn her of the intrusion.

The elevator door opened and they stepped out. Jim took the lead.

"Doesn't sound threatening to me," Lee said, following at a brisk pace with Hayley at his side. "Who's William?"

"Don't have a brain-pluckin' notion," Jim answered without

looking back. "But I'm not arguin' with a witch."

*How long has she been watching us?* The vision she'd had at Mr. G's came to mind, and she shuddered. "You're right, Jim," Hayley said. "Don't tell her you're not William. In fact, keep all your answers short. Yes or no. She's dangerous. One wrong word, and she might kill us."

"You really think there's a witch in his room?" Lee asked. "I've been a victim of Jim's tall tales more than once."

Hayley nodded. "At my home the other day, when I awoke, I found a feather on the floor at the foot of my bed. I shrugged it off. I had no clue where it came from. But I do now. Whatever she wants, it's urgent. And if I'm not mistaken, she's focusing on death. She wants to kill someone."

"I could've told ya that," Jim said.

They turned down the south hall toward the tower. Hayley looked up. Only minutes ago, she and Lee had been on the verge of losing themselves in desire in the room directly above Jim's. *She could've come for us herself.* The thought sent chills up and down her spine.

Before Jim opened his bedroom door, Hayley stopped him. "Remember, short answers."

They entered a room lit by recessed lighting, and although a fire danced in the fireplace, the room felt cold. Hayley rubbed her arms.

"I can tell Max to turn up the heat," Lee whispered.

"No," Hayley replied. "It might look like sorcery. Anyway, the witch is causing it. She's gathering energy."

He nodded.

Looking for the bird, Hayley glanced to her right toward the green wall above the bed with a fresco depicting a lush forest at dawn. She'd never been in Jim's room before now. The layout looked completely different than Lee's. She searched the rest of the room.

In front of the fireplace stood a beautiful Indian maiden, the firelight reflecting off her brown skin. Her black hair hung loosely down her back. She wore a sleeveless buckskin dress, her arms bare. But even though the transformation amazed her, Hayley's sense of danger kept her alert.

The witch waited, scrutinizing them.

Jim, Hayley, and Lee gathered in front of her.

The Indian maiden turned her gaze on Jim. "You have done well, my love. Speak freely, Sweet William. Be not afraid. My will is only to protect you from harm. Tell me, is she not a witch?" She pointed at Hayley.

Although Hayley had faced the same accusations from her peers while in school and from judgmental people throughout her life, this allegation surprised her. *Because of my abilities? What's behind this?*

"Who, Hayley? No."

"What say you of the corn-haired wench and the raven-haired woman. They be witches?"

*Kathy and Laura*, Hayley thought.

"No and no," Jim said.

"It has been hundreds of years since you and I bound and planted the evil deep within the earth. 'Tis then I made the promise to protect you and all humanity for eternity from the wickedness. When I died, the archangels gave me a second chance to prove myself worthy, allowing me to become a sentinel and keep my vow. Recently my promise has been threatened. When the forest was robbed of its trees and cleared of its growth, the rune spell I cast upon a stone and planted to imprison the evil was plucked from the roots of an old oak tree. This day I feared would come."

Her face grew pensive. She took a deep breath and released it as she shook her head. "Knowledge of the evil's escape and recapture must not be noticed by mankind. My impulse to warn you, Sweet William, put you and your friends in danger. I am deeply sorry." A soft smile brightened her face. "But I am also happy to see you once more." Her smile faded. "There is but little time, my love. Because the evil draws its strength from your realm, so must its downfall be earthbound as well. Soon, Sweet William, you and I again will send this evil to its grave. By sunset tomorrow, I will give you the knowledge to protect yourselves from the *seiðr*. You must take a list of items to Annie."

She looked at Hayley. "Tonight, in your dreams, I will guide you, seeress. Tomorrow, when you arrive at the place you'll envision, speak not a word of me." Her voice hardened. "This task I give to you in my stead while I attempt to deter the threat."

*What's a "seiðr?" Is it evil? Who's Annie?* Before Hayley could ask questions, a light blue aura began to swirl around the maiden. "She's gathering more energy," Hayley whispered to Lee. "Be careful."

The maiden's eyes turned blood red. Tiny bumps emerged, covering her neck. From each bump, barbs pierced her skin and evolved into small plumes. She held her arms out to her sides, and thousands of pea-sized bumps spread across her skin from her throat to her fingertips. Hollow shafts knifed up through the raised skin on her outer arms, and feathers unfurled as her arms metamorphosed into wings.

She stood in front of them part bird, part beautiful woman.

Hayley gasped, experiencing an array of emotions—wonder, trepidation, and a touch of fear.

"Holy moly," Jim blurted.

Lee took a protective stance in front of Hayley.

The sentinel smiled. "I am a lethal foe. But no harm will come to my Sweet William or his friends. My oath is bound by truth."

Ignoring the sense of caution growing inside her, not wanting to miss the opportunity to learn more, Hayley stepped around Lee. "What's your name?"

"I am Vara. A *volvakona* in my last life of flesh. As a spirit, I am now a sentinel." She turned to Jim. "Be quick to do as I ask, I implore you. Time is of the essence." With that, she instantly completed her transformation into a goshawk. Taking flight, she circled the room. Evanescing, she flew through the outer wall.

Jim trembled as he fell into a chair near the fire. Across from him, Lee and Hayley sat speechless on the couch.

*She's good, not evil*, Hayley reminded herself, pushing away the remaining doubts. *If that's true, why did she put us in danger?* She tried to use her gift to see the present in order to gather insight. *Nothing. This is frustrating.*

"What in the hell was that?" Lee asked.

Hayley gazed at the wall where she had last seen the goshawk, then back at Lee. "I've never heard of anyone like her." She attempted to find the answers by tapping into a phenomenon called Akashic—a divine universal library. As there were rules restricting her ability to see her own future, so too restrictions applied to accessing information from the library. *Apparently, knowledge pertaining to sentinels is out of the question, too—another hindrance.*

Lee stood and paced. "She just flew into my home like it was natural."

"It's not the first time she's been here," Jim said. "I was bewitched last night. Thought I was dreamin' that I was bein' seduced by a pretty young Indian gal. As we got to the good part, she up and disappeared."

*Why would a sentinel seduce someone?* "Did she say anything?" Hayley asked.

"Just before she vanished, she said, 'Do you not know me? I am Orkona.'"

"'Orkona.' Are you sure?" Hayley asked. "Why Orkona when she said her name's Vara?"

"Hell, I don't know. My mind was on somethin' else."

"And she expected you to know her?"

"That's what it sounded like. They were the only words she spoke. I'll never forget her voice." He closed his eyes. "As sweet as heavenly music."

"You really need a girlfriend," Lee said.

"She said a few words I didn't understand," Hayley admitted. "*Seiðr,* whatever that means, and *volvakona.*"

"You might take notes," Lee suggested. "Oh, and add 'Orkona.' I'd suggest we google their meanings, but it's late. We'll see Roger in the morning. He'll call the team together, and we'll do some research." He turned his attention to Jim, who sat calmly staring into the fireplace. "Don't worry, we'll figure this out."

Hayley rose from the couch, hesitant to leave Jim alone. "Think you'll be all right if we take off?"

"Sure. What do I have to be nervous 'bout? If somethin's comin' for me, it will have to get by Vara first."

"That's a good way of looking at it," Lee said. "If you need anything, tell Max to wake us."

# CHAPTER 3

Lee opened his bedroom door, and Hayley entered. *The lights are on, and the room's cool.* She sensed a presence. *Grams.*

Fully materialized, Grams, appearing to be in her thirties although she'd been in her eighties when she died, sat in the high-backed chair by the fireplace. She wore winter white stove-pipe pants, a yellow turtleneck cashmere sweater, and white ankle boots with sensible heels.

All of Hayley's childhood, while seeing the dead and visions of their deaths had frightened her, she'd noticed a woman standing nearby — in the park, on the street, in her bedroom. Over time, she learned the woman, Elaina, watched over her. After Grams's death, Elaina began training Grams as Hayley's guardian angel. *I've always been able to trust Elaina. But I'm so glad she chose Grams to be her student. Grams is always here when I need her. I love her so much.*

Lee tightened the belt of his robe and followed Hayley to the fireplace.

Eager for answers, Hayley sat in the overstuffed chair across from her grandmother. "Did you see what just happened in Jim's room?"

"Yes."

Lee stood behind Hayley's chair. "What in the hell was that?"

"She's a sentinel—a type of guardian angel. Sentinels stand watch over events that could alter the future, and they step in to prevent occurrences not meant to be."

Hayley remembered reading an article about an explosion at a high school. Teachers and students were held captive. When the bomb exploded, children reported seeing angels hovering over the heads of the confined.

"The classroom hostage situation," Hayley said.

"Yes," Grams replied. "It was a rare occasion when the sentinels were seen as angels."

Lee nodded. "I recall reading about that."

"Then Vara's a protector?" Hayley asked.

"Yes," Grams replied. "A sentinel's powers have no boundaries, and they're forbidden to kill an innocent. She's not a witch. Because their powers are pure and they're celestial beings, they're banned by the archangels from performing witchcraft. Its tools, spells, and potions are corrupted by death, eye of newt, heart of bat—impure, in other words."

"That seems to be an unusual rule," Lee said. "I wonder how many witches they recruit to be sentinels. And why would a sentinel need to use witchcraft if they have an abundance of power already?"

"Witchcraft hasn't always been used for evil doing," Grams replied. "It's the soul using the practice that chooses its purpose. As for the souls who used witchcraft all of their lives on Earth, it would seem like a natural tendency for them to use the power they're most accustomed to. Maybe that's the reason for the rule."

"If Vara's truly a sentinel, I'm confused," Hayley said. "She said she came to Jim to give a warning, but the first time she came to him, she almost seduced him and never mentioned the danger."

"You're right," Grams agreed. "She became personally involved, something a sentinel is forbidden to do. Perhaps she was assigned to be a sentinel too soon after her death, and is still emotionally attached to her previous life."

"Like me," Hayley said, reflecting on her childhood, her intense interest in the Victorian home a block from where she lived, and her pledge to buy it someday. "Drawn to the house I lived in before being reincarnated and linked to my friends I knew in previous lifetimes."

"Exactly," Grams said. "Her love for Sweet William is still strong after hundreds of years. It's understandable that her first reaction would be to hug and kiss him. But she remembered her intentions and returned to making her sentinel's mission her priority."

"That makes sense. I guess what's really bothering me is why she seemed so unconcerned about putting us in danger."

"I agree," Lee said. "And why is she waiting to give us protection?"

Grams raised an eyebrow. "I don't have answers to either question. Plus, Hayley received a vision of Vara standing at the foot of her bed. A sentinel's purpose is secret information, their missions are given to them by the archangels. Usually, all traces of a sentinel's presence are eliminated. I would think Vara would be especially covert since she knows Hayley can read residual energy. There must be a reason I'm unaware of for why Hayley's privileged to see and sense certain things, while others are forbidden the knowledge."

*Maybe that's why Vara wondered if I'm a witch.*

A log shifted in the fireplace. Lee strolled over, slid the screen aside, and added a few more logs to the fire. "Why haven't we known about her kind until now?" Lee asked over his shoulder.

"Long ago," Grams explained, "sentinels were believed to be gods in animal form. The Church executed the pagans who continued the practice. Since then, sentinels seldom appear in any form, animal or angel, and if noticed, once they have completed a task, they can erase the memories of those involved to keep their existence secret."

Lee rose, returned to Hayley, and eased himself down on the arm of her chair. "I've read about half-animal and half-human creatures that Egyptians considered gods."

"Yes, as did other cultures," Grams said. "Vara can appear in her natural form of an angel, but she chose to take the shape of a bird, giving her the ability to travel quickly on Earth. It's not uncommon among sentinels. Myths of half-human and half-bird creatures were once believed in Greece, India, Russia, Egypt, and other cultures. Even today, if a person sees something they can't understand, it's human nature to analyze it and come up with a theory. Your dictionary calls it 'agenticity.' That's why some cultures got it wrong. The sentinels were never gods, just God's hand in miracles."

"I'd like to know more about her and the threat we're facing," Hayley said. "Earlier this evening, I had a vision of someone wearing a dark hooded robe. I know now it couldn't have been Vara. Do you think a witch could be involved? Do you think it's the evil she mentioned?"

Grams shrugged. "Maybe, maybe not. In the past, witches had powers great enough to shake the world."

"I always thought witches were fabricated fairytales," Lee admitted.

"They were definitely real—and fierce," Grams said. "Still today, some keep their abilities hidden to protect themselves from condemnation. The Church tried to eradicate them during the sixteenth and seventeenth centuries. The witches who fled unnoticed hid their powers or stopped using them. Over hundreds of years, some of those abilities became dormant. Today, a witch's power is a fraction of those used in the past."

A knot of unease tightened in Hayley's stomach. "How much danger are we in?"

"I don't know," Grams said. "All I can do is wait and see, just like everyone else. You'd better get some sleep. Only heaven knows what's in store for you tomorrow." She stood. "I'll be close by."

She walked toward the door, fading with each step until her essence became undetectable.

# CHAPTER 4

Before Hayley awoke, her vivid dream played out in bits and pieces. She saw a sign that read "Interstate 40." Then she envisioned the turnoff and a town's name. Finally, a voice said, "It is here you must go."

Hayley opened her eyes to see Lee watching her.

"You were mumbling in your sleep," he said. "Something about the interstate."

"Vara showed me where we need to go." She rolled over, grabbed the notepad from the bedside table and sat up. While she wrote, she often paused, picturing what she had seen in her dream. "The information was scattered," Hayley told Lee. She finished writing. "Anyway, we need to take Interstate 40 through the Appalachians. I wrote it all down. It looks easy enough."

"Did she give you the list we need to take to Annie?"

"No."

"That's strange." Lee grabbed his cell phone that was ringing on the bedside table. "Hi, Roger." He listened. "We'll be right over." Lee returned the phone to the table, pulled back the covers, and stood. "Roger's freaked out about something. He didn't say what, but he wants us to come over."

Hayley sat on the edge of the bed and slid her feet into her slippers. "It's the list. It has to be."

***

On the way to Roger's, Hayley used her clairvoyance to perceive the danger Vara mentioned. She jumped when Lee placed his hand on her leg.

"You look like you're miles away." He returned his hand to the wheel.

"I was."

"Tossing out your psychic net?"

She nodded. "I was trying to sense the danger Vara spoke of."

Hayley didn't believe in coincidence. They were involved in this situation for some unknown reason, no doubt. But facing an evil great enough to concern a sentinel, she had to wonder what they could possibly do to help without being killed.

Lee glanced at her, then focused on driving along the winding road. She knew he could see the worry on her face.

"What is it?" he asked.

"I hate feeling vulnerable."

She thought about the many times while growing up she'd asked herself, *Why can't I be like everyone else?* About six months ago, when she'd joined the team of paranormal investigators, she'd received her answer. At the end of a case, she learned that she and her co-workers were born to rescue souls.

"Let's not worry until we have to," he said. "When it's necessary, we'll deal with it."

*He's right.* She cleared her thoughts, eased back into the rich leather seat of his SUV, and enjoyed the view of Lake Tales.

Lee knew when to ground her. They had grown so close

since they met in June. It seemed as though they could read each other's minds. At least that's what Hayley had believed until a few days ago. She thought about the costume ball, how in front of two hundred people Lee had asked her to marry him. Hayley mentally pinched herself when she gazed at her engagement ring. *I didn't see it coming.*

She knew she couldn't see her future. If she wanted to know about her own impending circumstances, she had to consult another psychic.

"Did Roger give ya a hint to what's so important?" Jim asked from the backseat. "He's interruptin' my beauty sleep."

Lee peered into his rearview mirror. "Beauty sleep? From the looks of you, that old wives' cure's a myth. No. All Roger said was, 'Come over quick. You've got to see this.'"

"No need to be insultin'. If I take off my shoes, I can count the minutes I slept last night."

"Sorry. We didn't get much sleep either," Lee said.

To clear her head of all the unanswered questions that had kept her up half the night, Hayley watched the sunlight filter through the fall foliage and dance on the colorful leaves carpeting the road. Peeking through a grove of pines, she tried to glimpse Lee's home across the lake. They drove along River View, one of North Carolina's older roads eight miles from downtown Sutterville.

Jim reached over, placing his hand on the headrest of the front passenger seat. "Can't ya use your hocus-pocus mind to see what's up, darlin'?"

"Hayley's not a magician," Lee said.

Folding his arms, Jim sat back. "She knows what I mean."

"I can't perceive what's bothering Roger. I've tried. I can only guess it has something to do with the list."

Ahead on the right, Hayley recognized a slightly tilted white pine, a landmark signaling the turnoff to Roger's mansion. She looked for the narrow, nearly invisible road on the left. Lee slowed then turned sharply, throwing Jim across the backseat.

Mumbling, Jim straightened and ran his fingers through his thinning brown hair. "Where in the hell did ya get your driver's license?"

"Sorry. I was listening to Hayley." Lee focused straight ahead and slowed even more as the road curved. "But Grams said witches today are harmless."

"She also said there are those who hide their powers," Hayley reminded him. "Apparently, there's someone out there that Vara's been assigned to keep an eye on who's capable of altering the future."

"Must be evil incarnate," Jim interjected. "Vara said in one of my past lifetimes, I helped her bury that someone."

"That person's threats are substantial enough to make a sentinel show herself," Hayley said. "We need to know what's going on. As long as Vara keeps that person's identity from us, we'll all be jumping at the slightest noise."

"Unless ya hypnotize me and do that past-regression mumbo jumbo to take me back to the time when I was Sweet William."

"Good idea," Hayley replied, wanting answers now, not knowing when or if they'd see Vara again.

"Vara's business has fallen into our laps for some reason," Lee said. "I think we need to treat this like one of our cases and find the truth so we know what we're up against. Agreed?"

"Yes," Hayley and Jim said in unison.

Lee pulled into a driveway lying between maples, poplars, and dogwoods adorned in fall colors. He stopped his SUV in front of a security gate, its wrought-iron arch rising above the flanking columns. "We're here," Lee spoke into the intercom.

To occupy her mind, Hayley read the mansion's name on a plaque below a sculpted bronze angel kneeling on the gate's limestone right-hand column. "Is there a story behind the name 'Angel Hall'?"

"It's a joke between Roger's father and Lee's," Jim said. "Roger's house is made of white limestone and has wings in the back, like an angel. Lee's, as you know, is made of red brick, and its wings and towers look like horns stickin' outta the front of the house. Roger's dad called it 'Devil's Hall.'"

*Doesn't sound like a joke to me.* "Bet your dad didn't like that," she told Lee.

Lee shook his head. "He ground his teeth every time our home was referred to by that name. I haven't thought about that in years."

Lee had told her about that long-ago tragedy that took the lives of not only his parents but Roger's as well. She knew how he felt, and didn't mean to bring up a painful memory of the plane crash. Her parents had died in a car accident when she was fourteen, and she still vividly recalled the memories.

The gates swung open. They drove through.

The driveway curved, obscuring the view of Roger's home. Hayley looked toward the north, remembering the first time she'd visited his estate in August and how the grass reminded her of green carpets beneath a field of trees. Now, as the fall winds blew, most of the trees except the white pines in the north shivered, and their colorful leaves littered the dormant lawns. To the west, evergreens stood like bodyguards, blocking the view of Angel Hall from Lake Tales.

Across from the three-story mansion, adjacent to the drive, seventy-foot-tall eastern junipers grew around a huge circular fountain. In its center rose a life-size bronze monument of five rearing horses. Hayley, surprised to see it, stared at the goshawk perched on a horse's head.

She pointed. "We've been followed."

They gazed at the fountain, and the bird took flight.

"Kinda comfortin' that she's protectin' us," Jim said.

Lee slowed the car as he approached the house. "Protecting us from whom, though?" Cummings, Roger's butler, the wind playing with his neatly groomed gray hair, waited while Lee parked near the entrance. When the engine stopped, Cummings opened Hayley's car door. "Mr. Hudson wishes to see all of you in the library."

As he offered his hand to Hayley, she slid out of her seat. "Thank you, Cummings." She stood and pulled her coat collar up around her neck. Although the sun shone brightly, the breeze felt nippy.

Cummings opened the mansion's hand-carved wooden front door, allowing them to enter. Once inside, he took their coats.

Hayley stepped onto the inlaid wood floor in the foyer, and residual spirit energy engulfed her. *She's been here.* "I'm sensing Vara's presence," she told them. *Why isn't she covering her tracks?* She hesitated in the center of the entry. "I want to see where this energy trail leads."

Staircases, one on each side of the entry hall, gracefully rose to the second floor. While sensing the sentinel's energy, she started up the left-hand staircase, taking each step slowly past the ancestral portraits hung on the pale yellow walls.

When she reached the top landing, she faced an oil painting of Jim. Being a close friend of Lee and Roger's families, Jim had stepped in to mentor Roger, then twenty-eight, and Lee, eighteen, after their parents' deaths. Each considered Jim to be his second father, Lee had explained to her. Seven years ago, Roger had commissioned the portrait.

In the painting, Jim wore a suit and tie. His thinning brown hair, touched with gray, appeared neatly combed. *Hasn't aged a bit,* Hayley thought. "The trail stops here, Jim. Vara studied your portrait. When were you here last?"

Jim stood with Lee in the center of the foyer, looking up at her. "Day before yesterday. I did some plumbin' in the kitchen."

She touched the painting. In her mind's eye, she saw the face of the Indian maiden. Hayley turned and peered down at Jim. "I sense an urgency, a longing to find you." Slowly, Hayley descended the stairs, her senses still scanning the stairway. "She must have followed you home."

"Maybe she's confused," Jim said. "I know I am. I need a drink. Let's get to the library."

# CHAPTER 5

They hurried along a corridor brightened by three immense crystal chandeliers and eight large windows looking out toward the equestrian fountain. Paintings from American impressionists hung regimentally on the walls.

In the corridor, Hayley again noticed the sentinel's residual trail and stopped to investigate while the men waited. "Her energy's more recent here."

She rejoined Lee and Jim. They continued on, turning the corner entering the west hallway. At its end, Cummings waited, and he stepped inside the library to announce them.

"Show them in," Hayley heard Roger say.

Inside, Hayley looked around the oak-paneled library, sensing the atmosphere. Across the room, she noticed Laura Song, Roger's girlfriend, and Clint Waverly, one of his two nephews, standing amid intensified traces of the sentinel's lingering energy.

"Glad you guys made it." Roger crossed the room toward them.

Jim walked to the bar. "So, what's so damned important that we had to stop everythin' and hurry over?" He pulled a bottle of beer from a small refrigerator below the counter, beneath a shelf containing bottles of Johnny Walker Blue Label next to Wray and Nephew rum.

Roger paced in front of Lee, glanced at each of them, and ran his fingers through his blond wavy hair. "Hell, I don't know whether to be amazed or worried."

"About what?" Hayley asked. From the energy in this room, she knew Roger's situation had something to do with Vara.

Roger took her hand. "Come. You've got to see this." He led Hayley across the room.

Lee and Jim, beer in hand, followed.

Laura stood by an artist's easel. The gold-colored drapes hung open, and sunlight flowed in through the tall windows, giving Clint the perfect well-lit location for drawing.

Roger released Hayley's hand, and the women hugged.

"Hi, stranger," Hayley said. During the last few weeks, she hadn't seen much of her tenant, and good friend since Laura and Roger became a couple. "Is everything okay?"

"I'm fine, but mystified."

"So what's going on?" Hayley followed Laura's gaze and looked at the easel.

"Since Clint's operation, Laura's been giving him art therapy," Roger explained.

Hayley ruffled Clint's short red hair. "Feeling better?"

"Yeah. No more headaches."

His hair had grown little since the surgery, his scar still evident.

"I'm getting rewired," he said.

"'Rewired'?" Hayley asked.

"Research has shown that following trauma, art helps the brain to rewire," Laura said. "When I successfully removed

Clint's tumor, his limbic system was unavoidably compromised. That affects his episodic and semantic memories."

Hayley knew through her psychic foreseeing, before Clint's benign lump had been detected, that he would recover completely. "Hang in there, Clint. You'll be fine."

"Good to know," Clint replied.

"I thought art might help." Laura's brows furrowed. "But look. I turned away from him only for an instant, and see what he did? Two pages of strange writing."

"Let me get out of your way." Clint rolled aside in his office chair.

Hayley studied the large sheet of drawing paper as Roger lifted it, revealing the next page, while Jim and Lee stepped behind her. *Vara has to know we can't read this. Why the mystery?*

Jim rubbed his chin. "Looks like chicken scratch."

Lee looked over Hayley's shoulder. "What is all this?"

"You tell me," Roger said. "Clint was totally unaware he was writing what you see."

"I can't even remember picking up the piece of charcoal," Clint said.

"What you did is called automatic writing." Hayley leaned closer, considering the characters. "I've read about it but haven't seen it before." She touched the markings and remembered seeing a documentary telling of this antiquated writing and its origin. While her hands remained on the canvas, she closed her eyes and used psychometry to perceive the author and to know the meaning of the message. *Vara.* "Runes. How odd. Why would she use runes?"

Jim, in midstream of taking a drink, lowered his beer. "What in the hell's a rune?"

"It's an ancient form of writing dating to the time of the

Vikings," Hayley said. "I'm guessing this is the list Vara spoke of."

"Wait a minute." Roger took a step back from the easel. "Who's Vara?"

"Jim had a visitation the other night," Lee said.

Roger scoffed. "What visitation? Have a few beers too many before bedtime, Jim?"

"Hell, no!" Jim told him. "A man knows when he's bein' seduced. By an Indian maiden. Good lookin' too. Found out she was an angel."

Laura stared at him. "An angel? Are you serious?"

"Her name's Vara," Hayley replied.

"As we entered the foyer earlier," Lee said, "Hayley sensed Vara's residual energy. Apparently, Vara saw Jim working here a couple of days ago and followed him home. Last night she called on him again, but this time Hayley and I were invited to attend." He glanced at Hayley, then back at Roger. "Maybe 'invited' is too subtle. 'Ordered' is a better term. It seems Jim's visitor is a spirit sentinel—a woman who takes the shape of a bird. We talked to Grams about her. She said sentinels stand guard and protect mankind from chaos. Apparently, Vara's a type of guardian angel."

"Let me explain." Hayley told them the details of Vara's visit, the threat of danger, and the sentinel's code of secrecy. "Vara said she'd send us a list of ingredients used for protection. I'm assuming it's for an amulet. She instructed us to take the list to a woman named Annie, who lives in the Appalachians."

"An amulet?" Laura asked. "Are we talking about witchcraft? Why would an angel use witchcraft?"

"She's not. Sentinels are forbidden to work the craft. She's only providing information and letting Annie do the conjuring,"

Hayley replied.

"We're about to face a threat great enough to worry a sentinel," Lee said, "and Vara thinks a simple amulet will protect us? I think we should see if Kathy can find someone to translate Clint's writings and do whatever it takes to find out what we're up against."

Roger pulled his cell phone from his pocket. "I'll call Kathy."

"I already did," Clint told them.

"What are ya, some kinda psychic now?" Jim peered at his empty beer bottle and headed to the bar.

"Don't jump to conclusions, Jim," Roger said.

"Where have I heard that before?" Jim asked over his shoulder.

Hayley recalled. When she first met Lee, Roger, Jim, Clint, and Kathy at Paranormal Search and Analysis, Hayley had been trained as a paranormal investigator. *Don't jump to conclusions is a ghost hunter's first rule.* Presently, after becoming the saviors of souls, they no longer went in search of ghosts—now, the ghosts and spirits came to them.

"When did you call her?" Roger asked.

"When you phoned Lee. I told her something weird happened and to get here quick."

"Perfect." Hayley knew from her experience working at PSA that Kathy couldn't be beat when it came to research.

Cummings came to the door. "Miss Lane, sir."

Kathy, in a pink sweater and white jeans, stepped past Cummings and crossed the room to Roger's side. "What's going on?"

"Take a look at this." Roger pointed at the easel. "Hayley says it's automatic writing."

From her raspberry leather purse, Kathy removed her

red-framed glasses, put them on, and leaned in, gazing at the characters. "Runes. I studied them some at the university."

"Can you read them?" Roger asked.

"No. I can sound out a few words, but I don't know their meanings."

Hayley told her about the visitation.

"Is there some way to get this translated?" Roger asked.

"I know just the person." Kathy retrieved her cell phone from her purse. "I had a professor who has her doctorate in ancient languages. I can call Duke University and see if she's there."

On her phone, Kathy looked up the university's number, called, and walked toward the fireplace as she spoke.

Hayley glanced past her, noticing an energy she hadn't previously perceived radiating from the mantle. She left the others and crossed the room. Lee joined her.

Hayley took a closer look, found new carvings in the mantle, and ran her hand across the characters.

"More runes?" Lee asked.

She nodded, still perplexed about the use of the ancient text.

"Roger, do you know about this?" Lee called out.

"Know about what?" He hurried to them and gawked at Hayley's discovery. "She defaced my mantle! Do you know how old this mantle is? It cost my parents a mint. Not to mention the time and expense it took to import it from Wales. Better be a damn good reason for this."

With a fresh beer in his hand, Jim joined them around the fireplace.

"Perfect etching," Hayley told them. "It almost looks laser cut. Clint didn't do this."

"You're right, I didn't," he said, touching the engraving.

Kathy strolled back to the group. "We're in luck. I talked to

Professor Rothschild, and she's free tomorrow afternoon."

"What will stop Vara from knowin' we're investigatin' behind her back?" Jim asked Hayley. "Do you think she'd care?"

"There's no harm in being discreet."

"Matilda's a sleuth when it comes to research," Kathy said.

Jim looked at Kathy. "Is the professor trustworthy?"

"Yes. I would trust her with my life. And vice versa."

"What's she like?" Jim asked. "When I took a few classes at Duke to catch up on the latest paranormal investigative technology, I noticed some of those professors there aren't any older than the spit on my boots. We need someone experienced who can read this chicken scratch before one of us gets killed."

"I'd say Matilda's near your age, Jim," Kathy said, plopping down on the couch. "early fifties. She may be a little hard to work with, but trust me, she's an expert in this field."

Laura sat on the opposite couch, facing her. "She sounds perfect."

"Does she have any background in the paranormal?" Jim asked.

Kathy glanced at Roger, a questioning look on her face. "I didn't think that mattered."

"She might fly outta here faster than a hummin'bird on steroids when ya tell her who wrote that scribblin'," Jim said.

"Kathy's right," Roger told them, joining Laura. "It doesn't matter. She doesn't have to know about Vara. She just needs to transcribe the runes."

"But if it comes down to it and she learns about Vara," Lee said, "you have to promise not to say a word if she scoffs. It will only make matters worse. Promise, Jim?"

"Okay, okay. I swear I'll keep my thoughts to myself."

"Thank you," Kathy told him. "Matilda has a habit of rubbing people the wrong way. So I have no doubt you'll be biting your tongue more than a few times while she's here."

"Thanks for the heads up, sugar," Jim said. "Looks like it's gonna be a painful evenin'."

"First things first," Lee said. "Before we follow Vara's instructions to deliver the writings to Annie, we should take photos."

"Clint, would you take some close-ups of both pages and the mantle?" Roger asked. "You can use my camera."

"Can do, Boss," Clint said. "I'll download the photos onto your laptop and have everything ready to print out in less than an hour."

# CHAPTER 6

After leaving Angel Hall, Hayley, Lee, and Jim piled into Lee's SUV. Hayley, sitting up front, sensed Vara's urgency once they turned off the interstate, heading into the Appalachian Mountains. In this first week of November, at higher elevations, fall had robbed the trees of their foliage. The lower elevation near Lee's had experienced nearly the same level of thievery. They followed the curved road covered with wilting leaves. To their left, the sun shone through naked tree branches and peeked through evergreens.

A short drive ahead, around one more bend, the road straightened, and Lee slowed as they reached a town.

Hayley refreshed their memories about the store's appearance.

"I'll keep my eye on the side streets," Jim said from the backseat, pressing his nose against his window.

When they passed the last building, a boarded-up gas station, its corrugated tin roof rusted, her hopes fell. She released the breath she didn't realize she held. "We can't be lost. This is the town Vara showed me. I'm sure."

Lee picked up speed.

The bare beech, birch, and basswood trees allowed Hayley to see deeper into the woods. *Nothing.* The trees gave way to a clearing after a mile. In the distance, Hayley saw a sign reading "Healer's Hollow" in the corner of an unkempt yard.

"Slow down. I think that's it."

Lee slowed. He turned up a dirt driveway leading to a clapboard house, its wood-shingled roof patched with tin, plywood, and a tarp hanging off the roof's right side. He parked beside the house. Before climbing out of the car, Hayley buttoned her coat and adjusted the scarf around her neck. Lee did the same.

"Okay, let's follow the yellow brick road," Jim said, unbuckling his seat belt.

They left the vehicle and walked a flagstone path through dead grass and past a garden, its herbs and flowers frostbitten by the cold November nights. Bowed steps led them to a covered porch extending across the width of the house, the sun shining through holes in its sagging porch roof, columns rotted. Its floor creaked and slanted.

A sign on its storm door read, "Come In."

Hayley used her gift of perception, searching for danger. *Not a trace of negativity.*

Jim pulled the door open and allowed Hayley and Lee to enter first.

A blend of unfamiliar scents greeted Hayley as she strolled to the counter. Behind the register, covering the wall, stood shelves filled with mason jars. She examined their labels: *Wishing beans, mugwort, barberry, angelica root, bat's head root.* Hayley stopped reading and gasped at the sight of dead insects and other jars filled with parts of creatures floating in preservatives. She turned away without reading the other hundred or so jar labels and looked to the right of the curtained doorway.

A sign on those shelves read "Remedies." The first shelf held labeled bottles of bat's blood, dove's blood, and potions for luck, money, love, infatuation, lust, and domination.

"Have a good look around. I'll be with you shortly," a woman's voice called from the back room. Before Hayley stepped away from the counter, she overheard the woman whispering. "Take it out of here. It's not safe."

*This might be a bad time*, Hayley thought.

With Lee at her side, Hayley strolled through the shop. On a long table lay shallow baskets filled with cedar bark, birch twigs, whole white sage leaves, cinnamon, and items Hayley didn't recognize. Below a hand-written sign reading "Smudge Tools" lay turkey, guinea hen, and goose feathers, alongside sweetgrass oil and sage smudge sticks. In the corner, she found an array of gemstones—tiger eye, garnet, black tourmaline, carnelian, and quartz crystal.

While Lee flipped through a book on gems and studied the stones in the basket, Hayley noticed shelves filled with other books across the room and wandered in that direction. She browsed through the collection, running her finger across books on rocks, minerals, and gems. Then she studied the categories on the shelf below—herbs, the making of candles, remedies, potions, and the *Book of Spells*. When she touched that book's leather binding, Hayley had a vision and stepped into the past as if time traveling. She watched a woman pull back the hood of her dark blue cloak, allowing her blonde hair to whip in the ocean breeze and trail across her youthful face. While balancing herself at the bow of a Viking ship, the woman held a wooden staff at her side and clutched a leather-bound book to her chest.

*A Viking witch*, a voice whispered in Hayley's mind. Tasting the salt in the air and feeling the sway of the ship while the men rowed in unison, Hayley knew her awareness stood witness without body or substance—no one could see her.

Hayley remained behind the witch, but close enough to the crew to hear the men grunt with each stroke. A step away, she saw a man with dirty blond hair, his face hidden behind a mustache and a bushy beard. He wore buckskin boots, tan hide trousers, and a long shirt topped by a three-quarter coat with a belt. He leaned toward another man wrapped in a dark brown cloak and pointed to the land on the horizon.

Her vision stopped abruptly.

*I think I found a clue.* She slid the thick brown leather-bound book from its cubbyhole, carried it back to the counter, and lifted its cover. Before she could scan the table of contents, Jim joined her.

He placed his hand on the lid of a huge pickle jar on the countertop and examined its content—a large colorful spider. "Almost looks alive," he said.

"It's blue," she told him. "It can't be real." Even so, Hayley's pulse quickened.

It moved.

She jumped back. Goosebumps covered her arms. The book she wanted to peruse remained open on the counter, but her arachnophobia kept her from returning to its pages.

A short woman in her mid-twenties, Hayley guessed, with waist-length brown hair, pulled the curtain aside, hesitated for a moment, and stepped to the counter. With a tender expression on her face, she opened the pickle jar and put her hand inside, allowing the creature to crawl up her arm. "Her species is called a Cobalt Blue. My father found her in Vietnam. I've had her since I was sixteen. Her name's Lovely." Gently she placed the tarantula back into the jar, returned its lid, and placed the jar under the register.

Hayley's racing heart began to calm. Watching the creature crawl up Annie's arm had almost sent her running out the door. She knew if the purpose of their visit had been insignificant, she'd be outside peering in through the window, putting a barrier between her and the eight-legged monster.

"Can I help you?" Annie asked, closing the book Hayley had placed on the counter. She pointed to the right-hand shelves. "A love potion, perhaps?"

"No," Hayley said. "Are you Annie?"

"Yes."

"We were told you can make amulets."

Lee walked over and placed the pages of rune writings on the counter and unrolled them.

The woman eyed them as if fitting pieces of a puzzle together. "A runic spell. In all the years I've owned this shop, I've never had a customer bring one to me." Annie raised an eyebrow. "Can I ask who sent you here?"

"We can't tell ya," Jim said. "It's kinda personal. But we were assured you could help us."

"The one who sent you is psychic," Annie said. "Only my relatives know I use runic spells." She fixed her attention on the *Book of Spells*. "And your friend told you about this book also?"

"Well, no," Hayley said. "I thought it looked interesting and pulled it from the shelf."

"It's a book containing witchcraft spells," Annie explained, flipping through the pages. "This is the only translated copy. The original's written in runes."

"The original must be very old," Lee said.

"Yes. The book and knowledge of runes have been passed down in my family since the 1600s." She closed the cover and crossed her arms. "It's difficult for me to believe you selected this book by coincidence. Is this a hoax? Did someone in my family put you up to this?"

"No," Hayley said. "And you were right. The woman who sent us is extremely gifted. She said our lives are in danger. We need your help."

Annie studied the writings again. "How unusual. A list of ingredients to make amulets."

*I was right. It is a list,* Hayley thought.

While Annie held her hand over Clint's automatic writing, she chanted words Hayley didn't understand. The writing vanished from the page, revealing an underlying spell also written in runes.

"Well, I'll be…," Jim said.

"I've never seen anything like this," Annie admitted. "It was written by a master. Extremely interesting."

Lee pulled out his cell phone. Leaning in, he took photographs of the underlying spell. He reviewed the images and snapped a few more shots. "How many amulets will it make?"

With another wave of Annie's hand, a shadow of the original runic characters appeared, gradually growing darker until again, cloaking the writing beneath. "Ten. They're twenty dollars apiece."

"We only need eight," Lee said. "And we'd like a complete translation of the entire script, please."

"Certainly."

"Is the spell to uncover the hidden text complicated?" Hayley asked.

"No. The writings on top include a list of items used in making an amulet and a spell that provides protection on the Earthly plane—the spell beneath shields against assaults from the spirit realm. What's interesting is the placement of the words. It's highly unusual, and each word has a meaning." A smile crossed her face. "I'm excited to be able to translate this. Then I must gather the elders and call upon the ancients to help us walk between realms."

"'Elders? Ancients'?" Hayley repeated. "Are you Native American?"

"Maybe a small trace is left in my family's blood over the generations. Our ancestor, a Keeper of the *Book of Spells*, was one of a few survivors of a lost tribe. Our stories tell that she and her people lived in the hills of Massachusetts before their extinction from smallpox."

Hayley reached over, opened the book, and scanned the table of contents. "Is our amulet spell in here?"

"No. If it were, nothing you could say would convince me that someone in my family didn't send you. Do you want the book as well?"

Lee glanced at Hayley. As if reading her mind, he pulled out his wallet. "Yes."

"In that case, you should be warned that the book has a spell attached to it and can't be used for malice, or it will return to my bookshelf."

"Hayley doesn't have a speck of evil in her," Lee said.

"I know," Annie told him. "If she were evil, she wouldn't have been able to pull the book from the shelf."

"Is the original protected as well?" Hayley asked.

"Yes. Each generation of my family has placed wards upon the book. The spells on each book are unbreakable." She turned her attention to Lee. "You can pay me for the amulets when you pick them up. As for the book, it's very expensive, I'm afraid."

He handed her his credit card. "We'll take it."

Annie rang up the sale. "Do you practice witchcraft?" she asked Hayley.

"No, but I'm very interested." She ran her hand across the book's leather cover and wondered if witchcraft had anything to do with the cover appearing so much older than its actual age. "What's the key to witchcraft? There has to be more behind the words of a spell."

"You're right. Clarity is necessary to create. Focus is used to direct intent. Discipline is essential. And practice makes perfect. But always remember that witchcraft is not a game. Thought is more powerful than most people realize. It's true what they say, 'Be careful what you wish for, or it may come true.'"

*Grams told me the same thing.* "Can I learn what you did to read the underlying spell?" Hayley asked.

"Yes." Annie walked over to the bookshelf, pulled out a paperback book, and brought it to the counter. "If you're serious about learning, *Basic Witchcraft* will teach you what you need to know. Practice, and by the time you return to pick up your order, I'll be able to show you the spell I used." She handed the book to Hayley. "Take it as a gift."

With a touch, Hayley felt the witchcraft book's energy as if each word held the writer's essence. She checked the author's name. *Annette Forte – Annie.* She placed it on the counter with the *Book of Spells.* "Did you write this?"

"Yes, while I was teaching my daughter, Zoey."

"Is she gifted like you?"

"Yes. It runs in my family."

Lee took two of Annie's business cards from a clear plastic holder on the counter, put one into his wallet, turned the other over and wrote his phone number. "Call me when the amulets are ready." He passed a card to Annie. "So, what are we looking at — two or three days?"

"Maybe four," she replied.

"Any way to rush it?" Lee asked. "It's extremely important."

"I'll talk to the elders tonight. If they perform a certain ceremony, and the ancients give us their guidance, I may have them ready sooner."

"Thanks," Lee and Hayley said in unison.

"I'm glad you stopped by." She brushed her hand across the scroll of pages, eyeing them fondly. "Fascinating," Annie said.

Lee picked up the books, and he and Hayley turned to leave. The hinges squeaked as Jim opened the storm door and followed them out.

Once in the car, Lee handed the books to Hayley. "Promise me you won't do anything reckless that might kill you or harm you in any way."

"Do you really think I'd do such a thing?"

Lee raised an eyebrow.

"Okay. I promise."

He started the engine.

"I noticed ya hesitated before takin' that book from the shelf," Jim said, from the back seat, "and I saw that spaced-out clairvoyant look on your face."

"I saw that look too," Lee said. He backed out of the dirt parking lot and headed for the street. "Envision something unusual?"

"Maybe," Hayley said. "Annie said the *Book of Spells* was handed down from the 1600s, but it's much older than that. I glimpsed the book's past. A Viking witch carried it on a voyage, probably around the eleventh or twelfth century. There's evidence placing Vikings in America during that time. Somehow it was passed to one of Annie's Native American ancestors — the

Keeper, Annie called her."

"Do you think the book has something to do with our case?" Lee asked.

"I don't know yet. I don't think it's a coincidence that Annie's ancestor, the Keeper, was Native American, and Vara is too. I'm wondering if they're the same person and if that's why Vara didn't want her name mentioned. Maybe Grams knows."

While Lee drove, Hayley closed her eyes and pictured herself with Grams at Lee's mansion in his sitting room by the fireplace.

*What did you think about the vision I sent you when you touched the* Book of Spells? *Grams asked in Hayley's mind.*

*Amazing. The book I bought wasn't the original.*

*Correct, dear. Yours is a copy made within the last five years. The vision I sent to you came from the original I located in the back room of Annie's shop.*

*Do you think Vara was also the Keeper Annie spoke of?*

*Maybe. I've found evidence that Vara knew of the book when I traced its history. Tonight in your dreams, I'll reveal what I've found.*

*Thanks, Grams. I can't wait.* Hayley said her goodbyes and her vision ended.

Hayley opened her eyes and ran her hand over the book's cover. "Apparently, Annie's original *Book of Spells* has an interesting history."

"What did Grams tell you?" Lee asked.

"She found something that might interest us. She'll show me tonight in my dreams."

# CHAPTER 7

While Hayley lay in the darkness of Lee's bedroom, the rhythm of his breathing as he slept lulled her into her own peaceful slumber. Disconnected images drifted through her mind, and she started to sleep.

In a dream as vivid as life, she saw dark clouds covering the sky. Lightning flashed. In the forest, a beautiful raven-haired woman, with staff in hand and the *Book of Spells* resting on a rock pillar in front of her, chanted in a language unfamiliar to Hayley. The woman reached upward as if beckoning the lightning to come to her. Rain pelted the forest, but not a drop touched her. Hayley saw that the woman stood in a bubble, protecting both her and the leather-bound book from the elements.

A small Indian girl hid behind a pine tree and watched. In a whisper, she repeated the woman's words and flicked her little finger as she touched her wet hair, then curved her hand into the shape of a bear's claw, mimicking the woman's gestures.

Hayley recognized the little girl—Vara, at around age six.

While the woman silently stood, the storm moved on. Vara turned and hurried away.

Hayley's dreams skipped ahead in time, and she saw the raven-haired woman with the *Book of Spells*, standing at the edge of the village where Vara lived. A young brave rushed through the village to advise the chief of her arrival.

"Tell her I wish to speak with her," the chief said.

"Do not let her approach," the medicine man, standing at the chief's side, said. "Hildr is evil."

"So you say, but did she not give twenty years of her life to heal my wife? Did our ancestors not accept her offering? I will put the decision in our ancestors' hands once more."

"Our ancestors spoke to me," the medicine man said. "They say the woman is evil, that she deceives us. In their wisdom, they rejected her offerings and banned her from our village. Would you go against their wishes?"

The chief raised his voice an octave. "Or is it your wish to denounce her because, when you could not heal my wife, Hildr could? Did you not see the healer's face when she left the hut? Hildr's youth had been taken, and my wife's heart beats strongly."

"The evil one's spirit has poisoned your mind."

"The love I have for my son is pure," the chief told him. "But if our ancestors wish to intervene, I will accept their decision." He left the tent and gazed at the dark cloudy sky as if waiting for a reply. The medicine man joined him, his face stern.

Moments later, Hildr, carrying the *Book of Spells*, stepped forward, entering the village. Lightning lit the sky. Thunder rumbled.

Stepping away from the chief's side, the medicine man began dancing and chanting. In a ritual call to the ancestors, the medicine man raised his arms to the sky. Then he turned to the raven-haired woman and shook his staff as if in warning.

"What do you bring to my village, Hildr?" the chief asked.

The woman held up the leather-bound book. "I bring the wisdom of the ancestors."

To the chief's left, from the hut of Vara's dying brother, the spirit of a wolf appeared. Vara huddled close to her mother. While his people spoke in whispers, the chief watched the spirit wolf lope across the clearing and sit beside Hildr. She crossed the center of the village to stand in front of the chief, and the wolf accompanied her.

Hayley looked at the darkened sky as lightning flashed high above the village, its bolt splitting into three, resembling an eagle's claw. For a moment, she thought she saw a shimmer over the village, much like the protective bubble she had witnessed the healer create in the forest to shield herself from the rain. From the look on Vara's face, Hayley believed the girl had seen it too. When the shimmering vanished, Vara glanced at the villagers. Everyone watched the spirit wolf.

"Our ancestors have welcomed you," the chief said.

"No!" the medicine man shouted, rushing toward Hildr. Before he could reach her, a bolt of lightning struck him. His charred body crumpled to the ground, while the remnants of his clothing smoldered.

Hayley watched Vara stare at Hildr's horrified expression. Suddenly, everything and everyone around her froze as if time stood still. In that instant, the mask lifted off Hildr's face, her eyes twinkled, and her lips formed a smile as she met Vara's gaze. In a blink, time seemed to continue, and her horrified expression returned.

"Once more," the woman said, "I have promised twenty years of my life as a sacrifice to honor the ancestors in return for granting me the power to continue to heal."

The chief led Hildr to his son inside the hut.

Later, when the healer left, she leaned heavily on the gnarled branch she used as a staff. Her face had aged twenty years. Her raven hair had turned to the color of smoke.

Vara cried when her brother, Taiho, stepped out from behind his healer. He wore his buckskin pants, his bare upper body showing no signs of the festering welts that had covered him. His eyes shone bright, and his step looked firm.

Hayley woke, rolled over, and turned on the bedside lamp.

"Grams's message?" Lee asked, shielding his eyes with the back of his hand.

"Yes." She grabbed a notepad and pencil from the nightstand drawer and propped a pillow behind her back. "She's found a way to perceive Vara's past life as an Indian child, living with her tribe. But now I have even more questions. Sorry. I have to write down my dream before I forget. In the morning, you can read what I've written. Go back to sleep."

"I don't think so. Unanswered questions have a way of weaving nightmares."

She nodded. "You're right. Okay, give me a moment." Once she finished writing, she returned the notepad to the drawer. "How about we go down to the kitchen, and I can tell you over a cup of hot chocolate?"

"Sounds like a plan." He followed her lead and threw back the bedcovers.

They dressed in their robes, strolled through the hallways, and took the stairs to the first floor. Along the way, Hayley noted the night-shift maids in the halls dusting the array of elegant antique furniture, huge mirrors, and masterpieces hung on the walls.

She remembered him telling her months ago how his and Roger's families became wealthy. In the late seventeen hundreds, a gold mine had been found on Franklin property. The Franklins partnered with the Hudsons, Roger's relatives. Using the profits from the mine, they invested in the railroads. Since then, the mine had run dry, leaving both families substantially wealthy, and their early investment in the railroad expanded with the growth of the country. This mansion, as well as Roger's, had been built with the yield from the partnership's endeavors, Lee had explained to her.

Ahead, she glimpsed the familiar black-and-white tiled hallway that connected to the enormous kitchen. Only last weekend, it had buzzed with chefs, catering two hundred guests attending the costume ball Lee threw to benefit the children's hospital. The black-and-white tiled floor continued throughout the kitchen. White ceramic tile covered the walls to the ceiling and between the white cabinets and the black marble countertops.

Lee gathered the ingredients to make hot chocolate and removed a small saucepan from the rack mounted above the island in the center of the kitchen. Once the milk heated, he served up the hot chocolate and topped it with whipping cream.

They picked up their mugs, and Hayley followed him through a doorway to a dining room normally used by the staff. They sat at the table while Hayley described her dream.

"So we've linked the *Book of Spells* to Vara, now what?" Lee asked.

"Unfortunately," she said, "Grams can only glimpse the book's residual energy, which allows her to see just bits and pieces of Vara's past."

Hayley stared into her mug and closed her eyes, allowing her psychic abilities to search for more answers. She opened her eyes and shook her head. "I can sense Vara's residual energy. She's not covering her tracks, maybe because we already know of her existence. But her mission is cloaked in mystery, so I can't envision her past, present, or future. Looks like the only information we'll get about her is what she allows us to know and what we perceive in the *Book of Spells*. Too bad. We need to connect more dots."

They rose from the table and took their mugs to the kitchen. While placing their cups into the sink, their hands touched.

Lee studied her face, picked up a linen napkin from the counter, and dabbed the traces of whipping cream on the corner of Hayley's mouth.

He kissed her lips. "I love you, Hayley Johnson."

She put her arms around him. "I love you too, Lee Franklin."

Lee feathered kisses across her neck. As his heated breath set her aflame, he loosened the belt of her robe, and his lips followed the rounds of her breasts.

In the midst of elation, Hayley froze at the sound of footsteps in the hallway. "A maid."

Lee stepped back. She covered up, pulling her robe closed and tying its belt.

He took her hand and led her out of the kitchen. They dashed down the long hallways to the elevator and ducked inside. When the door closed, Lee pushed the third-floor button, turned to Hayley, and continued caressing her.

She embraced his neck while he guided her against the wall, his kisses deep and sensuous. Beneath her robe, his hands surveyed her curves, while every cell in her body screamed for more.

He lifted her, and she wrapped her legs around his waist. "I'm going to make love to you in every room of the house," he said.

When the elevator door opened, he lowered her and took her

hand. "Room number one," he announced and led her to a guest bedroom across the hall.

Once inside, hunger filled his eyes. He turned and locked the door, then faced Hayley.

She dropped her robe.

# CHAPTER 8

In the morning, Hayley thought about the heated pleasure they'd shared the night before. Lee's home had a multitude of rooms, and the thought of making love to him in each made her giggle with anticipation.

Across the room, Lee stoked the fire in his sitting room's fireplace. Standing in her robe and slippers, Hayley glanced through the long windows encased in the tower's curved wall overlooking the rain-drenched sea of grass in the front lawn. She loved this room—walls as green as the apples on her tree at home just before they blushed red, carpet the color of the blue sky reflected in a crystal pond and drapes the shade of espresso with cream.

She turned when Lewis entered with a tray of coffee, bagels, honey, butter, and strawberry jam, and placed the food on the table next to her. After filling their coffee cups and removing the tray, Lewis stood aside, awaiting further instructions.

Lee glanced over his shoulder. "Is Jim up yet, Lewis?"

"Yes, sir. He stated he was unable to sleep last night and asked me to inform you that he's moving to Roger's for the time being."

"Has he left yet?"

"Yes, sir. He also requested placement of surveillance cameras in his room while he's away."

"Understandable." Lee added another log to the fire. "Take care of it, Lewis. Make sure the cameras cover every inch of his room." Lee replaced the hearth screen, turned, and crossed the room, joining Hayley at the breakfast table.

"Will that be all, sir?" Lewis asked.

"Yes. Thank you."

With empty tray in hand, Lewis turned and left the room.

Lee pulled out a chair for Hayley and sat facing her. He reached across the table, took her hand, and brought it to his lips. "Room number two tonight," he said with a sensuous smile. "But first we have to get to Roger's. I told him we'd be there before noon."

***

Hayley relaxed and gazed out Lee's car window on their drive to Angel Hall. The rain had stopped. Rays of sunlight streamed down through the billowing gray clouds, illuminating the colorful autumn leaves on the trees along River View.

Once they reached Angel Hall, they met Roger, Laura, and Jim in the library. When Clint and Kathy arrived, the team gathered, and Hayley told them about her dream and the conversation with Grams. Lee gave his phone to Clint to download the picture he'd taken of the underlying spell.

As their meeting concluded, Cummings stepped into the room. "Professor Matilda Rothschild to see you, sir."

"Show her in," Roger said.

A tall, slender woman with fair skin, auburn hair pulled back into a twisted knot, and wearing dark-framed glasses stood on the threshold. She smiled when Kathy, her former student, stepped forward. They hugged. "It's so good to see you again," the professor told her.

Kathy's smile broadened. "I'm so glad you came. Come join us." She led her into the library.

"I was surprised to hear from you. The last time I saw you, you had applied for that crazy job as a paranormal investigator."

Jim grimaced but didn't comment, keeping his promise to not make a scene.

"They hired me, and I'm still working with them." Kathy motioned toward the others. "These are my co-workers. The three founders of Paranormal Search and Analysis, Roger Hudson, Lee Franklin, and Jim Newton. And these are Hayley Johnson, our psychic; Dr. Laura Song, an authority on cognition and memory systems; and Roger's nephew, Clint Waverly."

"We're grateful for your help, Professor," Lee said. "I can understand how busy you must be."

She shook his hand. "Actually, I've taken a sabbatical. I've reduced my activities to giving guest lectures. A few of my engagements have canceled, leaving my schedule wide open." She turned to Roger. "Kathy told me you've stumbled across ancient writings. 'Runes,' she said. Three hundred characters or more. Does this have anything to do with one of your cases?"

"No," Roger said. "It's much more personal."

"Thank goodness. If the circumstances pertained to your line of business, I'd be called upon to exercise a choice."

"What choice would that be?" Roger asked.

"I owe Kathy my life, which is a story in itself that I won't go into. I'd hate to have to choose between damaging my reputation and turning Kathy down the one time she has asked me for help."

"You believe working with Paranormal Search and Analysis

would damage your reputation?" Roger asked.

"Yes, most profoundly."

Jim raised his fist to his mouth and coughed, camouflaging a chuckle.

"The job of interpreting in itself would not be questionable by your standards," Roger said. "The process in which they were written is."

The professor peered sharply at Kathy. "I wish you'd told me this involved the paranormal before I drove out of my way in the rain to get here."

Kathy clasped her hands together pleadingly. "You've always told me to seek and learn, knowledge is the slayer of ignorance, and an open mind leads to understanding. Please stay. We need your help."

Dr. Rothschild took a deep breath, letting it out slowly. "I won't make promises, but I'll take a look."

"Thank you," Kathy said.

"Please let me explain," Roger said, leading her and the others to the couches in front of the fireplace. "Maybe something to drink after your long drive?"

"Yes, please. Water would be fine." Matilda Rothschild sat on a couch, laying her purse beside her.

Roger grabbed his cell phone, paged Cummings, and sat across from the professor. "Several months ago, my nephew here, Clint, had a tumor removed and a plate placed in his skull. Laura, Dr. Song, was his surgeon and lead physician. After the operation, he developed some memory loss, so she recommended art therapy. While getting ready to create his masterpiece, he turned to the easel and found that he had unconsciously written two full pages of runes. This is a paranormal phenomenon called 'automatic writing.'"

"Automatic writing is a form of spirit communication," Hayley explained. "While the writer is in an altered state of consciousness, he channels the spirit energy and allows it to use his arm and hand as a tool."

"Interesting," the professor said. "So what you're telling me is that a spirit from possibly medieval times came to your home and took control of this man to write whatever this may be."

Jim glanced at Roger with an "I told you so" look.

To Hayley, the professor's sarcasm felt like a slap in the face. *Do we really need this woman, or can we rely on Annie's help instead?* Hayley asked Grams in her mind.

*Matilda has a key role in your case,* Grams replied.

*Care to elaborate?*

*Sorry. Her involvement is tied to your future, which I can't reveal.*

*Rules are meant to be broken.*

*Good try, but not this rule.*

The professor looked sternly at Kathy.

"Knowledge has no bounds, I believe you once said," Kathy told her.

"Is it possible for you to interpret the runes without worrying about how they were produced?" Hayley asked.

"If it were any other form of writing, I'd say yes. But in some cases, a runic character may have hidden meaning. It's important to know the writer's intent. To transcribe the runes to the best of my ability, I would need all the facts, believable or not."

"You'll have them," Roger said. "We'll pay you whatever fee you require. This is extremely important to us. In a few days, we should have the original pages back, but for now, we have photos. Care to see them?"

Matilda hesitated, taking a long, drawn out breath, then agreed. "Of course."

They rose, and he led her to table near the window where Clint sat in front of a laptop and continued downloading his photos to the printer. When the copies were made, he spread the pictures in sequence.

The professor studied the inscription. "Younger Futhark. A sixteen-character alphabet common in some countries from about AD 200 to 1100. It's derived from the Old Norse dialect universally well known in scientific circles. Only a person with knowledge of runes could have written this. Are you sure this isn't a hoax?"

Clint threw his hands up. "I had nothing to do with it."

Laura nodded. "I turned away from Clint no longer than two minutes. He's not acquainted with the dialect and has absolutely no expertise in writing runes. Anyway, we know the perpetrator. It was written by a spirit."

"I see." The professor straightened and faced the investigators. "I'll proceed with that fact in mind, as farfetched as it is."

"So, you'll take the job?" Roger asked.

"Reluctantly, yes — as a favor to Kathy. This may be the only chance I'll have to pay her back. I'll start with these photos, but I'll need to see the original writings."

Kathy hugged her.

"That can be arranged. Thank you," Roger said. "And there's something carved into the mantel as well." He led her to the fireplace. "It's here."

The others gathered around, while Cummings circulated with drinks, presenting the professor with a glass of water.

Roger ran his hand over the inscription. "It came to my attention shortly after the appearance of the other writings."

Matilda Rothschild focused on the carvings. "Also, Younger Futhark. I can interpret this."

"Go ahead." Roger retrieved a glass of wine from Cummings's tray and took a sip.

"Do you want details or the short of it?"

He lowered his glass. "Short if you don't mind."

"Summing it up, it's a blessing bestowed upon all who dwell in this home, protecting them from dark witchcraft or other evil."

Lee glanced at Hayley, standing at his side. "So, it's a blessing."

"Maybe," Hayley said, "but I'm sensing an underlying meaning."

The professor nodded, took a drink of her water, and cleared her throat. "Each runic character holds several interpretations and can be used with others as a secret code intertwining within the script. So what you read is not always what it appears to be."

Hayley didn't believe in coincidence. There had to be a reason why Vara would use this antiquated script instead of the language they were accustomed to reading. *But why would Vara encode secrets within the list? What could she possibly have to hide?* The whole idea made Hayley uncomfortable. *What in the world are we dealing with?*

Roger gathered the photos and handed them to the professor, who set her drink on a coaster on the end table near her purse.

While everyone reclaimed their seats on the couch, Jim stood by the fireplace, running his finger over the engraving on the mantle. "Have ya ever heard of a connection between the Vikings and American Indians?" he asked Matilda.

"You bring up an interesting subject," she said, placing the photos next to her drink. "There's a manuscript in the Annenberg Rare Book and Manuscript Library at the University of Pennsylvania. Roger Williams wrote it in 1645. He believed the Algonquin, a term used for a dozen distinct Native American tribes who speak related languages, spoke Old Norse or an older Norwegian dialect. He listed two thousand Algonquin words or phrases that sound alike in both Algonquin and Old Norse or Norwegian languages, and mean the same things."

"Did any of those Viking-language-speakin' Indians live in Massachusetts durin' the seventeenth century?" Jim asked.

"Yes. Stories from the elders of the Wampanoag tribes in Rhode Island, as well as Massachusetts, tell of Vikings mixing blood with their people about 1001-1016. Wampanoag means 'white Indian.' They're born with fair skin and many with red hair." Matilda raised a finger to her chin. "Witchcraft and runes.... If I had to make an assumption, I'd say the spirit who perpetrated the automatic writing was a Viking witch, which makes perfect sense if I were to believe such a thing."

"Would," Jim replied. "But the rune writer is an Indian maiden named Vara."

"'Vara'?"

"Yes," Lee said. "She's an Indian woman who, after her death, became a sentinel, a type of guardian angel. She told us something evil is coming. The runic writing is a list of items we'll need for protection."

With narrowed brows, Matilda looked at Kathy, seated next to her. "The thought of an angel creating spells and writing in runes is outrageous."

"My coworkers wouldn't exaggerate," Kathy replied. "I trust each of them with my life."

"Sorry," Hayley said. "We should've explained. Vara instructed us to take the original writings to a woman named Annie, who has the ability to create amulets and perform the spells. Hidden beneath the writings is another spell that can be read only by using witchcraft. The photos Lee took of the underlying spell are with the others."

"If you have someone else who can interpret the runes and has the ability to know the rune's secrets, why do you need me?"

"Havin' an angel appearin' in your bedroom and tryin' to seduce ya' is 'bout as strange as seein' Bigfoot goin' door-to-door sellin' Girl Scout cookies," Jim said. "To add to the weirdness, the angel has sent us to a witch, this here Annie, for protection. Almost sounds like a Grimm's fairytale. We need someone who doesn't have wings and never flies a broom. A person who's been recommended by someone we can trust: Kathy. Ya seem to fit the bill."

Matilda chuckled. "You have a unique way with presenting the facts, and I completely understand. Grimm's fairytale explains this situation perfectly. So what are you looking for?"

"We're hoping," Lee said, "if we can discover why she's allowing witchcraft to protect us, we'll find out what she's protecting us from."

"This is too bizarre," Matilda said.

*This woman is impossible.* Hayley relaxed, trying to calm herself. "This entire situation is difficult for all of us to believe. Nevertheless, we have to work with the evidence presented to us. Unfortunately, we only have bits and pieces to go on. When we took the runic writing to Annie, I came across a copy of a book of witchcraft spells. The original book, written in runes, was brought to this country by a Viking witch. In time, it was passed to another woman, a healer, who carried the book to Vara's village when Vara was a little girl. Eventually, the *Book of Spells* made it to someone called 'the Keeper,' a member of an Indian tribe somewhere in the hills of Massachusetts. Now Annie's the Keeper."

"I see," Matilda said. "And how are you tracing the book's

past?"

"Hayley's a psychic medium," Roger said. "She's able to visualize the past."

"Interesting," Matilda said. "In some cultures, you'd be considered to be a shaman, a term given to those who interact with the spirit world."

"Do you believe in such abilities?" Laura asked.

"I believe that primitive people's intuition played a major role in their survival. I also know that shamans have expert knowledge of medicinal plants. And some are known to use peyote, certain mushrooms, specially cured tobacco, cannabis, and other entheogens to induce an altered state of consciousness, allowing them to communicate with the spirit world."

"Do you believe in the spirit world?" Hayley asked.

"No," Matilda said with some authority. "I believe in hallucinations which contribute to myths. And that facts can be twisted and presented as truth." She lectured the team as if she were teaching a class. "During Roman times, priests used mechanical trickery to prove they were in the gods' favor. Holy men, as well, in 1856 used magic to deceive Algerian tribes to prove the Muslims had supernatural powers. In doing so, they swayed the tribes into joining their revolt against French rule. But Napoleon III matched magic with magic, hiring a magician of his own to show the Algerians the power of France. In doing so, Napoleon's magician squelched the uprising." She raised her chin. "I truly believe ignorance is responsible for belief in the paranormal and, or, magic."

*Another slap in the face.* "Interesting," Hayley said. "In that case, I'd like you to reserve your opinion of my abilities until you know me better. Until then, maybe you can consider yourself an advisor or a consultant to help us determine fact from fiction, what is feasible or unfeasible, and give us knowledge of terminology. For example, I'd like to know the meaning of a few words that confuse me — *seiðr*, *orkona*, and *volvakona*."

Matilda nodded. "I'll accept your offer. As for your clarity in terminology, easy enough. Let's start with the word *seiðr*, which roughly means the essence or act of witchcraft in the Old Norse language. In the same antiquated language, the root *kona* translates to 'wife.' *Volva* means 'witch.' Hence the meaning for *volvakona* is 'witchwife.' If it were a male, the term would be *vitki*, meaning warlock. But the prefix *or* in *orkona*, *orwife*, is a puzzle."

"Witchwife," Jim repeated, rubbing his chin. "Vara said, 'Do you not know me? I am Orkona.' Orkona, orwife…your wife," he sounded out. His eyes widened. "I'll be a lizard-lickin' jackass. My wife?"

"In your previous lifetime as Sweet William," Hayley said. "That explains Vara's knowledge of runes and spells."

"So, my past's past is catchin' up with me?"

"Looks that way," Lee said.

*How does a witch become an angel?* Hayley wondered. *That's another mystery.* Her mind wandered, recalling other times in the last few months when she'd seen a goshawk in the vicinity. *Was that Vara? How long has she been watching us?* Looking over the professor's shoulder and out the window, she noticed the rain had stopped, the darkened clouds moving toward the north. Marshmallow clouds trailed behind, sunbeams streaming between their meandering gaps. While the others questioned the professor, Hayley closed her eyes and cleared her mind, trying again to envision Vara's location and maybe get a glimpse of the danger she mentioned. But once more, she perceived nothing. When she opened her eyes, she found Lee studying her. She knew her frustration showed on her face.

Lee patted her thigh. "Patience," he said in a low voice.

She forced a small smile, turned her attention to the ongoing conversation, and recalled her dream about Vara's village, wondering if it would help to know the tribe's origins. "Is there any connection between runic writing and American tribes?" she asked.

Matilda shook her head. "The Norse and Germanic people wrote runes. American Indians never did. Although runestones have been discovered in several locations, including North Dakota, Massachusetts, and places in Oklahoma, nothing points to the writer belonging to an indigenous people. I believe, as do many others in the scientific community that the Vikings, as well as the Knights Templar, are responsible for the carved stones."

"That doesn't mean the witch didn't pass along the knowledge," Lee said.

"According to your facts," Matilda said, "she must have, considering the *Book of Spells* can be read by Annie and her relatives. As for runes used in witchcraft…. During the 1700s, in Europe, believers who provoked the magical and systematic power of the runes—using them as tools to call up deities that controlled crops, tides, love, fertility, healing, and curses—were burned at the stake. And of course, we know that the belief in witchcraft also made it to America, although the use of runes by the accused never came to light.

"Be it as it may, mystery and secrets are the true definition of the word *runes*. Some medieval runestones clearly refer to curses, oracles, and runic magic used to create amulets and other things pertaining to witchcraft. In any case, there is no proof that the Vikings' pagan magic, as well as their gods, were anything more than fabrications and superstitions born out of the necessity to explain the inexplicable."

*She needs proof that Vara exists. That might be impossible.* "In some cases," Hayley said, "the past stays a mystery."

Matilda raised a hand to cover a yawn. "Excuse me. It's been a long day." She picked up the photos from the end table, retrieved her purse on the floor by her feet, and placed the photos inside.

*Was it something I said? Is this her way of ending the conversation?*

"Did you find a hotel close by, Professor?" Roger asked.

"No, not yet. I was planning to ask Kathy for a recommendation."

"You're more than welcome to stay here."

"Thank you. I'd like that."

Roger glanced around at the rest of his guests. "Anyone care to stay for dinner?"

"I can't," Kathy said. "But thanks. I'd like to get to the library before it closes. I need to do some research on the Vikings' route to America."

"We can't stay either," Lee said. "We have reservations for dinner." He looked at the professor. "You're welcome to join us. We're dining at the Lion's Den. It's well known for its prime rib. We'll bring you back here."

"Thank you, but maybe another time," she replied.

"How about you, Kathy?" Hayley said. "The library's just around the corner from the restaurant. Bring your findings and meet us there at six."

"Great. I'd better get going." Kathy stood, retrieved her purse, and hugged Matilda. "See you in the morning. Have a good night."

# CHAPTER 9

At the Lion's Den, Kathy took the last bite of her chocolate cream pie and slid the plate to the side. She spread a map of the United States onto the table. "I've narrowed our search by following evidence and theories that the Vikings traveled down the St. Lawrence River and into the Great Lakes."

"I've recently seen programs on the History Channel discussing who discovered America," Lee said.

"Then you might know," Kathy said, "the Kensington Runestone was found in Minnesota in 1898, and recently has been dated to 1362. The stone's unique carvings and the translation connect the Vikings with the Knights Templar, who had fled Europe in the fourteenth century. After the Templar Order was declared unlawful and most were massacred in France in October, Friday the 13th, 1307, most survivors fled to Scotland, while others went farther north to what was then called Scandinavia, where they are believed to have joined the Vikings."

"This is interesting," Hayley said.

Kathy pointed to a few states. "Besides the Kensington Runestone, some runestones have been found in Maine, Rhode

Island, and Oklahoma, as Matilda mentioned. And in the 1950s, another carved stone believed to be linked to the Knights was discovered in Westford, Massachusetts, as Matilda also stated. So I've drawn a circle encompassing Newfoundland and a number of states in the United States to create a region where we can begin searching for the book's trail."

Hayley remembered her vision of the Viking witch's journey and how she'd clenched the book against her chest as if it were the most precious thing on board the ship. "I think we're going about this the wrong way. Instead of following the path of the Vikings, we should ask Grams to see if the *Book of Spells* can help us follow the witch's trail."

She and Kathy looked at Lee when his cell phone rang.

"Calm down, Lewis. Fire? Where?" Lee took his wallet out and fumbled with one hand, placing a hundred-dollar bill with the check on their table. "We'll be right there." He stuck his phone back into his pocket, stood, and shoved his chair back, almost knocking it over. "My house is on fire." He returned his wallet to his pocket and grabbed his coat and Hayley's, while Kathy picked up her things.

They hurried out of the restaurant.

***

Lee needed only twenty minutes to drive home from the restaurant. The security gates stood wide open. Once they drove through, Hayley saw flashing lights in the distance, and Lee sped up.

When Lee's car came to a halt, Lewis frantically ran to it. "Sir, please explain to the fire chief that I must have had a bad dream. This couldn't have possibly happened. But it seemed so real."

"Of course, Lewis. Let me find out what's going on first."

Lee left the car, ran around, opened Hayley's door, offered her his hand, and helped her step out. She stood by the curb, glanced toward the commotion, and saw publisher Frank Thompson snapping pictures for his newspaper, the *Sutterville Times*.

He shook his head when he saw them. "What a big waste of time," Frank called out.

"Looks like everything's under control," Lee said to Hayley.

Firefighters secured hoses onto their trucks, started engines, and turned off emergency lights.

Hayley turned to Lewis. "What seemed real?"

"One minute the place was on fire," he replied, "and the next it was as if nothing had happened. But I did see it. Max had alerted me, sounded the fire alarm so everyone could evacuate, and notified the police and fire department. Before I knew it, my room was filled with smoke, and water poured from the ceiling. After I called you, I hurried to the second floor to find the source and saw smoke coming from under Jim's bedroom door and filling the hallway. When the police and firefighters arrived, they opened Jim's door, and his bedroom looked normal."

*Witchcraft?* Hayley wondered.

The fire chief and a policeman walked up, looked at Lewis, and frowned at Lee.

"Mr. Franklin," the chief said, "apparently this has been some kind of bad joke. No laughing matter."

"Yes, yes, of course. There must have been some misunderstanding. Lewis is an honest person and doesn't pull pranks."

"It changes nothing, Mr. Franklin," the police officer replied. "It's a false alarm. Joke or no joke, there's a fine to pay."

"I understand. Send me the bill."

"We appreciate your cooperation," the chief said. He and the officer headed toward their vehicles.

Lee and Hayley walked up the drive to the home's open front door as Kathy parked. The fire trucks pulled away while Kathy sprang out of her GT, glanced around, and joined them in front of the house.

Frank Thompson, the last to leave, placed his camera into the trunk. "What happened to the cases you used to take? Why aren't you going to the office anymore? You have fans who read my paper that are eager for your ghost stories."

"Things have changed, Frank," Lee said. "We may not be going back to the office."

"There's going to be a lot of unhappy people if you don't," Frank told him.

"They'll get over it."

Frank climbed into his car and, with a scowl, sped away.

"So...what's going on?" Kathy whispered.

"False alarm." Hayley looked over her shoulder at the house and grabbed Lee's arm. "Look!"

A goshawk, wings spread wide, flew out of the doorway. Soaring upward, it circled the mansion.

*** 

Lewis led Lee, Hayley, and Kathy to the south wing. Along the hallway leading to the library, they entered the security room.

Thomas Hayes, the security guard and Kathy's love interest, sat in front of a wall supporting monitors. Computers dominated his desk. He held an icepack to his forehead and turned toward them, lowering the compress, his hands shaking.

Kathy knelt and brushed the hair from his forehead, examining him for wounds. "Are you okay, Tom?"

He blushed and winced when he smiled at her. "I'm fine, Kat. Just a little bump on the head."

"You look like you need a strong drink," Lee said.

"That sounds good, sir. This has been a nightmare."

Kathy stood up. "Jack, perhaps?"

"In my office." Lewis pointed to the adjoining door.

Kathy left the room.

While Lee questioned Thomas about the reason for the false alarm, Hayley opened herself up to the room's residual energy and gagged. She put her hand to her nose. The room smelled as if something that died in the pit of hell had recently been present. Shielding herself with white light, she left Lee's side and attempted to pinpoint the source of the horrid smell.

"I rushed in here when water started pouring into my bedroom," Lewis quickly explained. "All systems were down, and Thomas lay on the floor. I asked Velma to bring him an icepack and left her to attend to him while I ran upstairs, then outside, waiting for help. When the emergency vehicles arrived, the paramedics examined Thomas, and the firefighters ran to the second floor."

Hayley found where the intruder had stood in the corner of the room. The presence of evil almost shattered her protective shield. Layer upon layer of muddled words chattered in her mind. *"A seer?"* a woman's voice hissed. *"Slumber, vitki, but dream not of my coming to slay her Sweet William and feasting on his guts."*

*Vitki means "warlock,"* Hayley remembered. A vision came to her. She saw a woman pushing back the hood of her cloak, revealing sparse long blonde hair. Thin translucent skin stretched taut across her skeletal face, her ghastly open mouth devoid of lips, teeth, and tongue. Bile rose in Hayley's throat as she watched in horror. With her bony fingers, the witch reached out to Thomas as if cursing him.

*The monitors! She thinks Thomas is a warlock!*

His head tilted forward, and he began to snore.

With her chin raised, the witch sucked energy from the electrical equipment around Thomas. The monitors went dark one by one, their energy giving life to the ghostly apparition. Her waist-length hair turned thick and healthy. The thin skin covering her bones regained a youthful vibrancy. Full smiling lips formed around her mouth, showing perfect white teeth. Then with a flick of her wrist, she vanished.

Every hair on Hayley's body stood on end as she shivered in terror. *Had Jim been the intended target?*

Releasing the vision, Hayley quickly stepped to Lee's side.

"Did someone assault you?" Lee asked Thomas. "Did you see anyone?"

"No, sir. According to the paramedics, I'd gone to sleep, I hit my head on the desk when I fell forward, and again when I toppled to the floor. I don't remember a thing."

"We've got a problem," Hayley whispered to Lee.

"What is it?"

"You're not going to believe it, but the Viking witch did this. She came here looking for Jim. She wants to kill him."

"The one you saw in your vision at Annie's? Seriously? Kill Jim? What in the hell for?"

"I don't know why," Hayley said. "She came here first, probably drawn by the energy from the computers. When she saw the monitors, she thought Thomas was a warlock and put him to sleep so he couldn't stop her. She looked grotesque, like something you'd see in a horror movie. But after she sucked the energy from the electricity in this room, she regained her youth. Then she disappeared."

"This is damn confusing. What would a thousand-year-old ghost have against Jim? Lewis, if the system in here shuts down, would the cameras throughout the estate stop filming?"

"No, sir. If anything happens to shut down the system, the mainframe, Max, has a backup, and so do the cameras. In case something is disrupted in one area of the estate, the surveillance still continues."

Lee looked at the speaker above the file cabinet next to the door connecting with Lewis's office. "Max, systems check."

"Yes, sir," the computer replied.

"Good thing she didn't damage Max," Lee said.

After a moment, Max acknowledged, "All systems are online, sir."

One by one, the monitors displayed the estate. Jim's room appeared on the main screen. It looked the way Hayley remembered it from the other night. Nothing seemed disturbed.

"Thomas," Lee said, "rewind tonight's surveillance tape from Jim's bedroom. Play it back for us."

"Right, sir."

"Go back to seven o'clock," Lewis told him.

Kathy returned with a glass for Thomas and a bottle of Jack Daniel's Black Label. Thomas poured himself a shot, downed it, set the glass aside, and began displaying the footage on the forty-inch screen in the center of the array of monitors on the wall.

Hayley watched for signs of the witch's presence. She pointed at the monitor. "There. See it?"

"No," Lee said. "Play it back."

Thomas did.

"Watch the right-hand window's top corner. It's hardly visible, a tiny blue light."

"I see it," Lee said.

The speck of light repeatedly crossed Jim's bedroom, entered the bathroom, and darted out again to the center of the room.

"It looks like she's searching, maybe for Jim," Hayley said.

The pinpoint of light expanded into a small sphere, then grew, becoming a large bubble. A tall blonde woman lowering the hood of her midnight blue cloak stood in its center. She raised her hands. Fire streamed from her palms, setting Jim's bed ablaze.

The witch turned in a circle, igniting the dark green damask drapes at both windows. When she faced the fireplace and began setting the furniture on fire, overhead sprinklers came on, dousing her efforts. She hissed with displeasure.

"Thank God, Jim wasn't home," Lee said.

The witch's hiss grew into a curdling scream. While she spun the water into a raging funnel that reached from ceiling to floor, her blonde hair turned white, her skin wrinkling while she released her powers in rage. As the waterspout twisted in fury, Jim's charred bed and the rest of his room's furniture exploded into pieces. With a wave of her hand, the witch gathered the wreckage, hurling it into the whirling waterspout.

Hayley noticed the witch's face again become grotesque. She lowered her bony hands to her side, and the whirlpool ceased. Debris scattered about Jim's bedroom just when a goshawk ghostly entered through the windowpane. The witch looked up, became a wavering black vapor, and vanished.

Instantly the goshawk changed into Vara in human form and stood in the middle of Jim's room. Her long black hair flowed down the back of her deerskin dress when she tilted her head back and stretched her arms to the side.

Hayley and the others watched time reverse, and Jim's bedroom returned to its original state. After undoing the witch's destruction, Vara again became the goshawk and, ghostlike, flew through Jim's bedroom door.

Thomas stopped the video. "I think I'd like to give notice now."

"Please don't, Tom." Kathy touched his shoulder. "We need you. You're trained to protect this place. You know every inch of the estate. You'd know if something was wrong. We can't fight her without you."

"Don't put this on me, Kat. From the looks of it, no one can stop her."

"We have to." Lee reached for his cell phone. "I'll let Jim know about this right away."

"Yes, do so," Hayley said. "But first, I'm going to check out his room to see if I can get any insight into what just happened so we can answer his questions."

Hayley and Lee hurried to Jim's bedroom on the second floor. When Lee opened the door, the room's energy almost overwhelmed Hayley. She stopped in the doorway. Her skin tingled, and the hair on her arms stood on end. "I can't go in," she said, stepping back into the hallway.

Lee closed the door. "Why?"

"There's too much energy in the air."

"Like static electricity?"

"Yes. It's similar. When the witch cast her spell, she released negative energy. Just like static electricity, traces remain in the air. In order for me to see the past, I have to open myself up to the energy in the room. Right now, it's too overwhelming. I'll have to wait until morning once it dissipates to a level I can tolerate."

"That's disappointing," Lee said.

"Yes. But it can't be helped."

They returned to the security office.

"Kathy," Lee said, "you can stay here tonight if you want. It's late."

"Thanks, but no. I'm taking Tom home. We'll pick up his car later. What time will you be going to Roger's in the morning?"

"Sometime before noon."

Tom rose from his chair in front of the monitors and handed Lee a DVD. "I made a copy of the video to take to Roger's." He walked across the room and grabbed his coat from the rack. "I'll be back in the morning."

"Thanks for everything, Tom," Lee replied.

"Sorry you had to be involved in this," Hayley said.

"I'm okay for now. The whiskey helped. Thanks for that." He opened the door for Kathy. "Ready to go?"

"Yes." Kathy glanced over her shoulder. "I'll see you at Roger's."

Hayley and Lee followed them into the hall.

"Good night, you two," Lee said.

"Vara's probably hunting for the witch," Hayley said, watching them walk away. "Drive safe and try to get some sleep." She strolled with Lee to the elevator.

"This will freak Jim out," Lee said.

"Why don't you let him get a good night's sleep? He's going to be full of questions we don't have answers to. It's late. Call him in the morning. Hopefully, we'll know more by then."

Lee looked at his watch. "You're right. It's 1:30. Anyway, he'll need to see the video. Words aren't enough. Let's get to bed."

# CHAPTER 10

The following morning, Hayley and Lee took the elevator down to the second floor and went to Jim's bedroom. Lee opened the door and stood aside, allowing Hayley to enter.

When she walked into the room, she found the energy from last night had dissipated. Before she went farther, she shielded herself, envisioning a protective white light surrounding her.

*No trace of fire-or-water damage. Can Vara reverse time? Amazing.* She moved to the spot where the surveillance video, she'd seen Vara standing. Before opening her senses to the energy around her, Hayley surrounded herself with another layer of white light. Then she closed her eyes to perceive the lingering memories of last night, but instead, she experienced stillness, a serenity as if nothing had happened.

*Damn.* She joined Lee, who stood by the door. "Vara erased the room's residual energy," she told him.

They stepped back into the hallway.

"At least we found out one good thing." Lee closed the door. "Vara doesn't know about the surveillance equipment."

A sly smile crossed Hayley's face. "She doesn't know about

Grams either."

They strolled down the hallway.

At the elevator, Lee pressed the call button. When the elevator arrived, and the door opened, they stepped inside. "Speaking of Grams.... We should ask her what Jim did to deserve all this. And will the witch return?"

They rode to the third floor, heading to Lee's sitting room. Once inside, Hayley sat on the couch in front of the fireplace, while Lee, at the bar, poured two cups of coffee.

"We need you, Grams," Hayley called out.

Grams, wearing black skinny jeans, black boots, and a white cashmere sweater, materialized next to her.

Hayley jumped. "All this is getting to me."

"What can I help you with, dear?"

"I'm sure you witnessed what happened last night. What did Jim do to anger a Viking witch?"

"Unfortunately," Grams replied, "I don't have a clue. Not yet. Until I do, I suggest we implement Jim's idea of past-life regression."

Lee set Hayley's cup of coffee on the end table next to her and sat across from her and Grams, listening.

"Regression shouldn't be a problem," Hayley replied.

"Also, I recommend you and your friends investigate whether Vara knows or not," Grams continued. "And Annie was right. If you want to show Matilda the underlying writings, you'll have to learn how to cast the spell. You'll need practice. I'll start you off with something simple."

"Like what?"

"Something you're familiar with — residual energy. Once you learn how to place memories into an object, by using psychometry, you'll be able to determine your success."

"That's cool."

"Spells are written to help focus your intent. Take a look at the other spells in the book and try writing your own."

"If that's all I need to cast a spell, it should be easy. I've spent years learning to focus in order to control my gifts."

"Yes, dear. I believe Vara's aware of your capabilities, and that's why she requested your presence the other night. While she asked if you're a witch, I'm guessing she was able to read your mind and determine how much of a threat you may be."

"A threat? To her? Are you serious?"

"Vara, no doubt, has foreseen all your possible futures and knows what you're capable of. You could be powerful."

Hayley's eyes widened. "You know how many times I wished I was normal, like everyone else."

"Yes. And that's why you're not a threat."

"She asked about Laura and Kathy too," Lee said.

"To veil her concerns about Hayley, I'm guessing."

"What about Vara's powers?" Lee asked. "She has problems tracking the witch, and she didn't stop her from entering my home. Either Vara's powers are limited, or she's not using them."

"I have a suspicion she's holding back," Grams said. "I suspect that, because she knows the future isn't fixed, she's repeatedly choosing different plans of action and foreseeing their outcome in order to find a way to contain the evil without someone getting hurt."

"She better make up her mind fast," Hayley said.

"Do you think that witch will return?" Lee asked.

Grams shrugged. "There's no way to tell."

"That reminds me," Lee said. "I need to give Annie a call and find out when the amulets will be ready. I hope Vara's right about them protecting us. From what we witnessed, I'm more than skeptical."

"She'll call you," Grams said. "The last ingredient on the list has baffled her."

"What is it?" Hayley asked.

"Grains from a runestone."

"Does she know of such a stone?" Lee asked.

"Yes. A heavy stone was brought to her shop, and, when taken away, the bottom edge chipped. She'll find what she needs soon."

Lee raised a brow. "So, you've seen the outcome? Is she going to have the amulets ready for us before someone gets killed? Can you foresee the outcome of this entire mess we're in?"

"I can see Annie's future up to a point." Grams told him. "Once she becomes more involved with Vara, her actions will be off limits to me, just as Hildr's are. So no, I can't foresee the outcome of this predicament. That's why I'm searching for clues in the *Book of Spells*, trying to understand the way Vara thinks." She sat back in her chair. "It's all I can do for now."

"Hopefully," Hayley said, "the answers are in the *Book of Spells*. The visions you've shown me in my dreams so far have been helpful."

"For me also. One more thing, dear. If you intend to investigate, I'd suggest you introduce me to Matilda so we can share information."

"How should we introduce you?" Lee asked.

"I'll take care of that, and I promise to be sensitive."

"Okay," Lee replied. "We'll have a meeting at Roger's. I'll suggest including Matilda in our research. If she approves, we'll keep her in our employ."

Grams stood. "I'll join you for the meeting at Roger's. Warn the others not to tell Matilda I'm a spirit. I'll break it to her gently."

In that instant, she disappeared.

Hayley and Lee rose and strolled to the windows overlooking the front yard. Sunlight lit the long driveway, casting a soft glow on the Norway spruce lining both sides of the drive.

"This is disgusting," Hayley said. "My abilities are useless. I've always been able to foresee danger until now. I can't protect you or anyone else. That witch can attack us at any time, and I wouldn't see her coming."

Lee embraced her. "I love you, Hayley Johnson. That she can't destroy."

She felt his love radiate from every cell in his body. "I love you too."

He raised her chin, kissed her seductively, and scooped her into his arms. "You and I have the rest of the morning. Room number two," he said.

As he carried her out the door and down the hall, she felt a tide of longing flow through her, yearning for his heated passion.

# CHAPTER 11

Later that day, when she and Lee arrived at Roger's home a little after noon, they entered the library, expecting to find Grams but didn't see her. Jim and Laura sat at the end of the couch near the fireplace, talking with Roger, who stood by the mantle. He stopped in midsentence and hurried toward them.

"Where's Matilda?" Hayley asked.

"She's in her room, making a personal call."

Laura rose from her seat. "I'll go and get her."

"Thanks," Lee said. "We need to talk."

Across the room, Jim stretched his neck to look their way. They joined him on the couch.

"Grams plans on visiting us today," Hayley began. "She wants to ask Matilda if she'd assist her in researching Vara's past."

Roger's face paled. "Are you serious? It may backfire on us and send Matilda running to the nearest therapist."

"That's what we thought," Lee said. "We'd like to have a meeting. Grams said she'd be there, and doesn't want anyone to mention that she's a spirit. When the time's right, she'll reveal her secret to Matilda."

"Let's meet in another room," Hayley suggested. "I'd rather not fill the library with residual energy that would put a spotlight on our investigation."

"What's going on?" Roger asked. "Something must've happened."

Lee kneaded his hands, his gaze resting on Jim.

Jim straightened in his seat. "Somethin' tells me I packed my bags and hightailed it outta there just in time. What in the hell happened now?"

"You pissed off a Viking witch," Lee said.

Jim gasped. "Holy moly."

"How?" Roger asked.

"It's complicated," Lee said. "We have a surveillance video we'd like to show you." He glanced toward the door as Matilda and Laura entered.

"Good morning, Matilda," Hayley said.

"Good morning."

"We're having a meeting as soon as Kathy, Clint, and Julia arrive," Roger said. He checked his watch. "It's almost one." He turned to Cummings, who stood by the door. "We'll meet in the dining room and have dinner afterward. When Kathy and Clint arrive, please relay the message."

"Yes, sir."

Roger stood. "If you'll follow me, please." He led them to the dining room on the other side of the mansion.

"Wait for me," Hayley heard whispered before entering the room. After the others stepped inside, Hayley waited for Grams to materialize in the hallway and accompanied her inside. They sat across the table from Laura.

When Laura raised her hand to her mouth, Hayley

remembered Laura had met Grams a few months ago, and a second time when everyone else had been introduced to her not long ago at the charity costume ball. Hayley put a finger to her lips, cautioning Laura to say nothing.

Flames blazed in the fireplace centered in the ruby-colored wall on Hayley's right. Above the mantle hung a massive oil painting of Roger's father riding a black steed, while other oil paintings depicting the countryside lined the room. Across the table, the twelve-pane windows with their black velvet drapes pulled back allowed sunlight to brighten the room.

The men stood next to the fireplace talking and looked toward the door when Kathy and Clint entered. Roger hurried to greet them. Hayley assumed he explained the situation. Everyone looked toward Grams. Then they found their seats, except Roger, who stood at the head of the table.

"There appears to be a number of things going on related to the paranormal," he began. "First, I'd like Matilda to meet Julia Heartman. She has a unique perspective on historical events. You'll be working together to uncover a few mysteries involved in this case."

They greeted each other with smiles across the table.

"As you are aware, Matilda," Roger continued, "our case involves a sentinel by the name of Vara. She's been given the responsibility to protect humanity from an evil recently unleashed upon the world. In our research, we've learned that her mission is highly secretive. Vara didn't provide us with details of what or who this evil is, but by sending us to a witch named Annie, she gave us the means to create amulets. The use of witchcraft seems bizarre, but what's stranger still is she has written in runic the ingredients required for the spell, keeping what's written a secret from us as well. Because Vara has stated that our lives are in danger, all of us have agreed to investigate Vara's background in order to determine motives, and hopefully discover the evil Vara spoke of." He glanced around the table. "The video we'll be watching is from the surveillance cameras Jim had requested to be placed in his bedroom. Clint, would you mind starting the video?"

Lee passed the copy of the surveillance tape to Clint, who walked to the painting above the mantle and touched the bottom of the frame. The massive oil painting moved upward, revealing a large-screen TV.

"Before we start," Hayley said, "I want to direct your attention to the right upper corner of the video. You'll be looking for a small dot of blue light traveling to the center of the room."

Roger lowered the lights, with a remote closed the curtains, and started the video.

While the others watched Hildr conjuring fire and obliterating the room's furnishings, followed by Vara's intervention, Hayley and Lee studied everyone else's reactions. When the Viking witch showed up on the film, Jim focused on the flaming turmoil, his mouth agape. As the witch escaped and Vara entered Jim's bedroom, returning it to an undamaged state, his shocked expression froze on his face, and he swore under his breath.

After the video ended and Roger turned up the lights, Hayley watched Matilda and felt tension in the air, sensing the professor's outrage. "She'll storm out of here if we don't do something," Hayley whispered to Grams.

"It's going to be fine, dear. I'll talk to her." She rose and walked around the table.

Matilda stood, her lips pursed. She darted a heated glare at Kathy, who rose also. Grams joined them.

"Why am I here?" Matilda asked Kathy. "Am I being used as

a movie critic to see if your special effects look believable? How insulting."

"I know the video looked contrived, but it wasn't, I swear." Kathy turned to Grams. "I don't blame her. That scene had Hollywood written all over it."

A hush filled the room.

Matilda's face flushed with indignation. "This is a mockery. You really think I should believe what I just saw?"

"You know I wouldn't allow anyone to involve you in a hoax," Kathy replied.

"I'm an intelligent woman," Matilda told Grams. "How am I supposed to believe this?"

"Can you handle the truth?" Grams asked.

Matilda crossed her arms. "I'm not easily shaken. Please, enlighten me."

Grams called over her shoulder, "Roger, Matilda insists on knowing my secrets. May I reveal them to her?"

He lowered his head as if thinking about his answer, met her gaze, and nodded. "She deserves an explanation. But let her sit first, and don't go to extremes. You know what happened last time."

Matilda moved her hands to her hips.

Hayley remembered the last time too. Instead of fading away in front of the nonbeliever, Grams had aged her youthful appearance in a matter of seconds, time-lapsing into old age, causing the skeptic to faint.

"You're right, Roger," Grams replied. "Matilda, please have a seat."

Kathy stood aside while the two women sat.

For a moment, Hayley noticed an awkward silence until Grams said, "Remember, you asked for this. Try to keep an open mind."

With a raised brow, Matilda studied Grams's face. "We'll see."

"Let me start by telling you that my name is Julia, but I'm better known as Grams, Hayley's grandmother."

"Impossible. You look to be the same age."

Grams placed her hand palm-down on the table. "Watch carefully and know this isn't a trick."

Matilda nodded.

Grams's outstretched hand, beginning at the fingertips, slowly disappeared to the wrist, then gradually materialized once again.

Gasping, Matilda stared with wide eyes. "Do that again."

With her hand raised, Grams extended her index finger. It became ghostly transparent.

Matilda tried to touch the vague image. "It's not there."

Grams smiled. "Depends on the definition of the word 'there.'" Her finger reappeared.

"You're a ghost?"

"I'm a spirit, Matilda, not a ghost."

"But, you look normal, like everyone else."

"You'd be surprised at how many spirits you've seen in your lifetime without knowing it. Those who die and don't cross over remain earthbound and are known as ghosts. When I died, I walked into the light and entered Heaven. It's common for spirits to return and visit their loved ones."

Matilda shook her head. "I can't believe this. I mean, I do believe it, but it's impossible."

"Let's give it some time to sink in, shall we?" Grams said. "And I'd like you to consider assisting me with my research in this case. Please think about it. I really need your expertise."

She looked around the room at the others, all smiling, laughing, or chatting animatedly. "I know there must be more questions about the video, so I'm going to return to my seat, and we'll go on with our meeting, okay?"

"But I have so many questions. My head's spinning."

"And I'll answer them all in the following weeks. If you'll excuse me...."

Grams rose. Instead of walking around the table, she became slightly transparent, took a shortcut through the table, solidified once again, and sat next to Hayley.

Matilda, speechless, studied Grams from across the table.

"Okay," Roger said, "let's continue."

Kathy raised her hand and looked at Hayley. "You told us about how in your dream, the healer entered Vara's tribal village. Is this witch the same person?"

"No. The one we just saw is the Viking witch I envisioned when I touched the *Book of Spells*."

"Have you traced the book's entire past?" Kathy asked Grams.

"No. Because we're focusing on Vara, I'm examining only the book's memories of her."

"The book has memories?" Matilda asked.

"Yes," Hayley replied. "Holding an object and reading its residual energy is called psychometry."

Matilda glanced at Grams, then back at Hayley. "Interesting. So you and Julia have this ability?"

"Yes," Grams replied. "Once you and I spend time together, you'll learn more about me."

Jim raised his hand. "Grams, how soon will the amulets be ready?"

"There will be a short delay. Annie's having difficulty with the ingredients."

"We'll let you know when they're ready," Lee added.

Jim's brows narrowed. "She better hurry. Looks like we're runnin' outta time." He stared at Grams. "Is someone gonna die?"

"I don't know," she replied.

Jim swore under his breath.

*But it's possible,* Hayley thought. A knot formed in her throat.

"What did Jim do to deserve this?" Roger asked.

"That's what we'd like to know," Lee said.

Clint retrieved the copy of the surveillance footage and returned the oil painting to its original position, concealing the TV. He took the disk to Roger.

Roger set the disk on the table and took a deep breath. "How do we get out of this mess?"

"We're not circlin' the whirlpool yet," Jim said. "We'll have our amulets to protect us."

Hayley raised her hand. "I suggest we hire someone to perform past-life regression to take Jim back to his life when he was Sweet William."

"There's no need to hire anyone," Laura said. "I've performed regressions on several occasions while studying the paranormal and its effects on the human mind."

"How do you feel about that, Jim?" Roger asked.

"Hell, yeah. I'll do whatever it takes."

"It's settled then," Roger said. "Laura, will you need time to prepare?"

"No. I'll only need to be alone with him for a short time to put him under hypnosis."

Roger glanced at Cummings, standing by the door. "I need a voice recorder and a video camera, Cummings. Thank you."

"Yes, sir." He left the room.

Grams leaned toward Hayley and whispered, "I'm sitting in while Jim goes under, but don't let him know. In order for the hypnosis to work, he can't be distracted. I need to make sure he's regressing, and his imagination doesn't distort the truth."

"Will you be able to witness his memories?" Hayley asked.

"Yes. I'll see what he visualizes. If Laura's questions don't hit the mark, I'll still be able to learn everything I possibly can about his past-life's surroundings."

"Can I ask everyone to stand outside the door until I call you?" Laura asked.

Roger and the rest of his team left the room. When Hayley and Grams stepped into the hallway, Grams vanished.

After a short time, Laura opened the door. "Ready."

# CHAPTER 12

Jim, under hypnosis and regressed to his past life as Sweet William, sat quietly in a cushioned chair by the window, his eyes closed.

"You will only hear the sound of my voice," Laura said to him.

Once everyone gathered around, Cummings brought Roger a video camera and voice recorder.

"He's recalling memories of Vara," Laura explained.

Roger readied the camera and placed the voice recorder on the back of Jim's chair. "Okay, Laura."

At that moment, Grams materialized between Hayley and Matilda, who gasped and leaped behind Lee.

"My word, you nearly gave me a heart attack," Matilda said, her voice shaky.

"I wasn't thinking, Matilda. Sorry." Grams looked at Hayley. "It's okay. His imagination isn't interfering, so he's truly regressing."

Laura turned her attention to Jim. "When I count to three, everything surrounding you will become clear. One. Everything is coming into focus. Two. Your hearing is keen, and your sense of smell is sensitive. Three. Look around you and tell me what you see."

"The forest," Jim said, his eyes still closed, his body relaxed.

"Do you see anyone?"

"Vara and the witch," he mumbled, his words barely understandable.

"What accent is that?" Hayley whispered to Matilda.

"French."

Hayley leaned in closer, not wanting to miss a word.

"What time of day is it?" Laura asked.

"Night."

"Is it dark?"

"No. The moon is full."

"What month is it?"

"February. 'Tis the Snow Moon."

"I can hardly understand him," Hayley whispered to Roger.

"We'll have to listen to the recording later," he said in a low voice. He looked at Matilda. "Can you make out what he's saying?"

"Yes," she replied.

Laura glanced at them and raised a finger to her lips. She asked, "Do you know the witch's name?"

Jim mumbled.

Roger moved closer with his camera.

"Speak clearly," Laura instructed him. "The witch can't hear you. Do you know her name?"

"Hildr," Jim replied.

"Are you seeing what Jim is seeing in his mind?" Hayley asked Grams.

"Yes, dear. I have to concentrate."

"Relax. You're safe," Laura said. "Nothing will harm you. Why are you in the forest watching the witch?"

"We're going to kill her."

"Kill her? Why?"

Jim took a deep breath and let it out slowly. "Or she will kill me."

"Why?"

"To stop Vara from marrying me. She said Vara belongs to her."

"What's Hildr doing?" Laura asked.

"Chanting a renewal spell to regain her strength."

"Is she weak?"

"Yes. She has spent her energy causing havoc."

"What kind of havoc?"

"She put ergot in Salem's food, causing fits and hallucinations—for a diversion."

"Sounds like sixteen ninety-two," Kathy said to Hayley.

Laura asked, "Why did Hildr need a diversion?"

"To steal a child."

"Has she taken one?"

"Yes. The child is asleep in the cabin."

"Why?" Hayley whispered to Laura.

Laura nodded. "Why did she steal the child?"

"I don't know."

"That's okay," Laura said. "Is Vara still next to you?"

"No. She is gagging Hildr and binding her with witchcraft." His breathing became heavier. "I must get the coffin."

"Is the witch dead?"

"No. We must bury her alive."

"Can Hildr escape?"

"No. Vara is placing a cursed stone in the grave."

"Can you read the writing on the stone?"

"No. It's in the language of the witch."

"I think that's all for now," Laura said. "We've kept him under long enough."

Roger gathered his equipment and brought it to the head of the table.

"As I count backward from ten to one, you will slowly return to the present."

While Laura continued to bring Jim out of hypnosis, Hayley and Lee returned to their previous seats along with the others. After a few minutes, Laura and Jim joined them.

"How do you feel, Jim?" Roger asked.

"Like Jello. I'm formin' into the shape of this chair. Didn't know how relaxin' hypnosis can be."

"Did anyone have trouble understanding what was said?" Roger asked. He set the voice recorder on the table. "If so, Matilda said she can interpret for us."

He played the tape, turned up the volume, and stopped it when necessary to let Matilda clarify Sweet William's replies until the recording ended.

Grams spoke up. "He mentioned a stone. I could see it in his mind. It's the same runestone I saw at Annie's."

"So that's what they were talking about," Hayley said. "When we dropped off Clint's writings, I overheard someone say they had to move something because it wouldn't be safe in Annie's shop."

"Yes. It was loaded into a van and taken away moments after you left," Grams said. "I believe it's the one Vara spoke of being recently unearthed. But why it was at Annie's or where it is now, I don't know."

"Is there any way to track it?" Lee asked. "Maybe the spell

carved into it will give us a clue."

Matilda nodded. "I have connections. If the stone's out there somewhere, someone must know about it."

"Should we ask Annie about the stone when we pick up the amulets and the translation?" Lee asked.

"No," Grams said. "We shouldn't let her know we're aware of it or she'll ask questions. But the thing that confuses me the most is the different women in all my foreseeings. First, the young blonde Viking woman coming to America. The second, a raven-haired healer entering Vara's village. And lastly, the woman Vara and Jim buried, who resembled Vara. I'm led to believe Hildr can change her appearance and her age."

"So, you think they are all the same person?" Hayley asked. She thought a moment, analyzing the situation. "But that would make Hildr impossibly old."

"Yes, and maybe I'm wrong, but I don't think I am," Grams said.

"The kidnapping of the child sounds interesting," Laura said. "Hildr went to extremes to cause a diversion."

Grams agreed. "I'll try to find a clue in the *Book of Spells*."

"I guess that's it for now," Roger said. "Anyone who comes across anything interesting pass it along to Grams and Matilda. Anything else we need to discuss?"

Jim raised his hand. "I vote we retire to the library."

"How about lunch first?" Roger asked.

"That's the cue for me to be going, Hayley," Grams said. "Study the other spells and try to come up with one of your own to use to place a memory into an object. To save time, limit the memories to a specific event in your life. Otherwise, you'll be spending all night reliving your entire past. I'll return in the morning. My energy is low. Materializing takes so much out of me."

She said her goodbyes to everyone and walked toward the door, her image fading until she vanished completely.

***

After having lunch, Hayley laid her dessert fork across her plate and asked Laura, "Are you staying at Roger's tonight?"

"No. It's expected to storm this evening and tomorrow. The drive's too long from Roger's to the hospital. I don't want to fight the rain going to work, so I'm going home. I'm performing surgery in the morning."

Hayley turned to Lee. "I think I'll go home tonight too. I need to study the witchcraft book."

"Okay." Lee glanced at Laura. "Since I'm taking Hayley home, I'll give you a lift."

"Thanks, but my car's here, and I'll need it to get to work. Why don't I follow you and meet Hayley at home?"

"Sounds like a plan," he replied.

Laura stood and hugged Roger. "I have a tight schedule tomorrow. So, I guess I'll see you in a couple of days."

"I'll call you," Roger said, giving her a kiss on the cheek.

Hayley pushed in her chair. "I'm glad you decided to stay, Matilda. We really need your help." She looked at the others. "I won't be here tomorrow either. I have to study the *Book of Spells*."

"You're learnin' witchcraft?" Jim asked. "Facin' that butt-ugly witch with some half-baked mumbo jumbo is askin' for a death sentence. That witch will shred you like a woodchipper."

"I'm only dabbling," Hayley said. "I'm not crazy. Anyway, Grams wouldn't teach me anything that would get me killed."

A smile suffused Jim's face. "That was slicker than pig's snot the way Grams did that disappearin' act and then walked through the table. Pure genius. Made Matdie a believer."

*So he's calling her Matdie now?* Hayley watched Jim rise from his chair. "Where're you going?" she asked.

"Just chair hoppin'. Gotta a few ghost stories I wantta share with our new employee." He walked around the table and sat next to Matilda.

While following Lee and Laura into the hall, Hayley looked over her shoulder and watched Jim's mannerisms soften. *Is he flirting?* "I didn't think Jim liked Matilda," Hayley said.

Laura nodded. "That's what I thought, too. Just the other day, he said she's a snob. But today, I've noticed how he studied her from across the room."

"Knowing Jim," Lee said, "I'm pretty sure he's about to tell her 'I told you so' without saying 'I told you so.'"

Hayley laughed. "He said he's going to tell her a few ghost stories."

"It may be, but that 'I told you so' will be written on his face the entire time," Lee said.

# CHAPTER 13

Clutching the *Book of Spells* and *Basic Witchcraft* against her hooded brown coat, Hayley stepped out of Lee's SUV and said her goodbyes, while Laura exited her car parked alongside the curb. Once Lee pulled away, she and Laura walked toward the white picket gate.

Upon entering the yard, Hayley gazed lovingly at the old Victorian with its pale green siding, cream-and-eggplant trim, and gingerbread details. Overhead, the rain clouds appeared menacing. "Looks like we made it home just in time."

She closed the gate behind her and followed Laura along the walkway toward the front door when she noticed that autumn had robbed her garden of its summer beauty. The ground cover around the foot of the old apple tree had died back. The hollyhocks, white daisies, Virginia bluebells, foxgloves, and others usually lining the flowerbeds against the white picket fence now lay dormant. It made her realize how much time she had been spending at Lee's and how little she'd been home.

"Great weather for hot chocolate," Laura said.

"Definitely," Hayley replied, shivering.

They hurried up the stairs and stood under the roof of the wraparound porch just as heavy rain began to fall.

Hayley snatched the house keys from her coat pocket, unlocked the front door, and held it open for Laura. "I'll get the hot chocolate started." She hung her coat next to Laura's on the rack. "We can sit and chat for a bit before I shut myself in my room to study." On the way to the kitchen, she set the books and her purse on a hallway table.

Laura trailed her. "Why does Grams want to teach you witchcraft?" When they entered the kitchen, she went to the cabinet and pulled out two mugs. "If Grams knows how witchcraft works, why does she need to teach you? She can uncover the underlying writings for Matilda herself."

"True. It's me who wants to learn. Annie said it would only take a simple spell to reveal the hidden writings." Hayley took the milk out of the refrigerator, stirred in the chocolate syrup, and placed both mugs into a microwave on the kitchen counter.

"How will studying the spells in the book help?"

"It will give me an idea of how they're written so I can create my own."

"What kind? To do what?"

The microwave timer went off. Hayley removed the mugs and passed one to Laura. "Grams thought I could learn how to place memories into an object. It makes sense because when I cast the spell, I'll be able to touch the object and use psychometry to see how well I did."

Laura pulled a chair out from the small table against the kitchen wall and sat. "Sounds logical. Then what? Once you learn how to work a spell, will you stop there? You're not planning on doing anything foolish, are you?"

"No." Hayley sat across from her. "You and Jim must think

I'm crazy. I'm only curious. I was called a witch plenty of times while growing up, but I don't know anything about witchcraft. I'd like to get a better perspective about what we're up against, that's all. Besides, I promised Lee I wouldn't do anything stupid to accidentally harm myself before the wedding."

"And when will that be?"

Hayley wrapped her hands around the heated mug as her thoughts turned to the present circumstance. "I haven't given it a thought. There's been too much going on lately."

Laura, about to take a sip, hesitated. "Let's talk about something cheerful. I've heard enough about Vara and the witch."

Hayley remembered her birthday gift. "I almost forgot to show you." She held out her arm, her new bracelet dangling from her wrist. "Lee gave me this for my birthday."

"It's beautiful."

"Each charm symbolizes a memory, starting with my first day at work and ending with this charm representing a passport—another gift. He's going to take me anywhere in the world I'd like to go."

"Have you decided where you want to go yet?"

"No. I haven't taken the time."

She unfastened the clasp and laid the bracelet on the table. One by one, she explained what each charm represented.

Once they finished their hot chocolates, Hayley stood, gathered their empty mugs, and washed them, while Laura dried.

"I didn't realize how late it is," Laura said, glancing at her watch. "I have to get up early. When I get home from work, why don't we call Kathy? We haven't gotten together for a girl's chat night in a long time."

"Sounds like fun. I'll find out if she has plans." She picked up her bracelet.

Laura raised her hand to cover a yawn. "I'd better head upstairs."

"I'm going up myself. It may take a while to go through the spells."

When they left the kitchen, on the way to the staircase, Hayley grabbed her purse and the books from the hallway table.

Upstairs, after saying goodnight to Laura, she went to her bedroom, closed the door, turned on the lamp, set the books on the nightstand, and put her bracelet away in the jewelry box. Rain pelted the window overlooking the backyard. *The rain set off the floodlight's motion detector again.* She walked across the cool hardwood floor and stood gazing at the old oak. As rain drenched the massive tree, more leaves fell from its limbs. She could see herself as a child playing on a tire swing, hanging from a lower branch.

Her memories of growing up in this Victorian home, her dream house, had been born in her imagination during childhood when she lived down the street. She remembered the times she pedaled a bike past the house and imagined its interior — she'd envisioned the feel of the hardwood floors beneath her bare feet, the smooth surface of the railing that ended at the top landing just steps from the room she stood in now. *I couldn't have bought this without the inheritance Grams left me. Making it my own was meant to be.*

Hayley's thoughts flowed to her first case for Paranormal Search and Analysis. After that investigation, not long ago, she'd learned that what she had believed to be her fabricated memories were true. To her surprise, she, as well as her co-workers, had lived previous lifetimes together. And, she was told, she'd grown up in this house as the former owner's only son.

The sound of thunder returned Hayley's attention to the

present. She closed the drapes. Getting ready for a night of studying, she changed into her flannel pajamas, pulled back the white chenille bedspread, and propped pillows against the brass headboard.

Once between the yellow sheets, she lifted the *Book of Spells* from the nightstand, bent her knees, using her legs as a desk, then ran her fingers across the gold letters embossed in the brown leather cover. "*Book of Spells*," Hayley read aloud.

She opened the volume and flipped through the pages, peeking at the contents. *Love, memory, truth, phobias, blinding, invisibility, transformation, translocation, binding, breaking bonds.... How interesting.* She skipped to the back of the book. *Potions and Healing.*

She returned to the spells and began to study their composition. Although there were nearly a hundred, she read them all and shuddered while her imagination painted scenarios for the use of some gruesome incantations.

She glanced at the clock. *Nearly midnight. I'm sure to have nightmares.*

From the nightstand drawer, she removed a notepad and pen. She closed the book, flipped it over, and this time used the back cover for support. *Memories from a specific time in my life. How about the recent past?* After several attempts to create her own spell, she chose her last effort and read it out loud.

"Memories from June to November

"I store for safekeeping so I can remember.

"With each touch, I will recall,

"And in my mind, I will see them all."

Hayley took a deep breath, glad to put the book and her writings onto the nightstand. *I'll see what Grams thinks in the morning.* Yawning, she turned off the light and rolled over to go to sleep.

# CHAPTER 14

The aroma of coffee enticed Hayley to awaken the next morning, pulling her away from her nightmares of witches and spells. Scenarios of her worst fears plagued her recent dreams. Over and over, she had dreamed her friends had been killed or tortured by the old hag she'd seen in Jim's bedroom. This morning, she felt tired from tossing and turning all night.

She glanced at the nightstand. The books she'd placed there had been moved and replaced by a cup of coffee. Her thoughts flashed to Laura. Using her psychic ability to see the present, Hayley saw her friend performing surgery. *Laura didn't fix the coffee. It had to be....*

"Grams, you can show yourself. I know you're here."

Hayley propped a pillow behind her back and reached for the cup. As she brought the hot liquid to her lips, a bright flash in the fireplace ignited the kindling, setting the logs ablaze. With a puff of smoke, Grams materialized in the rocker by the hearth. Her blonde hair hung to just below her shoulders. She wore a lilac turtleneck mohair sweater, straight-legged blue jeans, and black boots. "I'm aware of your nightmares, dear. I'm sorry this whole ordeal is taking such a toll on you. I thought a bit of theatrics might put a smile on your face."

"It was very dramatic of you." Hayley held up her cup. "Thanks. Coffee is just what I needed."

"Yes, and you didn't flinch a bit—not even a ripple of coffee in your cup when I lit the fire. You passed your first test, total focus."

"That's it?" Hayley set the cup on the coaster, threw the covers aside, and sat on the edge of the bed.

"No, I was joking, dear. Thought creation takes time to learn."

"You mean witchcraft."

"Same thing," Grams said.

"I wrote my own spell like you suggested." She glanced around and saw the books on the dresser, the spell she'd written wedged between the pages.

"I read it, and I'm anxious to see how well it works," Grams said.

Hayley slipped her feet into the fuzzy yellow slippers by her bed and walked to the window. She pulled back the drapes and saw the clouds darkening the sky and a flash of sheet lightning on the early morning horizon.

Grams joined her. "Perfect. All this energy in the air will enable me to stay in shape, so to speak, for an extended period. It's going to be a long day—a morning with you, an afternoon with Matilda."

Hayley faced Grams. "I'm worried someone will be hurt, or worse."

Grams sighed. "I'm worried too."

*So someone could die.* Hayley's knees weakened. She walked to the bed, sat on its edge, and put her head in her hands. One by one, her friends' faces came to mind, and a tear trickled down her cheek. She looked at Grams. "Can I stop it from happening?"

"Yes. Their deaths would be considered inflicted and not meant to be." A tissue materialized in Grams's hand, and she passed it to Hayley. "That means we can stop it without interfering with their lives' purposes."

Hayley stood and paced the room. "Do you think Vara foresaw the future, and that's why she wants to protect us?"

"Yes. The difficulty I have is that each time she makes a plan to end this evil, it changes your future."

"Why? What do I have to do with all this? What does she envision herself doing?"

"That's the problem. I can't foresee her plans. As your spirit guide, I have to follow each choice you make and know the outcome it will produce. Up to a point, your future is clear, but beyond that, I believe your upcoming life will be decided by an outside force and not by your freedom of choice. Trying to figure this out is like putting a puzzle together while the picture keeps changing, and each piece takes a different shape. Without knowing what you'll be facing, I can't steer you in the right direction to avoid any pitfalls."

"Like death?"

"Yes. And if your future is somehow linked to her plans, it's bad news. I'll be just as blind as you are to your future. Whatever happens, we need to be ready to change the outcome if necessary."

"But how?"

"By doing exactly what we're doing, tracing Vara's and the witch's pasts to learn their motives and weaknesses. I feel one of the things perplexing her is how to bury Hildr again without using witchcraft. The rules she follows as a sentinel must be honored. It will be interesting to see how she intends to accomplish recreating the past without crossing the line."

"It will be interesting to know if her plans include me."

"Precisely," Grams said. "But we can't do anything except wait and see. Right now, in order for you to help Matilda in case I'm not available, I need to teach you how to uncover the hidden spell that Annie showed you."

*If only I can learn witchcraft, maybe I can protect someone.*

"That's not the reason you're learning witchcraft, dear. You wouldn't be protecting anyone, only putting them in more danger. So don't even think about it."

"You're right. Where do we start?"

"First, finish your coffee, get dressed, and we'll go downstairs."

***

In the living room, they sat on the couch.

"You're an expert at meditating," Grams said, "and you can tap into the universal knowledge to see the past, present, and future. While you are doing so, you'll notice how energy levels change as you expand your awareness. You'll also feel the faint pulse of the universe. At that moment, you must focus your intent."

"Okay. Tell me what to do."

"Clear your mind, expand your awareness, and focus on an object." Grams picked up a ballpoint pen from the end table. "The object can be anything, as you know, from your experience using psychometry. Let's just use this pen for now."

Hayley got comfortable and followed Grams's instructions.

Grams set the pen in front of Hayley. "Now, focus on the object, say your spell out loud, and think of the memory. Then say 'Be' to declare your intent while envisioning your memory flowing like a waterfall into the pen."

Hayley, remembering every detail about the first time she

and Lee kissed, did as Grams told her. *The kiss I had waited for. The one I would feel down to my toes that would arouse every inch of my body.*

She had to decide where to begin her memories: from the thank-you kiss she gave him on the plane to Hawaii in June, returned by his kiss and his promise of more to come later that evening. *Yes. That's when my passions were aroused, wanting more, hoping he'd keep his promise. Every minute of that day felt like forever, just waiting for that moment.*

Or should she start with the memories of their date that evening, dinner on the hotel balcony followed by slow dancing in the room? *My body melding with his as we swayed to the melody, my desires heightened by his sensual kisses between the musical notes.* "Be," she said, remembering each word, touch, and emotion of that evening, imagining them cascading into the pen.

She looked at Grams. "Now what?"

"Do as you always do when you search for residual energy."

Hayley picked up the pen. The memories she had placed inside played like a video in her mind. "This is cool." She set the pen down, counted to ten, and picked it up again. The same memories filled her thoughts.

"You'll need to practice," Grams said. "The stronger you focus, the farther away your target can be located."

*Practice?* Her cheeks still felt flush from the thought of Lee's kisses. *I'll have to remember something less arousing.* The memories of a meeting she attended at the Paranormal Search and Analysis office came to her—how she sat across from Lee and wondered if he could read her thoughts. Her cheeks flushed again, remembering how she had undressed him in her mind. *Stop thinking about him. The last time I thought about him strongly, I caused myself to astral project. I don't want to do that again. Think about Kathy instead.* "You said it can be anything. Can I put a memory or thought into someone else's mind?"

"Yes. I do it to you all the time."

"Grams!"

"Remember, your guardian angel is teaching me to be your guide. It's part of my job description, dear."

"Telepathy?"

"As you know, telepathy is mentally communicating with another person. But in this case, I believe you're speaking about 'nudging,' as I call it. That's when you put words or memories into someone's mind, but they'll see them as being their own ideas or imagination."

*Kathy,* Hayley thought. *I planned to call her anyway.*

"I know what you're thinking," Grams reminded her. "You'll need more practice than that. Work on storing memories. If you wish to wipe away your attempt and start over, you'll find the lesson in the twentieth chapter of *Basic Witchcraft*. Now I have to leave and join Matilda. If you need me, just give a shout."

"I will. Thanks, Grams."

*Memories,* she thought. The bracelet Lee had given her for her birthday popped into her mind. When Grams left, Hayley went to the jewelry box on the dresser and retrieved her gift. *Just what each charm is meant to hold. Perfect.*

\*\*\*

In her bedroom, Hayley lifted *Basic Witchcraft* from the top of her dresser and set it and the charm bracelet on the nightstand. Getting ready for a long afternoon of studying, she climbed onto the bed and placed a pillow between her and the headboard.

*How should I start? If I place two memories into one charm, will the second overlap the first, or will they run in sequence?* She opened her nightstand drawer, grabbed a notebook, and began jotting down the memories she planned to store in each charm. Next, following Grams's instructions, she meditated.

Hayley thought about her first day of work at Paranormal Search and Analysis, repeated her spell, imagined her memories of the past cascading into the mother-of-pearl ghost charm, and used psychometry to check the results. *The recollections are too broken up. I need to try again.* She referred to *Basic Witchcraft* to learn how to erase the stored memories and start over.

After many attempts, she found the process easier. Into the same charm, she placed her memories of Kathy describing the personalities of her new bosses, Roger, Jim, and Lee. Again she used her gift of psychometry and found the memories ran consecutively. *Good to know.* She finished with the first charm after adding her remembrances of her ghost-hunting training at Lucy's Restaurant and her ever-present desire for Lee. Then again, she read the results. *Much better.*

Into the charm resembling a sphere of Earth, she inserted her memories of the case on the island in Micronesia and her remembrances of Kathy at the Hotel Del. *Shopping with her, sharing a room, and when she told me that Lee was crazy about me — one of the best days of my life.* Over and over, she practiced until her thoughts flowed smoothly into each charm.

After the sixth charm, Hayley went downstairs to have lunch. While eating a ham-and-cheese sandwich, Hayley glanced at the kitchen phone. *Kathy. I need to call her. I wonder if I can....* She took the last bite of her sandwich and pushed her plate aside. Taking a deep breath and closing her eyes to relax, she began to meditate again. When she felt the pulse of the universe, she spoke the words, "Call Hayley," and said "Be," while envisioning the words flowing into Kathy's mind.

The phone rang.

*Kathy. Seriously? And I didn't recite the spell. I just said, "Be."* Hayley invited her over for a girls' get-together later. Then Hayley returned to her room and retrieved the bracelet. Saving time by eliminating the spell she wrote, she went through all the charms Lee had given her. Then she discovered three new ones—a bird, a witch's hat, and a book. *These weren't here before.*

*Happy belated birthday, dear,* Grams said, interrupting Hayley's thoughts. *Vara's the bird, Hildr's the witch's hat, and the book represents the* Book of Spells.

*Wow. Thank you, Grams.*

*You're welcome, dear. Just keeping your memories up to date. I'll check in with you later.*

Into the bird made of white gold, she placed her recollections of Vara's visit to Lee's home, starting with the first detection of the bird in the third-floor hallway while Jim ranted about a witch, and ending with memories of the next morning, going to Roger's home, learning about the runic writings, and the trip to Annie's.

Within the black obsidian charm resembling a witch's hat, she placed her remembrances of the fire in Jim's bedroom. She started with the phone call Lee received at the restaurant and ended with the memories of the next morning when she found Vara had erased all residual energy. She added the vision of the Viking witch, the healer in Vara's village, and the witch in Jim's regression, and made a note that they were all the same person. Somehow Hildr had found a way to become immortal.

To decide what to store in the *Book of Spells* charm, Hayley went through its pages. *It will take too long to store the entire contents, so I'll narrow it down to just the spells.* Taking her time for accuracy, she read the first spell, envisioned it cascading into the charm resembling a book, and visualized the results. Although it seemed to take forever, she repeated the technique until all the spells had been placed into the tiny golden charm.

She looked at the clock on her nightstand. In her psychic eye, she saw Laura's car turn the corner. *Good timing. I need a break.* She returned the bracelet to its velvet box, placed it with the rest of her jewelry, and stacked *Basic Witchcraft* on top of the *Book of Spells* on her dresser.

*I'd better get dinner started.*

***

Laura lifted her wine glass. "Here's to good friends."

Kathy and Hayley leaned in and the three clinked glasses.

"Do you think Vara will bury Hildr again by Christmas?" Kathy asked.

"The concept of Vara burying Hildr bothers me," Hayley said. "I'd feel better if she'd just capture her and take her to meet her Maker." She reached for a snack on the coffee table, piling cheese and ham on a cracker, then took a bite.

"But you told us Vara said that because Hildr's strength comes from the earth, so must her downfall come from the earth," Kathy reminded her.

Hayley finished chewing and took a sip of wine. "That may be. But why? And what is she waiting for?"

"I know," Kathy said.

Hayley and Laura set their wine glasses on the table in front of them, saying in unison, "What?"

"A full moon. Remember, Jim said there was a full moon when they buried Hildr."

"I think you're right." Hayley stood and hurried to the kitchen, removed the calendar hanging on the side of the cabinet by the phone, grabbed another bottle of Merlot, uncorked it, and returned. Flipping through the calendar until reaching November, she located the day of the full moon. "No wonder she gave us protection. We'll be dodging death for another ten days."

Laura shivered. "I hope the amulets work."

"So do I." Hayley reached for the wine, refreshing their glasses.

"It's commendable—Vara spending the rest of her life with William guarding Hildr's grave," Kathy said, "promising to protect humanity until she passed away. She deserved a test to prove herself capable of being a sentinel."

"I agree," Hayley said. "And her legacy of fighting against evil was passed down in her family. When Lee bought me the *Book of Spells*, Annie told me that if any of its contents were to be used maliciously, the book would return to Annie's bookshelf." She took a moment to pour herself some wine. "And if the person wanting to purchase the book was evil, they wouldn't be able to pull the book from the shelf at all."

"Can we see it?" Kathy asked.

Hayley went upstairs to her bedroom, brought back the *Book of Spells*, and handed it to Kathy. They nestled together on the couch and examined the pages as Kathy flipped through them.

"There's close to a hundred spells," Hayley told them. "I've read them all. Some are dark witchcraft. But there's a reversal spell on the opposite page for most, and I believe Vara was responsible for those. Grams told me the spells in the original book were written differently. Not only were they in runes, but each counterspell had been hidden beneath the dark spells, just like the one Annie revealed under Clint's writing."

"Does the original have the same spell protecting it from evil?" Kathy asked.

"Yes," Hayley replied. "Hildr, can't touch it."

"I wouldn't be too sure about that," Laura said. "It's Hildr's spellbook, after all. I'm sure she could find a way."

"Why would she need it?" Kathy asked. "She used it for centuries. She should've memorized the entire contents."

Laura sliced a roll of cheese, placed a piece on a Ritz, took a bite, and sipped her wine. "A person's remembrances become vague over time. After being buried for so long, she might need to refresh her memory."

"Good point," Hayley said. "Whatever we do, we can't let her get that book. I'll warn Grams that Hildr might try to steal it."

Kathy continued turning the pages and came to the spell labeled *Eternal Slumber*. "This is a long one."

"It's a spell in three segments leading to possession," Hayley explained. "It takes three days to cast, starting with sleep, followed by a coma, and then possession. Apparently, Vara or someone in her family created a counterspell to slumber, but there's nothing about how to reverse the other two."

"Understandable," Laura said, brushing a cracker crumb off her blouse. "She would've had to put someone into a coma and wonder what she would do if her counterspell didn't work."

Kathy's brow creased. "If the book has an evil-detecting spell, like you said, could it mean the book has psychic awareness?"

"I don't know how it works," Hayley said. "I do know that psychic abilities run in Annie's family. She has a gift similar to mine. Maybe when the book is opened, someone in the family is aware of the user's intentions. And maybe that someone is Vara herself."

"You think Annie and Vara are related?" Kathy asked, reaching, helping herself to a snack.

"I don't believe in coincidence. Both Annie and Jim, while he was hypnotized, mentioned the 1600s in Massachusetts. Yes, I have a gut feeling they're related, and that's why Vara didn't want us to mention her name to Annie."

"You think Vara was the Keeper?" Laura asked.

Hayley nodded. "I'm almost sure of it."

"In that case," Kathy said, taking the last cracker and piece of cheese off the plate on the table, "Vara would know you have the book."

"Maybe," Hayley replied. "And if she does, she doesn't seem to care. Grams told me the night Lee and I were summoned to Jim's bedroom that Vara really thought I could be a witch. But after she read my mind to determine my sensibility, she decided I wasn't a threat."

"Why would she care?" Laura asked. "If you were a witch, what difference would it make?"

"I asked myself the same thing," Hayley said. "Maybe she believes I'd foil her plans — that is, if I could foresee her plans — which she knows from her divine insight that I can't."

"And that's unfortunate," Laura said, finishing off the last drop of her wine and setting the glass down. "We're helpless without the amulets. When will we be getting them, anyway?"

"Tomorrow," Hayley said. "Lee's picking me up in the morning."

Kathy looked at her watch. "It's getting late."

"I'd like it if you stayed the night," Hayley said. "After what happened at Lee's, none of us should be alone."

"I'll be fine," Kathy said. "If we were in that much danger, Vara would've made sure we had the amulets by now."

"I hope you're right," Hayley said.

# CHAPTER 15

In the morning, Hayley climbed into Lee's SUV, and they headed to Annie's once again. At higher altitudes, they kept the car's heater running while snow hitting the windshield melted on impact. Lee drove his vehicle along the curved mountain road until he came to the small town they had passed through before. Beyond the boarded-up gas station with its rusted tin roof, about a mile down the road, he pulled into Healer's Hollow.

"I'm not sure if Annie can read minds," Hayley told Lee, "but in case she can, don't even think about the runestone or our investigation."

"Got ya," he replied.

Lee climbed out of the vehicle and ran around to the passenger side to open Hayley's door. When she stepped out into the cold, Hayley wrapped her scarf snuggly around her neck, adjusted her coat while her long hair whipped in the icy wind, and pulled up its hood. The drizzling snow stuck her face as she tailed Lee to the shop's entrance. Once under the leaky porch roof, he held the door for her and followed her inside. The dramatic difference between the snow-chilled mountain air and the temperature inside Annie's shop sent tremors of warmth through Hayley's body.

"Please, hang up your coats and stay awhile," Annie said from behind the counter.

Lee removed his fur-lined leather gloves, stuffed them into his pocket, and hung his jacket next to Hayley's coat on the rack by the door.

Hayley rubbed her hands together to warm her fingers, walked to the counter, and noticed the lid of the large pickle jar had been removed. Fear struck her. The hairs on the back of her neck stood on end. She nervously looked around.

"Lovely's been taken," Annie said. "She's my familiar." Her tears welled. "I looked everywhere. She's gone."

"Why wouldn't they take the whole jar?" Hayley asked. "Would whoever it was just reach in barehanded, or maybe they wore gloves?"

"You tell me," Annie replied.

Hayley's fear of a spider on the loose melted away, but her arachnophobia prevented her from touching the jar to envision Lovely's whereabouts. "I'm sorry for your loss. I wish I could help, but the thought of spiders terrorizes me."

"Thanks. But your abilities wouldn't help anyway. Whoever it was didn't leave a trace." Annie took a deep breath and let it out slowly. "I'll get your amulets. I'll be right back." She disappeared behind the curtained door.

Hayley heard Grams's voice in her mind. *I'm going to take a look at the original* Book of Spells *while we're here.*

*Okay. We'll keep Annie busy.* Hayley whispered Grams's intentions to Lee.

Annie returned, carrying the runic writings and a brown paper bag with handles. She placed the bag at arm's reach, unrolled the writings, and spread them across the glass countertop. "Have you been practicing?" she asked Hayley.

"Yes." She sensed Lee looking over her shoulder.

"Good," Annie said. "Let's see how well you did. First, you must be aware that the spell cast upon the writings sits like a dog waiting for your command. Speak to it with a clear vision of your desired outcome. Picture in your mind the words on the page vanishing and the underlying spell revealed."

"What should I say? Hopefully, a spell in English that I can pronounce."

"Just saying 'Reveal' should do it."

Hayley took a moment to clear her mind and, following Grams's and Annie's instructions, she expanded her awareness, felt the pulse of the universe, focused her intentions, and said commandingly, "Reveal." Her eyes widened when the runic characters on the page melted away, revealing the underlying writings.

A smile lit Lee's face. Hayley beamed.

"You're a natural," Annie said.

"So all your peers who teased you as a kid were right," Lee told Hayley. "You're a witch."

The prickling memories of Hayley's youth sprang into her thoughts, but she realized Lee meant well. He was buying time, and this might be a subject Annie could relate to. Hayley decided to play along.

"Why did people call you a witch?" Annie asked.

"When we were here last," Lee said, "we told you about the abilities of the woman who sent us to you. But we didn't mention Hayley's gifts to see the past, present, and future, as well as seeing and speaking to the dead."

A smile crept across Annie's face. "So we're cut from the

same cloth, it seems."

Hayley took a deep breath and released it. The memories of her past dampened her mood. "Kids can be cruel." She met Annie's gaze. "How did you fare growing up? Was your childhood painful?"

"No. I have lots of brothers and sisters with talents of their own. Did any of your ancestors have the same abilities as you?"

"Not that I know of." *Except Grams.*

"Sad. I believe I told you that witchcraft in my family has been practiced as far back as the late sixteenth century, when Vara Little Deer, my Native American ancestor and the Keeper of the *Book of Spells*, married a French trapper named William Depaul. Now, in my generation, we pass the knowledge to our children."

"You have a remarkable family," Hayley said. *I'm right. Vara was the Keeper,* she shouted in her mind.

*And I found something interesting myself,* Hayley heard Grams say telepathically. Hayley glanced at the bag of amulets on the counter, then back at Annie. "Is there anything we need to know? Maybe something we should say to activate them?"

"No words are necessary. Their defense shields are in place, and they're ready to protect." She rolled up the runic writings and set them down with their order. "Thank you for bringing the writings to me. It's been a delight I will not soon forget."

"Did you translate the script?" Lee asked.

"Oh, yes. I almost forgot."

She stepped into the back room. Annie returned, placing a yellow folder containing a few pages with text written in English into the bag. "If there are any questions about the translation, the ingredients, or anything else, please let me know."

Lee shook Annie's hand. "Thanks. It's been a pleasure talking with you." He helped Hayley slip into her coat, put on his own jacket, and grabbed everything from the counter, passing the bag to Hayley.

"With you as well."

"It's been extremely interesting," Hayley told her.

"Keep practicing. You're very talented," Annie replied.

"Thanks again." Lee pulled open the door, and they left the shop.

Although the snow had stopped falling, the wind continued to gust. Hayley flipped up her coat's hood, pulling it snug around her neck. On the ground, the melted snow had begun to turn to ice. Watching her step, she hurried to the car to get warm. Lee opened the passenger door of his SUV.

"I was right. Vara and Annie are related." She slid inside and took the rolled up writing from him. "And Vara was the Keeper of the *Book of Spells*."

"That answers a few questions." Lee shut her door, jogged around to the driver's side, climbed in, and started the engine. "I'll have you warm in just a minute." He adjusted the heat. "Did Grams find anything?"

"Yes," Hayley said, setting everything on the floor by her feet. She heard Grams's voice in her mind.

*Tell Lee to call Roger and gather the team. I'm in luck. Matilda's napping. While she's asleep, I'll slip the information into her dreams. As for you, rest your eyes. Simultaneously, I'll play back the memories I found within the pages of the book so you and Matilda can view them.*

Hayley told Lee as they drove away, "Grams found something in the book. I guess it's a lot of information because she wants to show me in a dream. So I'm going to take a short nap. Meanwhile, you're to call Roger and tell him to arrange a meeting."

"Right."

Hayley closed her eyes. Once Lee had completed his call, she relaxed, listening to the hum of the car's engine, and cleared her mind. While in a meditative state, she began to doze.

In a dream, Hayley saw a young child, Vara, peeking into a hut, the *Book of Spells* lying next to a sleeping little girl. "Sihu, Sihu, the clouds go over the mountains, and the lightning follows. You must wake." But the girl didn't move.

Vara gazed at the ground as the ash-haired woman brushed past her, entering the hut. Tears streaked down Vara's brown cheeks while she listened to the woman chant an incantation. Sihu's eyes remained closed, and her breathing shallow.

Then Hildr lifted Sihu's head, poured liquid into her mouth, stood, and began to leave. She hesitated at the doorway, glanced at Vara, retraced her steps, and snatched up the *Book of Spells* before exiting.

Vara followed Hildr to the chief's hut. Through a gap in the deer hide hanging across the entrance, Vara watched in silence.

"Your daughter will die tonight," the old woman said, sitting across from the chief. "I am old. My powers are greatly diminished. I have pleaded with the ancestors to take me instead and let her live in good health."

"Have they given their answer?" the chief asked.

"Yes. I will sleep next to Sihu. When the sun rises, you will know the ancestors' decision."

Hayley's dream flashed ahead in time.

In the morning, within the little girl's hut, two young bucks lifted a body wrapped in deerskin and carried it away. *Is it Hildr?*

A maiden waited in the hut while Sihu ate. When she finished, Sihu handed her the empty bowl, and the young woman left.

Vara's face beamed when she ran inside. "Sihu, Sihu, the sun shines, and you are awake."

Sihu smiled, her hand moving to her hair. Staring at the hand movements, Vara gasped. From a vision she'd seen before, Hayley knew that Vara had mimicked that hand gesture over and over while watching the old woman in the woods.

"How can this be?" Vara asked. "You live in Sihu's skin. What have you done to my sister?"

The old one looked at Vara through child-eyes the color of smoke.

Vara stumbled back.

Hildr lowered her hand from her hair. "You are a smart child." She glanced at the *Book of Spells* and smiled a little more sweetly. "I know your dreams. You wish nothing more than to wield the lightning and know my powers. I will teach you if you hold your tongue."

Vara stared at the new persona, who used to be her sister. "Bring Sihu back."

"Your sister sleeps and will never awaken. Her body belongs to me now. Think of what I offer. You know of my powers." She gave Vara a frosty glare. "You have no choice but to please me."

Vara's tears welled. She wiped her wet cheeks with the back of her hand, bit her bottom lip, and took a shaky step forward. "If I do not speak of this, you must teach me all you know, but also give oath that you will never harm me."

Hildr nodded, made a sign with her hand, and spoke words Hayley had never heard. "The spell is cast and binding."

Hayley's dream ended. She woke and looked at Lee. "I can't believe it. When Hildr gets old, her spirit sheds her body, enters a child's, and takes it for her own. Hildr's old body dies, but Hildr survives, living from childhood to old age, jumping from child to child, living endless lifetimes."

"Possession?" Lee asked, looking for traffic while getting

onto the Interstate.

"More than just a possession." She told him the details of the memories stored within the pages of the book. "Even though she doesn't kill her victims, she basically takes their lives. She puts the child into some kind of coma. The spell she uses enables her to step out of her own body and into the little girl's. Then Hildr takes control."

"Like a driver switching cars."

"Exactly," Hayley replied. "And the child's in the backseat or, more likely, the trunk."

"So, does the child live in the trunk forever?"

"Yes. In an endless sleep until her body's death."

"And Vara's been trying to stop her from finding another child," Lee said.

"I believe so. Now we know for sure how Hildr was able to be the Viking witch, the healer in Vara's village, and the witch in Jim's regression. She's lived for centuries. Can you imagine that?"

"Vara's got her hands full."

"Yes," Hayley said. "She's not allowing Hildr to have enough time to find a child and perform the necessary spell over three days. I think Hildr's attempts to kill Jim are just a distraction to sidetrack Vara."

"Or vice versa," Lee said. "Maybe Vara's distracting Hildr."

"That's possible too. Now that each of the team gets an amulet, Vara can concentrate on capturing her."

"That's right," Lee agreed. "The only thing left to answer is why Vara wrote the ingredients in runes. Kathy thinks Vara used them to involve Annie in order to avoid using witchcraft herself. And she believes whatever Vara has planned will happen during the next full moon eight days from now."

"That may be. Jim mentioned a full moon in his regression. So Vara intends to use Annie to bury Hildr."

"Looks that way," Lee replied.

# CHAPTER 16

Lee and Hayley drove straight to Roger's. Six miles from Angel Hall, Grams interrupted Hayley's thoughts.

*Vara's at Roger's. She waits for you to bring the amulets to the others. When you get there, go directly to the library. The others, except Laura, are already there. Matilda and I will watch on the surveillance monitors in Roger's upstairs sitting room.*

Hayley relayed the message to Lee.

\*\*\*

"The evil I had spoken of is a powerful witch named Hildr," Vara said, in human form, wearing a sleeveless buckskin dress and standing in front of the hearth in Roger's library. "Time is essential, Hayley. Please hurry to give each an amulet. Hildr could be watching us as I speak."

Hayley gave each of the team an amulet: a small two-inch-long glass capsule filled with the items on the rune list, sealed on each end with silver caps, and hung on a long silver chain. "Here's one for Thomas," Hayley said, passing it to Kathy.

"He's out of town tonight. I won't see him until tomorrow while he's at work. We're having lunch on his break. I'll give it to him then."

"He'll need it sooner than that," Hayley said.

"All right. I'll take it to his place and give it to him before he goes to work in the morning."

Hayley handed an extra one to Roger to give to Laura. "Will you see her before I do?"

"I'll see her tonight," he told her. "I'll give it to her then."

"Good to know." Hayley returned to her seat next to Lee.

"You must wear these at all times," Vara explained. "The energy from each item within will disrupt and dispel any curses Hildr may use to assault you. Never remove them, even when bathing. Until I expel Hildr's spirit from the face of the earth and imprison her for all eternity, you cannot take these off."

Kathy put Thomas's amulet into her purse, picked up her notepad and pencil, and began taking notes.

"I still don't get it," Jim said, hanging his amulet around his neck and stuffing it under his shirt. "Why's she after us?"

"She's after you, Sweet William, and to quench her wickedness, she will drink the blood of your friends."

Jim cleared his throat. "I've been meanin' to tell ya for some time that I'm not Sweet William, and this is a big misunderstandin'."

"I know in this reality you are Jim," Vara said. "But in another lifetime, you were my Sweet William. Who you are now means nothing to Hildr. To her, your soul is as much Sweet William as you are Jim Newton. In this matter, she is correct. You helped me kill her flesh and bind her soul. She cannot harm me now that I am a sentinel, but she knows if she captures your soul, she will crush my heart, and I will live with this heartache for eternity."

Jim frowned. "But—"

"I spent twenty-five years with Hildr. She confided in me

and taught me well. I had grown older while Hildr taught me all she knew. My time to have children had nearly passed. I met Sweet William, a trapper, in Salem, and fell in love for the first time. Hildr forbade it and threatened to kill him. But her powers had waned. I knew this. Over the years, each time Hildr used her *seiðr*, a toll was taken, her energy weakening, her powers failing. It was then, during her weakness, before she could regain her energy, that Sweet William and I planned her death."

"But my friends had nothing to do with it," Jim said. "What can we do to stop her?"

A sadness filled Vara's eyes as she paced in front of the fireplace. Then she said, "Hildr can do little as spirit. She must materialize in order to use her seiðr, but once she does, her energy will deplete, and she will lose solidity. I must capture her before she becomes flesh and blood, or she will be lethal. I will stop her evilness, I promise."

"What types of powers do you mean?" Lee asked.

"Spirit journey, shape-shifting, prophecy, control over weather-and-animal movements, altering minds, creating illusion, madness, and forgetfulness. These are but a few."

"Holy moly," Jim said.

"How old is she?" Kathy asked. "Where did she come from?"

"I can place her in her first life during the time when their king and the church forced Christianity on Hildr's people—the Vikings, you call them."

"There is written evidence," Kathy said, "that the Vikings combined their pagan beliefs with Christianity and became known as Celtic-Christians."

"Yes, but Hildr, a *völva*, denied this faith, and in the mountains, she hid in a cave while strengthening her *seiðr*. Once, while spirit traveling, Hildr happened upon a young girl, ten years old at most, who lay in a coma. This was when Hildr's spirit slipped into the young body and took control. It was then that Hildr recognized the possibility of transmigration, allowing her to live another life. By trial and error, she found a method to induce a coma, the body left without paralysis. This secret she did not reveal to me."

Hayley gasped. Kathy paled.

"Who would allow her to do such a thing?" Lee said. "Didn't the villagers know?"

"No one knew of the possession," Vara said. "Everyone believed the child recovered from her illness. While the possessed girl grew, Hildr kept her powers hidden. Nothing seemed unusual. Over time, the villagers believed her to be a revered healer."

Kathy scratched her head with the eraser end of her pencil. "I need a few more facts before I can pinpoint an age."

Vara touched a finger to her lips and nodded. "During that time, the Church condemned the Knights Templar for heresy. 'Tis then the king of France ambushed and decimated most of the Knights Templar, and placed a bounty on the heads of the survivors."

"That was Friday, October 13, 1307," Kathy said, looking up from her notes. "I believe that's where we get our belief that Friday the 13th is an unlucky day."

"Some knights with blood ties to the Vikings fled," Vara explained, "finding refuge with Hildr's people. Together they voyaged from Greenland to Newfoundland and throughout the Americas, as they are called now."

*Exactly,* Hayley thought.

Vara continued. "This was the time of Hildr's escape from Christianity. In her first transmigrational life, as a blonde-haired youthful healer in her teens, she traveled with her people and the Templar to the coast of what now is called Nova Scotia. From there, she migrated to what is now America."

Kathy made a few calculations and looked up from her notes. "I read about the Templar's connection to the Vikings. On a rock in Westford, Massachusetts, there's a carving of a man dressed as a Knight Templar. It's believed to represent Sir James Gunn. He died there one hundred years before Columbus was said to have discovered America."

"Yes," Vara said.

Hayley noticed Kathy adding and subtracting the years.

"So she came to America and kept killin' children," Jim said. "Disgustin'. No wonder we murdered her."

"Yes," Vara said. "Hildr possessed my sister, Sihu, and took her life."

Hayley felt stunned. *When she killed Hildr, she also killed her sister.*

Jim's eyes widened as Hayley believed he came to the same realization. "Ya mean to tell me we killed your sister?"

Vara took a deep breath, letting it out slowly as she stared upward. "Hildr took her life. The spells she cast prevented Sihu from wakening. Her thoughts and memories were taken from her." She smiled at Jim. "We did a good deed. When Sihu's body died, her soul was released and rose to Heaven. We didn't kill her, we freed her."

"I understand," Jim replied.

"I had no time to mourn when Hildr took Sihu's life when we were young, for as swiftly as a deer runs, a sickness swept through my village, killing my family and all who remained there. Hildr surrounded herself and me with protection, and we survived the illness by fleeing. I pleaded with her to save my people, but she said her *seiðr* was not great enough."

"The old mucus-faced hag," Jim said, his fist clenched.

"Over twenty years passed before she misspoke, forgetting where she had met me. After killing many tribes to the east for her pleasure by conjuring disease, she reminisced about the peoples she had once slain with the same sickness — my people."

Kathy nodded. "Our history states that the settlers who arrived in Massachusetts in 1620 brought the disease, which annihilated the indigenous tribes."

"Yes, it appeared so, for Hildr's *seiðr* was not perceived. I know not what year we placed her in the earth. The people who came to our lands from over the ocean had divided. Some joined with warriors from the tribes to the west and killed all who lived in the farmlands of Salem. This town, I know, for it is there that Hildr cast spells and created havoc."

"The Salem Witch Trials, 1692," Kathy said. Hayley remembered Jim had mentioned that as well while in regression. "I've got it," Kathy declared. "If Hildr was around eighty when she left her own body before she took her very first victim, a ten-year-old child, I'm figuring Hildr's somewhere around eight-hundred years old, give or take a few decades."

Vara nodded. "Now, I must leave to find Hildr." She began her transformation into the goshawk, but before Vara completed her metamorphosis, she warned, "Hold your amulets close."

She finished transforming, passed through the library windows, and flew into the early evening's gray sky.

Hayley looked up at the surveillance camera. "Grams, you and Matilda can join us now. We'll meet you in the dining room."

*** 

Roger stood at the head of the table and began the meeting. "Grams, would you like to fill us in on what you've learned?"

"Thank you, Roger." She told about the recent memories she'd found within the *Book of Spells*. "Layer upon layer of residual memories of those possessing and using the book led me to believe it had been passed down, until I found out Hildr's secret. I know now that she can be any of the women I envisioned throughout the pages."

"This was the first time she mentioned exactly what danger we face," Hayley said. "And something surprised me. She said she had to leave to locate Hildr." She looked at Grams. "Are we sure Vara's a sentinel? She should have the ability to know where Hildr is at any given moment, I would think."

"Yes," Grams replied.

"We were probably just a momentary distraction," Roger said. "But why she hasn't captured Hildr yet still baffles me. However, I have a theory. She might've been given the mission to only stand watch and alert the upper echelon of angels if the witch escaped back into the world. If that's the case, she's failed to follow instructions. But why?"

"Are you saying we shouldn't trust her?" Lee asked.

"Hold on," Jim said. "Don't start jumpin' to conclusions. Vara hasn't given us any reason to believe she's a danger. She's gone clear outta her way to make sure we're safe, or she wouldn't have given us amulets. Maybe she might think by capturin' Hildr she can prove herself worthy of bein' a full-fledged sentinel."

"That may be, too," Grams said.

"Shoot," Hayley said. "I forgot to ask her why she wrote the amulet ingredients in runes."

Matilda raised her hand. "I contacted a colleague, a state archaeologist in Massachusetts involved in the discovery of the stone Vara had placed on Hildr's grave. During construction, an old oak tree had been uprooted, and workers unearthed a runestone beneath it. They called him to the site, and he had the stone transported to a lab for further study. After workers excavated the site, they uncovered the remains of a female Indian. The Bureau of Indian Affairs became involved."

"They found Vara's sister's remains?" Sadness suffused Hayley as she thought about Sihu's shortened life.

"It appears so," Matilda replied. "With the consent of the BIA, experts conducted further skeletal analyses and determined the stone to be connected to the burial — which we already established. But during the process of dating the stone's inscriptions, the stone mysteriously vanished."

"Like poof, and it was gone?" Jim asked.

"No. It disappeared after the lab had been securely locked. No evidence of a break-in was reported, and an investigation is underway. I kept quiet about our knowledge of the stone being stored at Annie's shop. Julia and I believe someone in the Bureau of Indian Affairs knows of its present location. Julia suggested I go to Massachusetts and snoop around. She believes I'll find a lead to its whereabouts. So I've booked a flight for seven tonight."

Jim patted his pockets and pulled out his car keys. "I'll drive ya to the airport, if ya like."

"Thank you, Jim. I'd like that."

"No problem, Matdie."

Hayley glanced at Lee and whispered, "'Matdie'?"

Lee shrugged. "I wouldn't make anything of it. Jim's been a crazy man lately. One minute he's praising her, and before he can take a breath, he's calling her hardheaded."

Roger looked at his watch. "Anything else we need to discuss?" No one raised a hand. "Okay," Roger said. "Let's adjourn. I promised Laura I'd take her to dinner."

"Speakin' of Laura," Jim said. "I saw ya comin' out of London

Jewelry in Sutterville yesterday. Lookin' for something special?"

"What were you doing in town?" Roger asked.

"Don't change the subject."

Roger crossed his arms. "You're the town crier. Why should I tell you?"

Clint glanced at Jim's surprised expression and snickered. Kathy giggled.

Jim put his hand to his forehead and closed his eyes. "My psychic powers tell me you're plannin' a proposal." He opened one eye and peeked at Hayley. "No mockery intended."

"No insult taken." Hayley tried not to laugh.

He opened his other eye.

Roger unfolded his arms and darted a glance at Hayley. "Looks like the possum's outta the sack."

"Don't look at me," Hayley said. Relief swept over her. She and Lee no longer had to keep her psychic knowledge of the couple's impending wedding a secret. She whispered to Lee, "Funny how things work out."

Lee smiled. "It was hard keeping my mouth shut."

"Told ya, I'm psychic," Jim said.

"You're just a damn good guesser, that's all," Roger told him. "And no, I haven't found what I want." He looked around at everyone. "Promise, no one say anything to Laura or give any hints. I haven't bought a ring yet."

"What are ya waitin' for, Christmas?" Roger's eyes widened. He glared at Jim. "I'm right, ain't I?" Jim asked.

"We're not here to discuss my private life," Roger said. "Meeting adjourned, and remember what Vara said, 'Don't take off your amulet for any reason.'"

"I'm leaving now," Grams said. "Have a good evening. I'll keep in touch." She strolled around the table, spoke to Matilda, and turned to leave, evanescing with each step she took toward the door.

"I guess we should leave, too," Lee said to Hayley. "I've made reservations at D'Avanti's. We need to take time out from this madness and concentrate on our own wedding."

"I'd like that."

They met Kathy at the door.

"Thomas is in as much danger as the rest of us since Hildr believes he's a warlock," Lee told her. "Hildr might think he has the answers to Sweet William's whereabouts."

"I'll call and check on him when I get home," Kathy said.

"I can help with that." Hayley used her psychic ability to locate Thomas. "Everything's fine. Thomas is surrounded by family. He's a good man, Kathy."

"He is," Kathy said. "I'll call him anyway. I'd like to hear his voice. Well, good night."

While Hayley watched her walk away, she felt uneasy. "Wait." Kathy turned. "Why don't you stay the night at Roger's or Lee's so you won't be alone?"

Kathy pulled her amulet out from under her sweater and held it up to Hayley. "I'll be okay. I'm putting my trust in Vara." She turned and walked away.

"I'll use my psychic ability to keep an eye on everyone," Hayley said, "like I did checking on Thomas. It will ease my mind."

"I thought you had a problem foreseeing our futures," Lee replied.

"You're right. I'm limited. But the present isn't the future. It's the here and now. Unless Vara blocks my abilities for some reason, I won't have a problem."

Roger joined them before they stepped into the hallway.

"Laura wanted me to remind you that she'll be staying home tonight."

Hayley hesitated at the top of the stairs with Lee. "She won't have to worry," she told him. "I'll be there shortly after dinner."

"And I'll see Thomas in the morning when he comes to work," Lee said. "We'll set up a plan for Kathy so she won't be alone anymore."

"She's welcome to stay with me and Laura." Hayley placed her hand on her blouse, feeling the amulet hanging beneath. "We can look out for each other and make sure we keep these on."

"Maybe she'll consider the idea," Lee said.

Hayley walked with Lee down the staircase and through the hallway to the foyer, where Cummings retrieved their coats. When she stepped outside, Hayley noticed the sun would be setting soon. She nervously glanced around. The thought that Hildr could be watching their every move sent a quiver of anxiety throughout her body.

***

At D'Avanti's, Hayley and Lee sat at a window table facing the deck, which ran to the edge of the lake. The November nights had become too cool for Hayley to sit outside and, by the looks of the deserted patio, for others as well.

She and Lee watched the sunset beyond the trees. A break in the storm had left a semiclear early evening sky. Over the canopy of the pines, shades of pink, gold, and red tinted the clouds to the west.

She set her knife and fork across her empty dinner plate, then, with a linen napkin, wiped the traces of chicken Marsala from her lips.

The waiter cleared their dishes. "Would you like me to warm your coffee?"

Hayley looked at her half-full cup and shook her head.

"No, thanks. We're fine," Lee said.

Once the waiter turned away, Lee reached across the table and took Hayley's hand. "I have an idea I'd like you to consider."

"What is it?"

"What do you think about asking Roger if we can have a double wedding?" Lee sat back in his chair and chuckled. "I can't remember doing anything major in my life when Roger hasn't been right beside me. It would be great to share our wedding day."

"I think so too." Hayley sipped her coffee. "Remember, I foresaw that their wedding will be in June." She set her cup down. "But Laura has to decide on the month and date. If I influence her, she'll think I planned the timing in order for my prediction to come true."

"Did your clairvoyance show the location?"

"No. Now that you mention it, I only glimpsed them kissing as man and wife. If I had seen more, I might've witnessed my own future."

"Which I'm more than thankful you're not able to do," Lee said.

"Me too. You couldn't have surprised me more when you proposed. I wonder how Roger will propose to Laura. I hope he's not serious about waiting until Christmas."

"I'll speak with him and see what he's planning," Lee said.

"That reminds me...I need to see if Kathy made it home all right. Give me a minute." Hayley closed her eyes, cleared her mind of disrupting thoughts, concentrated on Kathy's whereabouts, and envisioned Kathy on the phone, talking and laughing with Thomas. "She's fine."

"Great to hear. How about Jim?"

Hayley focused on Jim and envisioned Matilda and him at the airport. "They're saying their goodbyes before she boards the plane. Jim's telling her to call him to let him know she made it to Massachusetts okay." Her vision ended.

"Let's go." Lee picked up the check. "I'll take you home. Laura's there alone."

# CHAPTER 17

When Hayley woke in the morning to the sound of rain pelting her bedroom window, she looked at the clock. *Nine. I didn't want to sleep so late.* She noticed the silence and remembered that Laura had to leave early for work. Hayley climbed out of bed, grabbed her cell phone from the nightstand, tucked it into her pajama pocket, and went downstairs to the kitchen.

After having breakfast, she sat at the kitchen table, relaxed, and closed her eyes to use her clairvoyance again to check on the others. Instead, she heard Vara's voice telepathically speak to her.

*Hildr has taken Kathy. I cannot act. I must wait for the right moment, or Kathy will die. Do nothing. Hildr is dangerous. I will contact you and your friends.*

A vision followed. In Hayley's mind, she received an image of Kathy, who wore her red parka over blue jeans and a white sweatshirt, her hair in a ponytail. Kathy walked to her car and climbed in. When she turned the key and started the engine, she glanced into her rearview mirror and looked over her shoulder to back out of the parking space. That's when Hayley saw Hildr's spirit sitting in the backseat.

Kathy did everything she was told.

Hayley gasped. *Is she under Hildr's spell?* Adrenalin rushed through her veins. Panic, frustration, and helplessness filled her. "Grams," she shouted.

*I'm on it*, she heard Grams reply.

Hayley grabbed her phone and called Kathy. No answer. She left a text. "Hildr's behind you."

No reply.

"Damn!" She speed-dialed Lee.

No answer. *This is unbelievable!* She left a voice mail. "Call me. It's an emergency."

She phoned Jim. He didn't pick up.

*What's going on?* Hayley paced the kitchen while dialing Roger, Laura, and Clint. No response from anyone. She sat on the edge of the chair and tried to think, one thought following another. *I can't contact anyone. Maybe Lewis.*

Hayley dialed Lee's butler. Lewis answered.

"Lewis, do you know where Lee is?"

"Yes, miss. He's with Thomas in the security room."

"He isn't answering his phone. Can you check to see if it's working and ask him to call me? It's urgent."

"Yes, miss. Right away."

Hayley hung up. Poised to answer, she stared at her cell phone. *Come on, Lee.*

It rang. She picked up. "Lee, Hildr kidnapped Kathy."

"No!" She heard Thomas in the background, asking questions, and Lee answering him. "I'm putting you on speakerphone," Lee said. "Wait a minute. How did Hildr get to her? We're all wearing amulets."

"Maybe not," she heard Thomas say. "Kathy came by my

place this morning to bring me one, but she left it in her car. So she took hers off and put it around my neck. She must have forgotten to replace hers when she went back to her car."

"Causing forgetfulness," Hayley said. "That's one of Hildr's powers."

"What can we do?" Lee asked.

"We need to tell the others. I tried to call, but I couldn't reach anyone."

"I'll get on it."

"Tell them Grams will find her. We just have to wait."

"I'm coming over."

When Hayley ended the call, her heart pounded as if it would leap from her chest. *I need to calm down, clear my mind, and wait for Grams.* She found herself pacing again.

In a cloud of despair, Hayley wandered into the living room and stared out the window, not seeing how the wind whipped the apple tree or rippled the rain puddles on the lawn because Kathy's image filled her thoughts. She remembered her first day at Paranormal Search and Analysis and how Kathy told her about the three bosses, Roger, Lee, and Jim, and of their personalities. She looked back at her growing friendship with Kathy. Hayley's heart ached at the thought of her friend being hurt, or worse, killed.

Thunder rumbled over the mountains. The notion of Kathy driving in this weather made Hayley queasy. *She must be freezing.*

The sound of Lee's car arriving distracted her from her troubled thoughts. As he climbed out, unfurling his umbrella to shelter him from the pouring rain, she dashed to open the front door.

Lee hurried toward the house, not paying attention to the puddles forming on the walkway, reached the porch, collapsed his umbrella, shook it, and wiped his feet on the welcome mat. He went inside. "Heard anything?"

"No." She closed the door behind him. "I'll fix you a cup of coffee."

His face filled with deep concern, he nodded, placed the umbrella and his raincoat onto the rack by the door, and followed her into the kitchen. "How long has Grams been gone?"

Hayley reached into the cabinet and retrieved a coffee cup. "She left a moment before I called you. I haven't heard a word. Where do you think Hildr would take Kathy?"

"Probably somewhere isolated. The Appalachians, perhaps."

"How could this have happened?" She lifted the coffee pot, poured him a cup, and handed it to him. "Why didn't Vara stop her?"

"I'm wondering the same thing." His nostrils flared. "This stinks! When's Laura coming home?"

"Sometime before noon."

They went to the living room. Hayley sat on the couch.

Quiet, seemingly in deep thought, Lee set his coffee on the end table and walked to the fireplace. "I'm staying here tonight if that's okay." He moved the screen and stoked the fire. "I don't want to leave you and Laura alone. We should all stick together from now on. There are too many unanswered questions."

"This waiting is killing me."

"Me too." Lee replaced the poker on its stand. "I need to let Roger and Jim know we still haven't heard anything." He placed the screen in front of the fire.

Hayley glanced toward the hallway. "Grams!"

Lee turned on his heels. "Where's Kathy?"

"In the mountains," Grams said. "Vara was on their trail, but neither she nor the witch sensed my presence. I stayed hidden."

She sat in the overstuffed chair while Lee sat on the couch next to Hayley.

"What's wrong with Vara?" Hayley asked. "Why didn't she stop Hildr?"

"I finally found the answer to that," Grams said. "It seems they both have the power to foresee the future. Each time Vara would go after Hildr, Hildr would translocate, taking Kathy with her. Hildr was always one step ahead, leaving Vara frustrated. She could chase her for eternity and never capture her. That's probably why she needs Annie's help."

Now Hayley understood. "That, and we believe Annie will be the one to bury Hildr. According to the calendar, we only have seven days before the full moon."

"Then we'd better do something fast." Lee swiped his hand across the back of his neck. "Is Kathy hurt?"

"No, she's okay."

"How far up in the mountains did they go?" he asked.

Hayley could almost read his mind—he planned to search.

"Quite a ways and I kept my distance."

"What happened after they left Tom's apartment?" Hayley asked.

"Hildr made Kathy drive to a deserted cabin back in the hills," Grams said.

"Where?" Hayley asked.

"Remember the photo of you and Gramps standing near a cabin in a meadow of wildflowers? It's the picture you hung in your room over the dresser after his death."

A chill went up and down the back of Hayley's neck. While having dinner with Lee on her birthday, she'd envisioned a woman, wearing a hooded robe, coming toward her in that meadow, and making her feel that her clairvoyance had been intrusive. Then the woman hurled Hayley's awareness back to the present. *It was Hildr.* "Yes," she told Grams and turned to Lee. "I know just where she is."

"I'll call Roger, and we'll go find her," Lee said.

Panic gripped Hayley. "We can't confront Hildr. It would be suicide. Besides, Vara said to do nothing."

Lee stood and wandered to the window. "Do nothing? That's impossible." He looked toward the mountains. Then he turned with a shrewd look on his face. "We'll drive in, distract Hildr, and then grab Kathy."

"The road's flooded," Grams said.

"How did Kathy make it through?" Hayley asked.

"Hildr used her witchcraft. She floated small stones lying beneath the trees and dropped them on the road, covering the mud, giving the car tires traction. But she reversed the spell, and now the road's impassible."

"It doesn't matter," Lee said. "We'll load the ATVs onto the trucks. Once we're close enough, we'll unload them and travel offroad."

"Won't Hildr hear us coming?" Hayley asked.

"No. The ATVs are electric, quiet."

Hayley looked at Grams. "What do you think?"

"I've seen all your options. This is one of those times when I'm walking a fine line. The choice is all yours."

"Can you tell me if our choice will save Kathy?"

"If I tell you that I'll be telling you your future. You know I can't do that, but I'll ask if I can give you a hint." Grams closed her eyes, opened them again, and nodded.

Hayley sensed Elaina's presence, her spirit guide since birth, teaching Grams to be a guardian angel. Although Elaina kept out of view, she always stayed on the periphery of Hayley's awareness.

"I can tell you this: Going after Kathy now will alter your perception."

"That's cryptic," Hayley said.

"It's meant to be."

"But, you're allowed to steer me in the right direction."

"I'm your voice of reason, the intuitive nudge that suggests you to take one path over another. But it's only a suggestion. I can't tell you how to live your life."

"I know." Hayley thought a moment. "Lee, text Roger. Tell him we'll be over as soon as Laura comes home. This has to be right. Kathy's not meant to die."

# CHAPTER 18

"Confrontin' Hildr will be as bad as comin' face to face with Jaws," Jim said, sitting with the others on the cluster of sofas in Roger's library. "Ya know she'll eat us for dinner. We need to come up with a distraction that will grab her by her wart hairs and get her outta the way."

Clint raised his hand. "What are we looking at? Where exactly are they?"

"In a cabin in the mountains," Hayley said. "I know where it is. I've been there. There's a meadow in front, an old forest, probably as old as the witch, around the back and left side, and a road in and out to the right, coming off the main road a half-mile away."

"We'll need a map," Roger said. "I'll text Cummings."

"How big a cabin?" Clint asked.

"There's a main room with a kitchen, a bedroom, bathroom, and a screened-in porch in the back. I glimpsed it for an instant in a recent vision. It looks rundown."

"How will we know which room Kathy's in?" Lee asked.

"It doesn't matter," Hayley said. "I can astral project, find her, and be back in my body in a blink."

"Now we're diggin' where there's taters," Jim said. "And while that's happenin', we should get within a gnat's whisker of the cabin so we can load her into the bed of Roger's utility vehicle if she can't walk."

"Will it work?" Lee asked Hayley.

"It has to. Kathy's one of the reincarnated like the rest of us, born to be one of the saviors of souls. She's not meant to die like this."

"What if Hildr sees your spirit?" Lee asked.

"I've had lots of practice. I can do this, I'm positive. But I'll need a distraction."

Jim raised his hand. "I'll volunteer. This is all my fault. I'll approach the cabin from the front without wearin' this here amulet. I'm sure if Hildr tries to kill me, Vara will prevent it. I can count on her."

"You'd better damn sure hope so," Roger said. "She's not gonna like our interference. We can count on that too."

"I'm sure Vara's not going to be happy," Hayley replied. "After all, she told us to do nothing. But Grams said since Vara and Hildr can foresee the future, each knows where the other will be before the move is made. And Hildr translocates before Vara can grab her, allowing the chase to go on forever. Now there seems to be a standoff. Vara needs another plan. And that's why we think Annie's involved."

"In the scheme of things," Lee said, "it looks like that's why we're involved too—to help Vara save the world from Hildr's evil."

"The saviors of souls," Hayley said softly. "I wish the title came with a manual."

"Has anyone told Matilda that Kathy has been kidnapped?"

Laura asked.

"I did," Jim replied. "She wanted to fly back, but I told her to keep lookin' for the runestone." He rubbed his chin. "I kinda fudged the importance of the stone just a bit to keep her outta harm's way."

Cummings entered the library, handed Roger a map, and went to the bar. He filled a tray of glasses with wine and beer and circulated the room.

Roger spread the map on an ottoman in view of each of them. Hayley leaned in and pinpointed the location. The others studied the area.

"It's about a half-mile from the main road." Hayley accepted a glass of red wine from Cummings. "There's an old forest, like I said, on the cabin's two sides—to the left and along the back. Beyond the trees, the dirt road has a fork—one way leads to an abandoned gold mine. The other cuts through the forest and leads to the cabin."

"So we have a plan," Roger said. "Jim, you'll distract Hildr from the front. Clint and I will help Kathy escape out the back. Remember, Grams told us the dirt fork leading to the cabin is washed out, so let's keep the trucks out of the mud and leave them parked alongside the main street. Laura, I'd like you to stay with the trucks. Bring your medical bag in case you need it." He looked around at the team. "Any questions or suggestions?"

"When will we be ready to go?" Lee asked.

"Six in the morning." Roger hesitated while Cummings handed him a beer. "We'll pack up my ATVs, head over your house to get yours, Lee, and go from there."

"What about the weather?" Lee asked.

"The storm's moving out of Sutterville tonight," Laura told him. "But, it'll be freezing in the mountains."

"Will Kathy survive the night?" Clint asked.

"Hildr will take care of her," Hayley said. "She kidnapped Kathy for a reason. And I'm sure it wasn't to kill her, at least not yet, or she already would have. The good thing is, Hildr's been human often enough to understand what the body needs, including food and warmth. The problem is, if Vara doesn't keep Hildr occupied, Hildr will be able to gather what she needs to create the potion that will put Kathy in a coma. Then she'll possess her body and become flesh and blood again. The spell takes three days. We can't let that happen."

"You're right," Roger agreed. "What about clothing or gear? Do we need anything?"

Laura and Hayley sipped their drinks and glanced at each other.

"This seems like a good time to add to our wardrobe," Hayley told Laura.

"You're right. All my hiking clothes were bought in Oahu. I have nearly nothing for cold weather."

"I think a trip to Sports Unlimited may be in order," Lee said.

Roger stood. "We'll meet you there."

When Hayley stepped out the front door at Angel Hall, she glanced at her watch—*a little after one*—and then toward the mountains. In the distance, the clouds still looked dark and threatening. "If there's a thunderstorm, Lee, the energy in the air would increase Hildr's powers."

"Not a problem. Remember, Laura said the storm is moving on."

He opened her car door, and she slid into his Cayenne. Laura and Roger climbed into his Audi Q7.

On the ride to the sports shop, Hayley couldn't stop thinking about Kathy's safety. "It's times like this I wish we'd never made

that pact limiting me to see any of the reincarnated's futures,"
she said to Lee. But she'd learned when each of her friends — Lee,
Roger, Laura, Jim, Kathy, and Clint, as well as his cousin — came
together before they were born into this lifetime that the decision
had been made out of necessity. Time caused the problem. While
her acute abilities allowed her mind to travel to the past and
future, past-lifetimes mingled with the present, causing déjà vu,
confusing past memories to intertwine with the present. As for
their futures, they were wound closely to hers, and a divine rule
forbade her from seeing her own. The rules were in place. She
couldn't change them if she wanted to. *At least I'm allowed to see
the present, what they're doing in the here and now.*

"We're the saviors of souls," Lee replied. "Our purpose in
life is unique, and focus is essential. Rules had to be set."

"I know. It's just frustrating sometimes. If I had the ability, I
could've foreseen the kidnapping and stopped it from happening.
Now I wish I could foresee the outcome so I can be sure Kathy
and everyone else will be okay."

"It's hard, I know."

*Hard, yes. Someone may die, including you or me.* A list
of her friends' names scrolled through her mind like the
acknowledgments at the end of a movie. *List. I need to find a future
list that they'll all be on.* Hayley thought about the ball. *A guest list.*
She looked at Lee. "Are we spending Christmas at your house?"

"No. Why? What's that have to do with anything? We're
going to Roger's. Every year he invites his friends and family.
There's usually around thirty guests."

"Will everyone receive an invitation?"

"Yes. Why?"

"Maybe I can foresee the guest list. If everyone's name is on
it, then I'll know none of our friends will get seriously hurt. And

if Kathy's on it, that would mean we saved her."

"That's a little roundabout," Lee said. "It won't tell us how to save her."

"I know, but I'll foresee the list before we hatch our plan, and I'll see if she's on it. If she's not, we'll change the plan until she is."

"Smart thinking," Lee told her. "Have you ever driven an ATV?"

"No."

"I'll give you a few pointers when we get back to my place."

# CHAPTER 19

When Lee drove up to his home, he reached inside the glove compartment, retrieved a remote, pulled forward to the north fence alongside the front of the house, and pressed the remote control's button. The fence, Lee had explained to Hayley at the costume ball, retracted like a gate, allowing valets to drive guests' cars to a meadow beyond the trees.

He pulled his SUV forward, drove down a narrow road flanked by white pines, across the meadow, and stopped before a garage. The garage doors rose. Hayley checked out the cars parked inside.

"How many cars do you own, Lee?"

"Only two right now. All the rest are Jim's."

"He has five? I've only seen him drive his Ram and his Rolls."

"He likes to keep a low profile, and only drives his Rolls once in awhile. That's the reason he always drives his truck. It's been a while since he's driven his antiques. Lately, he mentioned he might sell them."

"He has good taste." Her grandfather had liked old cars. He had magazines full of them. She'd spend hours flipping through the pages. Jim had some of her favorites: the brown 1931 Cadillac coupe with its black fenders, chrome front end with a multitude of headlights, whitewall tires, and tan ragtop; the gold and maroon 1959 Bently coupe with its chrome front end and its whitewalls; and lastly, the steel gray 1931 Duesenberg J with all its chrome, whitewall tires, and tan ragtop. "I think he should keep them. They're beautiful."

"All you have to do is ask, and he'll give you a ride in whichever you chose," Lee said. "But for now, let's check out my ATVs."

She climbed out of the passenger seat as Lee left the vehicle and met a man wearing jeans, a fleece-lined coat, a tan cowboy hat, and boots. After a short conversation with Lee, the man turned and called to another hired hand, who wheeled out two quad ATVs.

She stood next to Lee and assessed her vehicle. *At least it has four wheels. Must be easier than riding a motorcycle — which I've never done.*

"Normally," Lee said to her, "we'd be suited up. But for now, we'll only wear partial gear."

The man who wore a cowboy hat went back inside, returned with two helmets and two pairs of gloves, and handed them to Lee. While Hayley slipped on gloves, Lee placed a black helmet over her head.

"We'll take a ride through the forest." He pointed to the north woods beyond another large building. "There's a course Roger's nephews designed."

"They're multitalented," Hayley said.

He nodded. "I'll take you through it. First, let me show you how this beast works." Lee pointed to a square screen between the handlebars. "The digital speedometer is here. Below that is the odometer, and off to the side is a graph showing the battery's energy level." He turned the key below the screen. "Once the ignition is switched on, you'll trip the tork on the left-hand grip. I'll set it at fifty percent for now, since we'll be riding slow until you get the feel of things. When you want to back up, you'll push this reverse button on the left-hand grip. Now, climb on board."

She threw her leg over the ATV and got comfortable on its black leather seat.

"Put your hands on the grips."

She followed his instructions.

"The brake is on your right handgrip, similar to where the brake-and-shift is on a bike. The lever near your thumb is the accelerator. Just above that is the button used mainly for hills, allowing you to use the brake and accelerator at the same time when you come to a stop to prevent you from rolling back."

"Good to know," Hayley said.

"Yes," Lee agreed. "Who knows what terrain we'll be driving over." He flipped down her face shield and took a step back. "Okay, slowly give it some power, using your thumb on the lever, and drive around in a circle to get the feel."

Hayley eased away, the electric motor soundless as she drove about twelve feet. Before turning, she braked, getting accustomed to the controls. Carefully she added power, made her way back to Lee, put it in reverse, and pulled forward again. *Easy enough,* she thought. She glanced into the woods beyond the meadow. "Okay, I think I'm good to go. But I have a question. If we'll be driving ATVs, how will we be able to transport Kathy to the truck if she's hurt?"

"Roger has a UTV, a utility terrain vehicle. It's used for maintenance and has a flatbed to carry lumber, supplies, or in our circumstance, a cot, just in case. In rough terrain, the police department uses them to rescue injured people. It'll be perfect."

"Sounds like it."

He mounted his vehicle and drove slowly, glancing at her over his shoulder. In the woods, he led her up and down small hills and over downed trees, and as they drove, he explained what to avoid, such as twigs, that would alert Hildr of their approach. "It's important to learn these things, especially when you're trying to be stealthy. But most of the time, you can just follow me." At the end of the course, he stopped, removed his helmet, and looked back at her. "What do you think? Are you up for this, or do you want to ride with me instead?"

She thought about it. "I'm okay driving slow, but if I'm trying to keep up and I get into trouble for some reason, I could ruin our mission. I think I'd rather ride with you."

"No problem," Lee said. "Since we're out here, let's drive around a while so I can show you the boundaries of my estate. We have all afternoon before we'll head back."

She straightened in her seat. "I don't know. I'm anxious to use my clairvoyance to locate the Christmas dinner invitation list to see if Kathy's name will be on it."

"What if Cummings uses last year's list? It sounds logical."

Her plan deflated, along with her confidence that it would work. "Now what will I do?"

"Riding around might clear your head," Lee said. "By the time we get home, maybe you'll find the answer."

"Okay." She put her hands on the grips. "Lead the way."

***

*Lee was right.* By the time they arrived home, Hayley had the answer. After showering, having dinner, filling her wine glass with Merlot, and sitting in front of the fireplace in Lee's sitting room, she decided to give it a try.

"I'll concentrate on Cummings writing Kathy's invitation," she told Lee.

"I knew you'd figure it out."

He sat cross-legged on the white shag carpet while she placed a pillow in his lap. Getting comfortable, she stretched out on the floor in front of him with her toes warming in the fire's glow and resting her head on the cushion. He leaned and kissed her before she closed her eyes.

She relaxed, clearing her mind. *Christmas dinner invitations,* she thought, and let her mind wander into the future.

In her clairvoyant vision, she saw Cummings writing an invitation in exquisite calligraphy, inviting Kathy to Christmas dinner. But instead of placing it on the pile with the others, he set it aside. Then Hayley's vision ended.

She told Lee what she foresaw. "Why did he set it aside?" Taking in a deep breath, she sighed.

"Maybe she will already be at Roger's," Lee said, "and he's going to give it to her personally instead of sending it."

Hayley felt frustrated, wanting a clearer understanding. "How do we know for sure if Roger's plan will work or if we need to change it?" She scrutinized the vision. "He set it aside. It could mean just about anything."

"Why would he make out an invitation for someone he knows can't attend?" Lee asked.

"You're probably right," Hayley said. "We'll stay with Roger's plan."

"Right," Lee replied.

She stood, retrieved the cushion, and placed it back on the couch. "Let's get to bed. Tomorrow may be more difficult than we imagine."

"Why would you think that? Do you foresee problems?"

"No," she replied. "Maybe it's just nerves."
"Hope so. I'll set the alarm for four a.m."

# CHAPTER 20

The clouds blushed pink as the sun rose. Leaves dampened from last night's rain littered the main road adjacent to the grassy clearing where the team gathered in the mountains.

Frosty air prickled Hayley's face, but the rest of her body felt toasty beneath the extra layers of clothing. She wore the same high-topped hiking boots and mud-colored camouflage outfit as everyone else.

With leather-gloved hands, Lee slipped a black helmet over her head and then put on his own. The ATVs had been unloaded from the trucks, and some of the team had mounted their vehicles.

Lee put his arm around Hayley's waist, and she stepped into his embrace. "Ready for this?" he asked before closing her visor.

She nodded. Adrenaline shot through her veins, and a knot formed in her throat when she thought of Hildr and imagined Kathy. By using the methods Grams had taught her, she sent a "nudging" to her friend — *Everything's going to be okay.*

Clint, driving an electric UTV, stopped next to her. "I saw that look on your face. Did you get a vision of Kathy? Is she all right?"

"I sent her a message letting her know we're coming."

"Will Hildr know you're using telepathy?" he asked.

"No. It's a little different from that. It's called nudging. Hildr shouldn't sense it. If she does, it'll appear to be Kathy's own thoughts. I showed Roger and Jim how it works."

"Nervous?" Lee asked Clint.

"More pissed off than scared."

Jim, on his ATV, pulled up beside them and lifted his visor. "When you're up to your ass in gators, it's hard to remember that you came to drain the swamp. So no matter what happens when I confront Hildr, keep focused."

"Will do," Lee replied.

Clint gave him a thumbs-up.

After talking with Roger, Laura climbed into the Ram's cab to stay with the trucks and trailers.

Roger started his vehicle and appraised the team. "Ready? Let's do this."

Moving forward in his seat, Lee adjusted his position, leaving enough space behind him for Hayley. He gripped the handlebars. "Get on and hold tight."

She did as told and wrapped her arms around his waist. He accelerated, quietly pulling away from the clearing next to the road. They crossed the asphalt and headed into the woods. Stealthily, they weaved between the trees and stayed downwind.

The urge to use her psychic gift to locate the room Kathy was in tempted Hayley. *It's too risky. She might sense my mental probing like she did that night at Mr. G's.* Hayley shook off the impulse. *Nudging's different. It will appear to be Kathy's thoughts, not mine. It's going to be okay. This has to be right.*

After a quarter of a mile, they spread out and hid within the trees at the edge of the meadow. Roger signaled for Clint to follow him through the woods behind the cabin, and gave Lee and Hayley a thumbs-up to stay where they were. They all looked at Jim, who seemed to be praying. Then he gave Lee, Roger, and Clint a wave and rode away as planned to find a strategic place to confront the witch.

When Hayley lost sight of Jim, she felt frightened for him until remembering what he had told them — focus. She removed her helmet and glanced toward the cabin in the clearing to their right, three-hundred yards away. Smoke rose from the chimney. All appeared serene.

They dismounted from the ATV.

Looking for Vara, she searched along the outer edges of the woods and gazed into the cloudless sky. *No goshawk. Not even a sparrow. She has to be somewhere. She'll protect Jim, I'm sure of it.*

Lee stood beside her, concern written across his face. Summoning all her courage, Hayley said, "I'm ready."

She shook off her doubts and fears, closed her eyes, and thought strongly about Kathy, intending to use her ability to astral project. In a moment, her spirit stepped from her body and soared along the edge of the woods until reaching the cabin's screened back porch. The trees' shadows made it difficult to see inside. She edged closer and saw Kathy sitting in a chair, her arms behind her. Cautiously Hayley's astral spirit passed through the screen door, and she studied her friend.

Kathy sat like a statue, her wide fear-filled eyes darting to her left. From behind her platinum locks, a blue tarantula peeked out, crawled into plain view, and perched on Kathy's shoulder. Kathy's face paled. Her breathing became erratic.

*Well, Annie, I know who has your pet.* Hayley tried to stifle her phobia, knowing if she let her fear escalate, she'd return to her body. It took all her strength to control her emotions and focus.

*Look toward the door.* Hayley nudged the thought into Kathy's mind.

Kathy looked her way. Then her body convulsed, her head jerked, her eyes rolled back. The huge spider scurried down her arm, ran down her leg to the ground, and hurried away.

Hayley, believing Kathy had been bitten, drew nearer. From a foot away, leaning in, she examined Kathy's shoulder. When she glanced at Kathy's face, she saw the whites of her friend's eyes had turned black. Terrified, Hayley jumped back.

"You're too late," the witch's voice hissed from Kathy's mouth. "She's mine now."

Terror consumed Hayley. Her astral spirit soared across the meadow and snapped back into her body. Trembling and crying, she fell into Lee's arms. "We're too late. Hildr possessed her."

"No!" Lee cried.

"Kathy, where are ya?" Jim's voice echoed off the trees.

Hayley gazed toward the meadow and gasped. "We have to stop him. She'll kill him."

Kathy, possessed by the witch, stood on the porch glaring at the man Hildr wanted to kill.

Jim strolled toward her. "I'm here to rescue ya." He looked around. "Where's Hildr?"

Frantically, Hayley sent him a nudge. *She's Hildr. Kathy's possessed.* Jim stopped in midstride and took a few steps back.

With a sweet innocent smile, the woman who appeared to be Kathy asked, "What's wrong? Where are the others? Are you alone?"

"So it's you," Jim said. "What? Think I've got gnat balls for brains? It's me ya want, not her. Take me instead and let her go."

Hildr reached up and petted Annie's familiar that once again perched on Kathy's shoulder. It crawled onto her arm. "Feed," the witch said and pointed to Jim.

With each step downward, the spider grew. At the size of a rat, it leaped off Hildr's/Kathy's arm, scurried down the stairs, and kept enlarging as it rushed toward Jim.

Wide-eyed, Jim turned to run but stumbled. When he raised his head, Hayley saw a gash over his eye. Blood flowed down his face. He rolled over, shielding his face with his arms, and swore as the monstrous spider reared on its hind legs and hovered above him.

Shuddering in horror, Hayley screamed.

Before she could stop him, Lee pulled a hunting knife from its sheath at his waist and ran past her.

She watched in terror.

# CHAPTER 21

At sunrise, Hayley cuddled closer to Lee as they stood looking through his bedroom window at the overcast sky.

"Good day to stay home and make love," Lee said. He softly kissed her and groaned when his cell phone rang.

"I suppose you have to get that," she said.

Lee sighed, walked to his nightstand, and answered the call. "Sure. Is something up? Okay. You're more than welcome." He ended his call. "We need to get dressed. Jim's joining us for breakfast."

"That's unusual. Any reason why?"

"He doesn't want to talk about it over the phone."

***

Hayley sat with Lee at the small table by the window in the sitting room, stirring her coffee and waiting for Lewis to bring breakfast. She glanced toward the door and gave a startled gasp when Jim entered.

Lee bolted from his seat and hurried to his side. "What happened?"

"I was hopin' you'd know." Jim looked at him through two

black eyes, the right eye black and blue, swollen closed, the left bruised and bloodshot. "The throbbin' pain woke me up. When I saw myself in the mirror, I looked like I'd fallen out of the ugly tree and hit every branch on the way down."

Lee led him to the table and pulled out a chair for him. "I don't recall seeing you last night. Did you go somewhere?"

Jim eased himself into his seat. "Damned if I know. But a woman called me twice this mornin'. The first time I told her she had the wrong number. When she called again, I told her I didn't know anyone named Matdie or Matilda. Maybe I got into a fight over some woman."

"That's highly unlikely," Lee told him. "Maybe you fell down the stairs while sleepwalking."

Hayley examined his face. "No cuts or abrasions." She placed her hand on his shoulder and closed her eyes, psychically trying to find the answer. "Nothing." She opened her eyes again and glanced at Lee. "Can I use your phone?"

"Sure." He passed it to her. "Who are you calling?"

"Laura."

"Good idea," Lee said. "This looks bad."

Once Hayley made the call, she handed Lee's phone to Jim, and he put the call on speaker. When she answered, he explained the situation.

"I don't have to be at the hospital until this afternoon," Laura said. "Why don't I come by and take a look?"

"I'd like that. Thanks, Doc."

Once the call ended, Lewis arrived with their meals sitting on a cart draped in white linen. After setting Jim's breakfast in front of him, Lewis stepped back. "My word, sir. From your grotesque appearance, I must conclude that your rescue efforts didn't go smoothly."

"What rescue?" Jim asked.

"Oh, my. It went that badly? Were you successful? Is Kathy safe?"

"Who's Kathy?" Jim asked.

"Sir, your attempt at humor is troubling."

"He's not joking, Lewis," Lee said. "Who's Kathy? What rescue?"

Lewis looked at Hayley. "This is extremely baffling."

"Did we miss a meeting with a client?" she asked.

"No, miss." Lewis hesitated for a moment. "I believe this is a misunderstanding. If I may, after you finish your meal, I'd like to escort you to the security room. I know of something that will clarify the situation."

"Sounds like a setup," Jim said. "What's up your sleeve?"

Lewis turned to Lee. "Sir, I don't mean to be mysterious. I simply want to make a point."

"Okay, Lewis," Lee said. "After Laura examines Jim's eyes, we'll be free."

"Dr. Song may wish to accompany us," Lewis replied. "It involves her, as well."

"This had better be good," Jim said. "You're confusin' the hell outta everyone."

"Trust me, sir. Words are simply not enough."

"That's a first," Jim said. "Words have never failed ya yet. Must be one of those seein'-is believin'-things." He touched his swollen eyes and winced. "If nothin' else, maybe the surveillance cameras will show me gettin' home last night. If I came home drunk, there's a couple of places I might've been. I'd sure like to know how I got these shiners."

***

Even though the sun shone brightly through the tower's

twelve-pane windows after the clouds moved off to the north, Hayley knew the wind rustling the trees felt cold. She peered at the long drive lined with Norway spruce and toward the wrought-iron security gates until she saw Laura's Lexus come into view.

"She's here," she said over her shoulder to Jim. He mumbled an incoherent reply as he lay on the couch with a cool cloth over his eyes.

When Laura entered the sitting room, she quickened her step. Jim sat up and lowered the compress. "My word, Jim. What in the world happened?"

"Don't remember a damn thing, Doc. The impact mustta scrabbled my brain."

She led him to the table by the window and examined his face in the sunlight. Hayley stood out of the way and winced every time Jim recoiled.

"I won't know about any damage to your vision until the swelling goes down," Laura said. "Until then, ice it. You might try using a bag of frozen peas. It works really well."

He held up the wet cloth he had clenched in his hands and set it aside. "Will do."

She handed him a small bottle. "You'll take only one of these every four to six hours for pain. They're fairly strong. Don't drive. If you want to go somewhere, have someone take you." Laura closed her medical bag and set it aside.

"If we're done here," Lee told her, "Lewis has something he'd like to show us." He called Lewis on his cell phone, then addressed the others. "He wants us to meet him in the security room."

They walked down the hall to the main corridor, followed it to the elevator, and rode it to the first floor.

Lewis met them in the hallway in front of the security room door. He clasped his hands together. "Sir, you know I'd never deceive you. This will be hard to believe." After opening the door, he allowed everyone to enter. Then he approached Thomas, who sat at the control desk. "We'll need to see camera nine's footage from last Wednesday night."

"There's not a hookup on nine, sir," Thomas told him. "It's an extra line in case we need to add surveillance."

"So you don't remember either," Lewis said. "Interesting. Check it anyway."

"Okay, sir." Thomas went to camera nine, and instead of a *signal not located* message, footage of Jim's bedroom came up on the main monitor. "This is news to me," Thomas said. He reversed the video to Wednesday. "What time, sir?"

"Seven."

Thomas found the surveillance time and date and pressed play, as Lewis requested. The large screen in the center of multiple small monitors displayed detailed footage of Jim's room. They watched silently.

In the center of the screen, a speck of light settled in the middle of the room. It grew into a small sphere and expanded into a large bubble encasing a tall woman wearing a dark blue cloak.

"Hildr," Lewis told them. "The witch."

They watched the drama unfold.

"Holy moly," Jim said.

While Hildr ignited the furniture and drapes at both windows, Lee looked questioningly at Lewis.

"It's real, sir. I was here when it happened."

Hayley's heart pounded like a drumbeat. Wondering if they were safe now, she darted glances around the room but didn't sense a threat.

Laura's eyes widened as she stared at the footage. "This is impossible."

"Why haven't we seen this footage before?" Lee asked.

"You have, sir," Lewis said. "Your memories have been wiped clean. You mentioned that this could happen. Keep watching, sir."

When another entity appeared out of nowhere in the guise of a goshawk, Hildr became a wavering black vapor and vanished.

"Vara's the bird," Lewis said.

With mouths ajar, they watched Vara change into human form and reverse Hildr's spell.

Thomas stopped the video. "This has to be a joke."

"I'm afraid not," Lewis said. "This is extremely complicated. But one of the women in the footage is responsible for your forgetfulness."

"Was I here when this happened?" Thomas asked, his voice shaky.

"Yes," Lewis replied.

Lee put his hand on Thomas's shoulder. "It's okay. We'll figure this out."

Stunned, Hayley tried to use her ability to see the past but felt blocked. *What's going on?* She followed Lewis and the others out of the room, leaving Thomas at the controls.

Lewis closed the door behind them, joining everyone in the hallway. Lee's cell phone rang, breaking the nervous tension in the air.

He put the call on speaker. "Hi, Roger. What's up?"

"Something crazy's going on here. A woman named Matilda arrived and claims she's a guest here. Odd thing is, her belongings are in one of my bedrooms. And she knows each of us by name.

She insists on seeing Jim and is in tears, speaking about a woman called Kathy. Do you know a Kathy?"

Lee looked at Hayley. She stared back at him, befuddled. Then she turned to Lewis. "Who's Kathy?"

"Oh my, you don't remember her at all?" Lewis asked. "Hildr kidnapped her, and Vara told you to do nothing. But you went against her wishes and attempted to rescue her nevertheless. That's when your memories were erased."

"I wish I could stay," Laura said. "This is all too unbelievable. But I have to get to the hospital. You'll have to fill me in later."

"Without a doubt," Hayley said.

# CHAPTER 22

On the drive to Roger's, Hayley felt uneasy, as if hidden eyes watched them every inch of the way. *How much danger are we in? Why don't I know?* When they reached Angel Hall, she, Lee, and Jim stayed vigilant.

Once Hayley entered Roger's library, she psychically scanned the room's past energy, flipping back through each day until she found traces of present activity. "Seven days of nothing, as if the room had been stripped of its residual energy," she told Lee.

"This is beginning to worry me," he told her. "What's going on?"

Roger and Matilda greeted them.

"Glad you're here," Roger said. "Matilda showed me a copy of the security footage from your place. It looked like a scene out of a horror movie. Did you see it? Do you think it's true?"

"Yes," Hayley replied. "Lewis assured us it's real."

Jim strolled in behind them, wearing sunglasses. Removing them, he revealed his swollen black-and-blue eyes.

Matilda gasped and ran to his side. "Oh, Jim."

"Excuse me, do I know ya, miss?" He stuffed the glasses into his shirt pocket.

"Oh, my heavens," Matilda said, studying Jim's face. "You don't remember me either." Tears welled in her eyes.

Roger led them to the couch.

"You have to remember," Matilda said, sitting. "Kathy's been abducted, and we need to find her."

"Who's Kathy?" Jim asked.

"She's my friend and a member of your team."

"Do you know where she's being held?" Hayley asked.

"No," Matilda replied. "I wasn't in town the last few days. Apparently, your memories were taken when you tried to save her."

"Who did this, the witch or the woman who turned into a bird?" Roger asked.

"That's not clear," Matilda said. "Vara's a celestial being, a sentinel, a type of guardian angel. Hildr's a witch in spirit form. Both have the ability to erase your memory. But Vara can restore the past. You saw her do it in the security footage. And I believe she's done it again. When Vara came into your lives, Jim moved from Lee's home to Roger's. But now the room he lived in upstairs shows no trace of his stay."

Hayley tried to remember her recent past. *We went to dinner, and Lee gave me a charm bracelet for my birthday. When we arrived at Lee's, I undressed and took a shower. We were playing hide and seek in the upstairs bedrooms, and when Lee found me, we made love.* Those intimate moments now seemed vague. *I don't remember the entire evening.* "Do you know when Vara first appeared?" Hayley asked Matilda.

"On your birthday—eight days ago."

A chill rippled through Hayley's body. She looked at her purse on the floor next to her feet. She placed it on her lap and peeked inside. The velvet case containing the birthday gift Lee had given her lay exactly where she had placed it that night. *Was it that long ago?* She retrieved the case and showed it to Lee. "I put it in my purse before I showered that night after dinner. Think back, Lee. What are the last things you remember before this morning?"

"We were playing hide and seek. And I found you." He smiled. "Need I say more?"

"That was eight days ago," Hayley said.

He thought for a moment. "You're right. I can't remember anything since then."

"Vara's responsible for your memory loss," Matilda said. "I'm sure of it. We counted on her and Annie to protect us. Now that you've been robbed of your memories, I don't know who to trust."

Hayley returned the case to her purse and set it next to her.

"Who's Annie?" Roger asked.

"She's a witch living in the Appalachians," Matilda said. "Vara had given you a list written in runes and asked you to take it to Annie so she could make protective amulets for your team."

"Why runes?" Hayley asked.

"When you took the list to Annie, she showed you a spell, hidden beneath the original, that's accessible only by using witchcraft. You wondered then why Vara wrote the list in a language you couldn't read, and if there were more secrets she meant to keep from you. So you hired me to transcribe the writings and to see if there was more to the list than meets the eye. I've examined the photos you had taken of the original list, and I found a coded message within it."

She picked up a large manila envelope on the seat next to her, opened it, retrieved the photos, and handed them to Hayley.

"It calls for the Kindred Keeper of spells to fulfill an oath and gives the time — the Frost Moon at midnight. I couldn't find the meeting place. Annie would know, but I don't trust her. She gave you the amulets but didn't tell you about the fulfillment of the oath."

"Who's the Kindred Keeper?" Jim asked.

"I believe it's Annie or someone in her family," Matilda replied.

"So, within the list and the hidden spell, you found another coded message?" Lee asked.

"Yes. A message Annie concealed from you."

"When's the Frost Moon?" Hayley asked.

"Before this gets any more confusing," Matilda said, "let me give you a timeline. It was seven days ago when Vara first appeared at Lee's home. A few days later, Hayley. Laura and Kathy brought to our attention the full moon would be in ten days. That is five days from now."

Roger walked across the library to a desk between bookshelves. He picked up the calendar and flipped through the days. "She's right. In five days." He set the calendar down and returned to the couch in front of the fireplace, where a fire blazed, warming the room.

"How did we know about the full moon?" Hayley asked.

Matilda told everyone about Jim's past-life regression, how Vara still referred to him as Sweet William, the three-day possession spell, and about the runestone's present circumstance.

Hayley studied the photos again. "Where are the original writings now?"

"They were kept here in the library while Julia and I investigated Vara's background," Matilda told her. "And there was a blessing recently carved into the mantle of this fireplace.

Both the carving and the original writings are no longer there."

*She can't mean Grams.* "Julia, who?"

"Your grandmother."

"Well, ain't that a jaw dropper?" Jim said. "Grams doesn't appear outta thin air to just anyone."

Hayley turned to Lee. "She wouldn't involve herself unless my life's at risk."

"Everyone's life's at risk," Matilda said. "The protective amulets all of you were told to wear have vanished too."

"Our memories, the rune list, the amulets, the blessing— anything else missing?" Lee asked Matilda.

"Hayley and you had purchased the *Book of Spells* from Annie so Hayley could learn to cast spells in order to reveal the hidden text if I needed to study it when Julia wasn't around. Annie also gave you a book of basic witchcraft. Julia said all Hayley needed was a little practice. By placing memories into an object, Hayley would improve her focus."

"Where are these books now?" Hayley asked.

"Your house. Julia had told me that you were practicing casting a spell by placing residual energy into a charm bracelet."

An eerie feeling filled Hayley when she removed the velvet case from her purse. She gently lifted the bracelet by its clasp, glanced at Lee, then touched the first charm, the ghost made from mother-of-pearl. Using psychometry, Hayley envisioned the memories of her first day at work. A blonde woman greeted her when she entered the office. *Is that Kathy?* Hayley let the memories encased in the ghost charm continue until they ended. "You're right. Memories are stored inside, but they're not the same as I recall."

"They wouldn't be," Matilda said. "The threads of Kathy's existence have been removed from your mind."

"Why haven't your memories been affected, miss?" Jim asked.

Matilda grimaced. "You used to call me Matdie."

"You're the one I spoke to on the phone," Jim replied. "Sorry. I had no idea."

"It's not your fault," Matilda told him. "Vara didn't know about our involvement. We kept our investigation a secret."

Lee reached for the other end of the bracelet. "Wait a minute." He placed it across his palm. "What's this? I didn't give you these charms—not that I recall."

"A bird, a witch's hat, and a book." Hayley held the bird between two fingers and closed her eyes. Suddenly she envisioned the first time she, Lee, and Jim met Vara. The memory jumped to their visit to Annie's when Lee received Annie's business card. "Look in your wallet, Lee. Do you still have Annie's card?"

He retrieved his wallet from his back pocket and began shuffling through its contents, stopping halfway through when he found a card containing the image of a *Y* with a line down the middle of its fork, and Annie's business information. "Well, what do you know?" he said, pulling it from the stack. "I guess Vara didn't know I had this." He gave it to Hayley.

"Hmm," she said, and turned to Matilda, passing her the card. "What does this symbol mean?"

"It's called *Algiz*. To summarize its meaning, I'd say it symbolizes communication with the Higher Realm, leading to the understanding of the Divine Plan and the ability to channel protection to use against harmful forces." She returned the card to Hayley. "Sounds about right. Apparently, Vara has a plan, whatever that may be, and she's giving Annie protection to fight against Hildr. And by the way, we also learned that Annie and her family are related to Vara."

"That's interesting," Hayley replied.

"Why would Vara need Annie's help?" Roger asked. "It doesn't make sense. Vara's a sentinel. Why can't she capture Hildr on her own?"

"Both Vara and Hildr have the capability to foresee the future," Matilda said. "They know each other's moves before they make them. As it stands, the two of them are evenly matched. Unless Hildr makes a wrong turn somewhere, Vara may be chasing her for eternity."

Roger shook his head. "If Hildr can foresee Vara's every move, then it makes perfect sense that she can foresee Annie's. She could outwit Annie as easily as she has Vara. What's the advantage?"

"You're right, Roger," Hayley said. "There's more to this than we know." She read the phone number. "Why don't we call Annie? If she won't tell us Vara's plan, maybe she'll be able to help us with our memories."

"How ya gonna tell if you can trust her?" Jim asked.

"I'll ask her to meet with us here," Hayley said. "It's easier than all of us going there. When she arrives, I'll sense if she's telling the truth." She looked through her purse but couldn't find her cell phone. "I must have left it at home."

Lee took his phone from his shirt pocket and handed it to her. After dialing the number, she placed the call on speaker. Annie picked up on the second ring.

"This is Hayley Johnson. Do you remember me?"

"Yes, of course. I've been thinking about you all morning. I was about to call you. Is everything all right?"

"We're fine, but we need your help. Something strange has happened, and we think it may involve witchcraft. If I give you directions, would you be able to come by?"

"No problem. I'll close the shop early and be there around five."

Hayley gave directions to Roger's home. "Thanks so much. See you then." She ended the call and passed the phone back to Lee. "That went well."

# CHAPTER 23

A log shifted in the library's fireplace while the fire licked freshly placed wood.

"You might want to leave before Annie arrives," Hayley told Matilda, "to continue keeping your involvement a secret."

"Yes, of course. I'll wait in the other room."

"Leave the door cracked so you can hear our conversation," Roger suggested.

Matilda rose, left through a side door leading to a conference room, and kept the door ajar. A short time later, Roger and Hayley greeted Annie when she entered the library.

"You have a beautiful home," Annie said.

"Thank you," Roger replied.

She turned and gave Hayley a hug.

While placing her arms around Annie, Hayley foresaw Annie standing alone in a clearing surrounded by a forest. Hayley looked up at the star-clustered sky and saw the full moon, its bright light illuminating the meadow. Along the edges of the forest, she could make out only the gray shadows of trees in a fog she sensed to be unnatural. *A spell to keep everyone out.*

On the far end of the clearing near a makeshift limestone altar, Hayley saw a little girl holding a large leather-bound book in her outstretched hands and standing with Kathy. Annie's face hardened as she called to the girl, "Zoey, come to Mama." But the child remained statuesque with eyes closed. Annie clenched her hands, then raised them. Fireballs shot from her palms, flying at Kathy, her daughter's captor.

With a brush of her hand, Kathy misdirected the flaming spheres.

Hayley's vision ended. *Kathy's possessed by Hildr, and Annie's going to kill her.* Deciding to keep the information to herself, for now, Hayley stepped back, controlling her emotions, forbidding Annie to sense her alarm. "I'm so glad you came," she told her.

"I've been worried about you," Annie said. "What can I help you with?"

"It's really strange, but when we woke up this morning, we found our memories had been tampered with. We're hoping you can help us."

Roger led them to the couches and introduced her to Jim. "I'm assuming you've met Lee."

"Yes, and I've also met Jim," Annie explained. "It won't take long to find out if it's a curse. If it is, I'll be more than happy to reverse the spell. I'll start with you, Hayley."

Hayley, arms at her side, stood in front of her.

Annie ran her hands about an inch away from Hayley's body. Then she closed her eyes and placed her hand on Hayley's right shoulder. She shook her head. "It's not a curse. How did this happen?"

"That's what we want to know," Hayley said. "Please, sit down."

Annie made herself comfortable.

Hayley sat next to her. "Let me be honest with you. I'm sure you're aware that Vara has been protecting us." She watched Annie's face and body language, noticing only a raised brow. "Do you know from whom or what?"

"Hildr," Annie said without hesitation. "My ancestors have expected this moment when she would escape from her grave. Since Vara's death, the *Book of Spells* has been passed down through the generations. Each child has been told the story of how Vara and William buried the witch. All have been taught the spells within the book, and have given an oath to stop Hildr from killing again."

*She's telling the truth*, Hayley thought.

"I can sense how frustrating your memory loss is," Annie said. "But I'm baffled how to find a solution. Let me try a couple of spells to see if that will help. Lee, would you mind if I tried them on you? I promise no harm will come to you."

"Yes, of course." He and Annie stood.

"Come, stand in front of the fireplace." She led him away from the others. "Just relax."

He took a deep breath. "Okay. I'm ready."

Placing one hand on a crystal on her necklace, Annie spoke in a language Hayley didn't understand. "Did it help?" Annie asked him.

Lee hesitated, then replied, "No."

"I have one more spell. If that doesn't work, I don't know what will."

Lee stood still.

She took off her necklace, clenched the crystal in her palm, and recited a much longer spell. "Anything?"

"Afraid not."

Annie frowned. "Sorry. I don't know what else to do."

Lee returned to his seat.

Annie sat again. "If this has to do with Hildr, the remedy could be intentionally kept from us."

"I was afraid of that." Hayley bit her bottom lip. *She's not going to like this, but I have to tell her.* "We believe Vara's the one who took our memories because we got in her way. She told us Kathy had been kidnapped and asked us to do nothing. But we went against her wishes and tried to rescue her."

Hayley sensed Annie's adverse reaction. *I knew it. How could I think she'd go against her family to help us?*

"Sorry," Annie said coldly. "I can't betray the Keeper." She stood and, without hesitating, walked away.

"You can't go," Hayley said. "There's more. I had a vision of your daughter, Zoey. She was with Kathy in a forest. She seemed to be in a trance. I don't know how long in the future it will be, but I'm sure it will happen."

Annie stopped on her heels, her face pale. She retrieved her cell phone from her purse and made a call. "Zoey, are you all right?" She listened. "I'll be home soon." She returned her phone to her purse and came back to the couch. "She's safe. What did you see?" Annie asked, clearly shaken.

"Wait," Jim said. "Did ya see Hildr? Doesn't that mean ya can psychically find her and Kathy?"

Hayley felt a knot in her throat as she replied, "That's not all I envisioned. Kathy's been possessed."

"Bring her back," Lee said to Annie. "Return Kathy to us."

She shook her head. "Too late. If Hildr has possessed her, she's already dead."

"What do you mean, 'she's already dead'?" Lee asked.

"The spell Hildr uses puts the victim into a coma—one she'll never awaken from."

"Did you and your family know Kathy would be the victim?" Hayley asked. "Could you have stopped this from happening?"

"No. But it has been told by our ancestors that the one who will be taken has given her permission. It is said that the Keeper approached her before she was born into this lifetime, and a deal was struck. I don't know the details, only that she gave her consent to help put an end to Hildr's evilness. Your Kathy should be remembered as a martyr."

"No. I won't believe that," Roger said.

"I'm not buying it either," Lee agreed.

"You're a murderer," Jim said.

Annie's face reddened. "I'm not evil, and neither is the Keeper. The only way to save your friend now is to imprison Hildr and bury her in Kathy's body. Once the body dies, your friend's soul will be freed."

"It's not logical," Lee said. "I don't believe anyone would volunteer to die by asphyxiation."

"Vara wouldn't lie." Annie straightened. "No matter what you believe, I can't go against the Keeper."

"Sounds like you're doin' whatever the Rice Krispies are tellin' ya," Jim told her.

"I'm sorry you feel that way, but this isn't up to any of you."

"If what you're saying is true," Hayley said, "it won't make a difference if you keep our meeting to yourself. Vara doesn't need to know. Nothing has changed. Our memories are gone, and we're not a threat to anyone."

The glare in Annie's eyes softened. "I'm sorry this is difficult for you. But you're right, you're not a threat. I find no reason to mention this to the Keeper. She needs to focus. In time you will accept your friend's decision. Enough talk. I'm sorry, but what's done is done." She headed toward the door and without looking back, brushed by Cummings and left.

"You can come out now," Hayley said loudly over her shoulder.

Matilda returned to the room and sat on the couch. "I heard everything." Tears filled her eyes. "We have to do something. Hayley, can you locate Kathy again?"

"I'll try."

Before Hayley could close her eyes, Grams materialized by the mantle. "Not a good idea," she said. "Remember how your vision at Mr. G's ended, dear? Hildr sensed you probing and flung your consciousness back to the present. Next time she could kill you."

"So what now?" Hayley asked.

"I don't believe your memories were removed permanently," Grams said.

"What gives you that idea?" Lee asked.

"If that were the case, Vara would have erased the remembrances of Kathy's existence completely. But she didn't. Matilda, Lewis, Cummings, and all of her other friends, not to mention *The Sutterville* archives, continue to hold memories of her past. No, I believe you've been delayed, pushed aside until Vara can complete her agenda."

"You mean until she kills Kathy?" Matilda replied.

"We don't know for sure if that's her plan," Grams said. "The divine work in mysterious ways. But there's good news."

Matilda raised her brow. "How's that possible?"

"I was there when Hayley used her gift of astral projection and found Hildr had possessed Kathy. It frightened Hayley, and she returned to her psychical self. That's when Hildr went to the front porch, appearing to be Kathy, and confronted Jim. I watched from afar and saw Lee run out into the field to rescue him. Before any bloodshed occurred, Vara flew into the clearing and changed into human form to save Lee and Jim's lives. She turned to Hildr and attacked. From then on, it became comical."

She chuckled. "When Hildr reached out to hurl a spell at Vara, Kathy jarred her arm. The spell was diverted and singed a pine tree. Hildr swore. And each time she attempted to attack Jim, Lee, and Vara, Kathy reacted. Finally, Vara called for a truce and took everyone's memories to convince Hildr that all of you would no longer be a threat."

"That means Hildr didn't have time to evoke the coma spell before possessing Kathy," Hayley said.

"She couldn't," Grams told them. "The spell takes three days. Vara's been on her tail day and night. Instead, Hildr chose to possess Kathy without using any part of the spell. Now Hildr has to share Kathy's body and mind."

"When Vara attacked, she could've harmed Kathy," Hayley said. "I thought she couldn't harm an innocent. Plus, she hasn't told Annie that Hildr didn't cast the coma spell. Isn't she supposed to be truthful?"

"Just because you're keeping information from someone doesn't mean you're not an honest person," Grams replied. "I do it to you all the time. It's part of my job. Maybe it's part of hers as well."

"But this is different," Lee said. "By not saying anything, she's allowing Kathy to be murdered."

"So, what's Vara's intention?" Hayley asked. "Is this the plan she convinced Kathy to go along with? Is Kathy really going to be a martyr like Annie said?"

"If Vara has her way," Matilda told her.

"What do you mean?" Roger asked.

"According to Jim's regression," Matilda said. "Hildr was in

Sihu's body when she was buried."

"Who's Sihu?" Jim asked.

"She's Vara's sister. Hildr possessed Sihu when she was ten. That seems to be the age Hildr likes her victims to be."

"And?" Roger asked.

"And that's the key to Vara's plan," Matilda said. "Only by keeping Hildr's spirit within a host's body, and placing the cursed stone over the grave, will her spirit be imprisoned. If it's true that Zoey is Vara's relative, Vara will save her life and sacrifice Kathy by allowing her to remain the host. Unless Vara stops Annie, when the time comes for Annie to repeat the full moon burial, she'll bury Kathy without remorse."

"It does sound like Vara intends on letting Annie perform witchcraft and kill an innocent," Grams said. "If she thinks permitting someone else to cast the spell will exonerate herself from breaking the forbidden rules, she's wrong. She'd be just as guilty."

"No matter what," Matilda said, choking back a tear, "Kathy will die."

"Do we know anything about the clearing—any clues to its location?" Roger asked. "How can we pinpoint where the battle will take place?"

"When the runestone was found," Matilda explained, "it was taken to Harvard University, where a test was being run to analyze the rock's origin and the age of the text. Unfortunately, the stone was stolen before any results could be made. I flew to Massachusetts to meet with a colleague and to follow a lead on its recent whereabouts, but the trail led nowhere. I only arrived back here this morning."

Pieces of a plan came together in Hayley's mind. "Was a sample of the rock taken?"

"Yes," Matilda replied. "The day before it vanished."

"Can your colleague get his hands on it?"

"I can ask him."

"What are ya plannin' to do now, darlin?" Jim asked Hayley.

"I plan to track the stone by using the sample piece."

"How's that possible?" Matilda asked.

"Like a person has his own fingerprints, the stone has its own signature energy. Every place, each person it's come into contact with, and the dirt that covered it for centuries has imprinted its energy into the stone. If I can get the sample and sense its energy pattern, I'll be able to psychically find the runestone."

"How interesting," Matilda said. "Will it work, Julia?"

"The theory is correct. But she needs to keep her distance. Vara still believes all of you are no longer a threat."

"Do you think Annie and her family have the stone?" Lee asked.

"Yes," Grams told him. "Recently, I detected it being moved from Annie's store. Since then, I haven't been able to locate it."

"Grams, would it be possible for you to pop over and get the sample?" Hayley asked. "Or will we have to wait until they arrive by mail?"

"I can't. To research Vara's intentions is something I needed to do anyway as your guardian angel. I have to know what and who is a threat to you in every variation of your future. The rest of the investigation is up to you. I have limits."

"I understand. You've been a great help."

"And you know when I discover Vara's plan, I may also have limits if it involves your future. Rules are rules."

"You've been so immersed with our case, as Matilda has said, I'd forgotten about that stupid rule—you can't tell me my future."

"I almost forgot too, dear."

"Did you foresee our memory loss?" Hayley asked.

"Yes. Why do you think I nudged Lee into buying that charm bracelet for you and then taught you the spell to place memories into an object? But that's the extent of it. I didn't influence you into placing them into the charms."

A spark of understanding lit Hayley's eyes. *And you knew that would happen too.* "The bracelet.... You found a way around the rules."

"Like I said, it was your idea to place your memories into the bracelet. I only provided a logical place to store them."

"Clever, Grams," Lee said. "You tricked me into buying the perfect gift. I had no clue."

"'Nudging,' I call it—placing into someone's mind a thought that appears to be their own idea. And no, it was your choice," Grams said. "You could've decided on another gift."

"Good thing I didn't."

"From now on, you have to be double careful making decisions," Grams warned. "Especially in solving this case. If you're not, one of you could die."

"Someone might die?" Roger asked Grams.

"From the moment you lost your memories, I became unable to foresee Hayley's future. And that scares me. Anything can happen, and if it's meant to be, I can't interfere."

"Dangerous or not, we'll move forward with the rescue," Roger said, "as soon as we find the runestone."

"I'll call my colleague in the morning and see if he can overnight the sample," Matilda told them.

"I'll tell Cummings to expect it," Roger replied.

"Well, I'm still trying to find a way around the guardian's rules of secrecy," Grams said. "So, I'll be going."

"Thanks, Grams, for everything," Hayley said.

"Just be careful, dear." She vanished as quickly as she'd appeared.

Lee turned to Matilda. "Do you think there'll be a problem getting the sample?"

She glanced at Hayley. "Can you foresee my future?"

Closing her eyes, Hayley cleared her mind and allowed her clairvoyance to search. "Matilda's future," she whispered. She saw a vision of Matilda and Jim locked in an embrace, kissing under the mistletoe. She glanced at Jim, then at Matilda, knowing she couldn't tell them without it affecting the outcome. Things had to happen on their own.

She tried again. "The sample," she said softly. She envisioned Matilda opening a package and finding three pea-sized fragments in a petri dish. "Yes. They'll be sent here."

"Thank goodness. We need to find Kathy quickly." Matilda stood and wandered to the window, staring as if looking out at the remnants of the storm. "I'm so worried about her."

Hayley joined her and noticed the winds had died down. Only a few lingering clouds remained. She put her arm around Matilda's shoulder. "We'll find her in time."

"She saved my life, you know," Matilda said. "One night, when I was working late at the university, I left to go home and walked out to my car. I didn't hear the man who grabbed me from behind. I struggled. When he raised a knife to end my life, Kathy attacked him with pepper spray, beat him to the ground, and held him there until security came. I didn't know she'd been sitting in her car, answering a text when she noticed me walking across the parking lot. If she hadn't been there, I would've died that night."

"Kathy's one hell of a woman," Hayley said. "And we won't

let her die either."

"Wish we could just call the police or FBI," Matilda said.

"That would be one variable. But it wouldn't work. We don't know where she is, and if they did find her, Hildr would put up a fight."

"You mean Kathy. That's who the police would see. If Hildr killed someone, Kathy would be taken to jail."

"Yes. Hildr's spirit would leave Kathy's body to find another victim, and Kathy would be convicted of murder."

Matilda wrapped her arms around herself and shuddered. "I hope she's warm and dry. I can't imagine how cold it must be sleeping in the wilderness."

"One thing's for sure, Hildr would take good care of her since she needs Kathy's energy to fight Vara."

"Until Annie buries Hildr and Kathy alive." Matilda covered her face with her hands and cried. "How is it possible to fight Annie, Vara, and Hildr?"

Hayley couldn't allow herself to give up hope. She left Matilda to join Lee and looked over her shoulder to see Jim stroll to the distraught woman's side. He stood tentatively, shifting his weight from one foot to the next, his hands entwined behind his back.

"Don't cry, little lady. We've been waist deep in donkey dung before, and we came out smellin' like a petunia."

Matilda glanced up at his two black eyes. "Oh, Jim," she said and smothered her face in his chest, sniffling.

Gingerly, Jim put his arms around her, glanced at Hayley and Lee, and gave them a thumbs up.

"Guess we'll leave him here," Lee said. "She's in good hands. Let's head home."

"Precisely what I was thinking."

After saying goodbye, Hayley grabbed her purse and walked with Lee through the hallways to the front door. Once Cummings presented them with their coats and scarves, they left.

"I want to study every memory I placed in the charms," Hayley told Lee when he opened the Cayenne's door for her. "If there are any answers to what we should do, I'll find them."

"Good plan. I'd like to have a clearer idea about what's been going on myself."

***

Hayley and Lee strolled into the dining room. She'd always loved this room and enjoyed dining here as much as dining in Lee's sitting room. Hayley glanced around as if getting reacquainted.

A grape leaves-and-vines design embossed each cornice, and double-crown molding framed a coffered ceiling. Three chandeliers, each around four feet in diameter, hung throughout the room — the largest above the dining table. On the north yellow walls, five twelve-foot-tall windows, dressed with green velvet drapes, looked over the garden pond. Above the huge carved marble fireplace hung a portrait of Ben Franklin. The lengthy table with seating for thirty-two had been set for two.

They took their time eating dinner. Between each nibble, Hayley reviewed the memories stored inside the charms and discussed them with Lee.

After the table had been cleared, the drapes had been drawn, and the day staff had been dismissed for the night, Lee looked at his watch. "It's almost ten."

"We'll save the last three charms for morning." Hayley raised her hand to her mouth and covered a yawn. "I haven't found anything to help us yet."

He stood and pulled out Hayley's chair. They leisurely walked down the hall to the elevator across from the ballroom.

She glanced at the ballroom's double doors, then down at her engagement ring, remembering the night Lee proposed to her.

He took her hand, lifted it to his lips, and tenderly kissed her. "We've been sitting all night. How about a little exercise before we retire?" Lee offered her his arm and led her inside the ballroom. "Lights on, Max," he said.

The computer responded.

The five chandeliers lit. The largest hung in the center of the rectangular room, which spanned nearly the width of the mansion. The walls, painted shades of pale green trimmed with gold, rose to meet the frescos ceiling, depicting the gardens of Florence.

The ballroom's grandeur still filled Hayley with awe. "So beautiful. But it looks empty without the white linen tables bordering the dance floor and the hundreds of costumed guests."

"Nothing a little imagination can't fix," Lee replied. "Max, Strauss."

When *The Blue Danube* began, they gracefully swirled around the dance floor. Lee dipped her, and while she relaxed in his arms, he said, "You are my heart, my soul, my happiness, and my love." He brought her to her feet and pulled her near.

A breath away from his lips, she whispered, "For eternity." Then she kissed him tenderly.

They continued to waltz, turning and gliding. The music ended once they reached the double doors.

Lee bowed to her, straightened, and said over his shoulder, "Max, lights out."

The room fell into darkness as he led her from the room and closed the doors. Hand in hand, they walked across the hall to the elevator, heading to his chambers.

# CHAPTER 24

That night, in a dream as real as life, Hayley found herself standing alongside a narrow paved road. Where the asphalt ended and a dirt road began, another unpaved road forked toward the west through the trees and down a hill. She turned in a circle, trying to get clues to her location. By a stone wall in disarray beneath dead leaves, fallen branches, and encroaching plants, a sign read, "Private property. Keep out." To the right, a bridge arched over a creek. Nothing gave her any idea to her whereabouts.

Hayley again faced the wooded trail in front of her. Like giant gray ghosts in a fog, tulip trees, hemlock, and pine looked foreboding, as if to whisper, "Do not enter." She squinted into the mist but saw nothing beyond. Her senses, however, told her that only steps away a forest full of century-old trees existed between her and the meadow where Annie would confront Hildr. When she began to wonder how she'd get to the field through the fog, instantly, she found herself at its edge under a massive hemlock and knelt behind its wide trunk, the forest now at her back.

As Hayley watched, Annie and her two sisters strolled out

of the mist and into the clearing. Each wore dark blue full-length robes with hoods covering their heads and hiding their faces. *Something's different,* Hayley realized. *Annie's not alone this time.*

Across the moonlit field, Hildr, possessing Kathy's body, stood near the limestone altar. By her side, Zoey, Annie's daughter, appeared as still as a log, her black hair hanging over her shoulders, her arms pinned at her sides, her head drooped as if she were sleeping, and the *Book of Spells* at her feet.

Annie took her stance between her siblings. "Zoey, come to Mama," she cried out.

The child didn't move. Her head remained lowered.

Annie's familiar, Lovely, perching on Hildr's/Kathy's shoulder, scampered down the witch's arm, jumped to the ground, and scuttled toward her rightful master. As the tarantula approached Annie, Hildr cursed, raised her hand, and flung a fireball, striking the spider. Lovely shrieked while the flames consumed her.

Annie swore. Her eyes filled with rage, and she took a step forward. Raising a hand, she signaled to her siblings, and they encased themselves within protective shields. Once safeguarded, Annie cast her first assault.

Vines emerged from the ground surrounding Hildr, each stalk spiraling her torso, pinning her arms to her sides, entwining its tentacles around her chest and shoulders, coiling her neck until licking her face.

Before the creeping plant engulfed her, Hildr spoke a spell turning the vines into slithering snakes. She grinned while they hissed, each losing their grip around her as they struck out at one another and dropped to the ground near her feet. With a twitch of her finger, she turned the snakes into lances and flung them at Annie and her siblings.

Annie froze five spears in midair inches before they pierced her shield. As they dropped to the ground, another whizzed by her right shoulder, shattering her sister's protective shield and striking her sister, puncturing her heart. She collapsed, lifeless.

The sibling on Annie's left ran to the slain sister, knelt next to her, then rose with hatred in her eyes and joined Annie. Side by side, they retaliated with blasts of energy hitting Hildr, slamming her backward, bashing her against the altar.

Appearing dazed, Hildr/Kathy stood and stumbled, taking a stance in front of the child. In an instant, the sisters struck again, sending a long line of golden rope lashing around Kathy's/Hildr's body, binding her from head to foot.

Standing in the woods behind Hildr, Hayley saw everything.

Once Kathy's/Hildr's body fell to the ground, Annie rushed forward and cried out. "Zoey!"

When Zoey raised her head, Hayley screamed and woke trembling.

Lee jumped out of bed and reached to turn on the lamp on the nightstand. "What's wrong?"

Hayley sat up, opened the drawer in the table beside her, and pulled out a notepad and pencil. She started to explain, making notes and telling him everything she'd envisioned. When she reached the end of what she'd foreseen, she told him, "But Annie will be standing at the wrong angle and won't see Hildr's spirit leave Kathy's body and possess Zoey. Annie and her family will bury Kathy, believing she's Hildr."

"You've always said the future isn't fixed," Lee said.

"It's true. What I dreamt wasn't the same as I envisioned when I hugged Annie. Then, she was alone when she confronted Hildr. In my dream, she was with her sisters. It's as if I'm foreseeing variations of Annie's future." Hayley thought a moment. "If I only knew exactly what will take place—who'll be there, how they'll attack—maybe I could change the outcome somehow."

"That would mean we'd have to be there when it actually takes place. And in order for that to happen, we'll have to find the runestone."

"That's too much to think about right now," Hayley said. "We'd better get some sleep."

# CHAPTER 25

In the morning after Hayley dressed, she retrieved her bracelet from her purse and sat cross-legged on Lee's bed while he showered. After he'd finished in the bathroom and dressed, he sat with her on the bed. To get a better perspective on what they'd be facing, she used psychometry to review all the memories she'd stored within the witch's hat charm.

"This is a nightmare." He stood and strolled to the fireplace. After lighting a fire under the logs, he looked over his shoulder. "Grams didn't appear to be very worried. Sure, she mentioned danger, but I got the sense that she thinks we can handle it."

"I agree. But that doesn't mean it's going to be easy. We need a plan."

Anxious to find the spell she had used before to place memories into her bracelet, she grasped the golden book charm. Again using psychometry, she flipped past the pages of the *Book of Spells* stored within the charm and found what she'd been looking for. *Storing.* "I found it," she told him. "I want to store the memories of my dream so I can visualize it over and over."

"Good time for me to leave and let you concentrate," Lee

said, pulling a sweater over his head, adding another layer for warmth. He strolled to the window near her side of the bed and looked out. "Good. The rain has stopped. I told Roger I'd go with him to pick out an engagement ring for Laura."

Hayley's eyes brightened. "Finally."

"Guess your prediction's about to come true."

"Did you have a doubt?"

He leaned across the bed and kissed her. "Never, my love." He walked around to the nightstand on his side of the bed, picked up his wallet, tucked it into his back pocket, and grabbed his keys. "Roger's coming by to get me. He's dropping off Jim. He said Jim's taking Matilda to dinner tonight to get her out of the house."

Hayley remembered her clairvoyant vision of Jim's and Matilda's future and nodded. "Good idea. Did he say where he's taking her?"

"To dinner at *The Hamlin*."

"Way to make a good impression. She's going to think he's rich."

"It's a rare occasion, that's for sure. He never flaunts his wealth." He slipped on his high-top sneakers and began to lace them.

She raised an eyebrow. "'His wealth'?"

Lee chucked. "I'm sure I told you." He leaned across the bed and kissed her again. "See you later."

"Yeah. I'll have something interesting to tell you when you get back," she said, remembering she hadn't told him about Jim and Matilda's future.

"Can't wait," he replied, walking away from her.

"Did Roger say when he's going to ask her?" Hayley asked.

"No," Lee replied. "But I'm sure it'll come up. I'll call you and let you know."

"I'd like that."

He hesitated before opening the door and turned to her. "What do you think about making it a double wedding? Roger's like a brother to me. It would be great."

"Perfect. Let me know what he says."

A faint feeling of déjà vu washed over her as if this had been discussed once before, but she dismissed it as a car honked outside.

"Will do," Lee said, hurriedly opening the door and closing it behind him.

Hayley turned her attention to the last charm. She touched it lightly, closed her eyes, and allowed the lessons on *Storing* and the reversal spell to be revealed.

After envisioning the techniques over and over, Hayley took a break for lunch in Lee's sitting room. Lewis had lit a fire in the fireplace for her as she cuddled at the end of the blue suede couch, nibbling a tuna sandwich and sipping milk.

She placed her empty dishes on the end table, stood to stretch her legs, and drifted to the window overlooking the spruce-lined drive leading to the mansion. Hardy trees still held on to their brightly colored leaves, while others, naked and colorless, waited for winter. She jumped when her cell phone rang, snatched it out of her pants pocket, and revealed the caller. *Laura.*

"What's up?" Hayley asked.

"I'm taking Matilda shopping for a dress to wear this evening. Jim asked her out."

"I heard."

"Anyway, I stopped at home. The books you bought from Annie are gone."

"I figured they would be. But Vara doesn't know about my

bracelet or Matilda and Grams's research."

"Won't Annie tell her that you asked for her help?"

"It doesn't matter. We kept our secrets from Annie as well. All she knows is that we know about Kathy. She doesn't know we'd uncovered the hidden message and found the plans for the confrontation during the full moon, or that we know about the runestone. Neither she nor Vara will expect us when we show up to spoil their plans to battle."

"Do you have any idea how we're going to do that?"

"Not yet, but I'm working on it."

"I'd like to give Vara a piece of my mind if I ever see her again," Laura said. "Today, I found that during the days I can't remember, I performed surgeries. If it weren't for the calendar on my desk, I wouldn't have known, and their recovery would be in jeopardy."

"That sounds horrific. Vara's got a lot to explain. Good thing we found out about our disorder as quickly as we did. Now we're one step ahead of her. Anyway, hope you have a pleasant day with Matilda and hang in there."

"Thanks. Just wanted to let you know about the books."

"Glad you called. Talk to you later. Tell Matilda to have fun."

Hayley ended the call and shoved her phone back into her pocket. She thought about last night's dream, imagining if she'd been possessed and how desperate she'd feel to have her life back. *Kathy must know what Hildr's thinking. She has got to know that Vara and Jim buried Hildr alive. I'm sure she can feel Hildr's fear of it happening again.* Hayley felt compelled to find the answer — the right moment when she could say or do something that would change everything and save Kathy. *I'd better get back to work.*

She crossed the room, settled on the couch, picked up the new notebook she planned to use as an object, turned to the first page, and thought back to last night's dream, going through each detail. Then she started casting the spell.

When she read the results of the first few efforts, she realized the memories she tried to store in the pages of her notebook appeared distorted and scattered. *Focus. If I did it before, I can do it again.* She wished for Grams's guidance.

Taking a deep calming breath, she tried again. This time the memories flowed smoothly but not perfectly into the empty page.

She thought about Lee. He'd been gone half the day. *When will he be home? I wonder if this spell would work on a person.* Hayley relaxed, said the words "Call Hayley," and visualized the thought flowing into Lee's mind.

As if he had received her message, Lee called. *Well, what do you know?* She pulled her cell phone from her pants pocket and answered.

"We're on our way home from Greensboro. He didn't find a ring he liked, so he's having one custom made. Should be ready by the end of the month."

"How did he like your great idea?"

"It made his day."

"When's he going to ask her?"

"Christmas."

Again she felt a sense of déjà vu. *Did we talk about this before? Am I on the verge of getting my memory back?* "I wish he'd tell her sooner. I can't wait to help her pick out a dress."

"As well as your own. How are you doing with casting spells? Are you a witch yet?"

"I've finally got it."

"Promise you won't get any crazy ideas that would get you killed."

"To use witchcraft against another witch? Seriously, Lee?

That would never happen."

"I'll take that as a promise. I'll see you in a bit."

She ended the call, focused again on casting spells, cleared the residual energy from the pages of the notebook by using the reversal spell, and continued to practice until the spell came naturally to her.

*Okay, I just found out the spell I used to store memories into objects can also place thoughts into a person's mind – 'nudging,' Grams called it. If I use nudging to place a thought into Kathy's mind, maybe I can coax her into reacting, interfering with Hildr's attacks again, taking control of certain movements that will let Annie see that Kathy's not comatose. I'm sure when Annie recognizes Kathy can be saved, she'll realize she's about to kill an innocent and back off.*

She flipped through her notebook to an empty page void of stored memories, grabbed a pencil lying on the end table next to her, and began to write.

*First, if I tell Lee I'm going to send messages to him, he may think every thought he has is a nudge. That would be too confusing. So, I won't use him for the experiment. But everyone else can help.*

*Secondly, they would have to be in the room with me so I can see how fast they react or if they react at all.*

*I have to be precise. What I visualize must be in focus. Since I've forgotten my memories of Kathy and what she looks like, I'll have to go through the charms until I can imagine her face distinctly, or my efforts to place thoughts in her mind will fail.*

*Then I have to work on speed. Sending a nudge to Kathy has to be instantaneous for her to react quickly.*

Hayley took a deep breath after reviewing her list. "This is going to take a lot of work," she said aloud. She unclasped the bracelet on her wrist and started with the first charm, the ghost made from mother-of-pearl. Over and over, she sought memories of Kathy, trying to etch her friend's image into her mind. *When I close my eyes and picture her, she's still a stranger. No matter how hard I try, my reflection of her is flawed.*

She looked up when Lee entered the room.

"You look frustrated," he said.

"I am. I've found a way to disrupt Vara and Annie's plan. But it'll take witchcraft."

Lee raised his hands. "That's out of the question."

"Hear me out first. I'm planning to use nudging. It's what Grams used on you. Hildr will think it's Kathy's thoughts."

"It seems harmless enough. What about Vara?" Lee asked. "Will she know?"

"I hope not."

"Can you do it?"

"I'm almost positive," Hayley replied. "I'm going to experiment on the rest of the team. If I'm doing it right, none of them will suspect a thing."

"What nudge do you plan on sending to Kathy?"

"I'm going to get her to fight like she did when Vara saved Lee and Jim, or react somehow to let Annie see she isn't in a coma. If Annie sees she's about to harm an innocent, she'll stop her attack."

"What makes you think Kathy won't redirect Hildr's spells on her own as she did before?" Lee asked.

"Because in each of my dreams, she didn't. I don't know why. But I can't leave it to chance."

"Understandable," Lee said. "Nudging. I know how I responded. Sounds like it will work. But no more witchcraft other than that."

"Promise. There's hope. There has to be, or why would we be involved?"

"Precisely. Now, how about we have dinner and put this nightmare aside for a while?" He took her hand while she rose from the couch. "Maybe some wine. There's nothing more we can do tonight."

"Great idea." Hayley put her arm around his waist and walked out of the room with him.

They wandered through the hallways and took the elevator to the dining room on the second floor. Lewis awaited them with cream of broccoli soup and pan-seared salmon alongside grilled asparagus.

Hayley lifted her glass of chardonnay and took a sip, nearly choking as she swallowed when Jim entered the room. He wore a tailored dark navy suit, his mustache had been trimmed, his face was shaven, and his hair was cut short, straight, and formal.

Lee whipped around in his chair. "What the hell?"

Jim threw up his hands. "I made a big mistake by tellin' Lewis where I'm takin' Matilda for dinner. Damn fool got all giddy on me and called Mario."

"My tailor?" Lee asked.

"Yeah. Seems those two have been talkin' 'bout me behind my back for years. Before I knew it, Austen was there."

"My barber?"

"Yep. In two shakes of a gnat's ass, I looked like this." He blushed. "They even put makeup on me to cover my black eyes. Ambush makeover, they called it. Hell, Matilda won't even recognize me."

Hayley noticed the swelling on his face had gone down. "You're handsome, Jim," she said. "She's going to love your new look."

"You'll have a great night," Lee told him. "Talk to Halister when you get there and ask him to recommend a dish."

"No need. Lewis called and took care of everything."

"Taking your Rolls-Royce?" Lee asked.

"Yep, but Lewis won't let me drive 'cause of that medication I'm takin', so he's gonna chauffeur. Hell, it's as if I haven't dated before."

"Well, not with someone as sophisticated as Matilda," Lee said.

"What do you mean by that? Lolita looked classy — whenever she had her teeth in. And boy was she patriotic. She had a flag pole in her bedroom. You know, she could — "

Lee cleared his throat. "I'm sure Hayley doesn't want to hear about that. Tell Matilda we said to have a good time, and we'll be over in the morning to check out the samples."

"Will do," Jim said. He turned and headed out the door.

"Have fun," Hayley called to him.

Lee shook his head as Jim left the room. "Don't believe everything he tells you. If he knew a woman named Lolita, I'm sure I would've heard about it."

"What about his wealth? Is that fabricated too?"

"No. He and Lewis have been playing the stock market together for years. They're both well-off. I thought I told you about that."

Hayley thought a moment and nodded. "You're right. I remember." He had told her a few months ago about the two's common interest. Vara or whoever had cast the amnesia spell erased hers and the other's memories from only the night of her birthday to the day of their attempted rescue. Thinking back and actually remembering something felt great.

"It's my good luck that they haven't moved on," he added. "I don't know what I'd do without them."

"It might happen. I had a vision of Matilda and Jim kissing

under the mistletoe. I have a feeling that their relationship is going to be more than a casual fling."

Lee straightened in his chair, a smile lighting his face. "Seriously?" Hayley nodded and grinned. He filled their glasses with wine and made a toast. "Here's to 'happily ever after.'" They clinked glasses.

After a couple more helpings of chardonnay, they strolled to the elevator. When the doors opened, Lee followed Hayley inside. Once he pushed the third-floor button, he turned to her, pulled her close, and seductively kissed her. As the doors opened again, he swept her off her feet and cradled her in his arms. "I'm going to make love to you in every room in the house," he said, stepping into the corridor and walking toward a bedroom across the hall.

Again she experienced the feeling this had happened once before. "Lee, have you been experiencing déjà vu lately?" she asked with her arms around his neck.

He hesitated a moment. "No. Why? Are you getting your memory back?"

"Not that I'm aware of."

Lee continued. "So, you think we're reliving the past?"

"It's just a feeling."

He opened the bedroom door and carried her inside. When he set her on her feet, he embraced her and whispered, "Maybe this will trigger your memories." His lips met hers.

As his kisses enflamed her, she could think only of this very moment, and barely noticed how he blindly reached behind him and shoved the door closed.

# CHAPTER 26

After frolicking with Lee until midnight and now back in his bedroom, Hayley fell asleep as soon as her head hit the pillow. She dreamed again of the thick fog and Annie and Hildr in the clearing. Once again, things were different.

Annie stood in the center of the meadow. When she glanced over her shoulder toward the woods where ten of her siblings waited, she gave a signal. Concealed in dark blue cloaks with hoods pulled forward covering their faces, they stepped from behind the tall pines, took their positions behind her, and postured for combat.

Again Lovely crawled down Hildr's arm, jumped to the ground, and scurried to her master. But this time, Hildr ignored the blue tarantula. To Hildr's side, Annie's daughter stood stone still, her head down, the *Book of Spells* at her feet. With a flick of her wrist, Hildr shielded herself inside a bubble. Then she attacked.

A stream of energy whizzed past Annie's head, striking one of her brothers. The force hurled the man backward, throwing him to the ground. As he staggered to his feet, his hood fell away, revealing his shoulder length hair. His hand held his stomach.

Grimacing, he steadied himself.

Hildr released another spell, striking Annie with full force. Fighting to stay on her feet, Annie caught her balance and planted her feet firmly on the ground. She struck back, flinging daggers, but Hildr's shield deflected the assault.

Hildr cackled, raised her hand, and spoke a spell. A fireball appeared in her palm, but as she released it, her arm jerked, and the ball missed its mark. Hildr hissed. Hayley realized Kathy had intervened. She watched Annie's face, hoping she had caught the gesture too. But Annie's determined expression showed no sign of softening, no acknowledgment that Kathy lived.

Annie's siblings came forward, joining her. Side by side, they raised their hands and cast a spell. A cyclone of blackbirds descended around Hildr's shield. While flapping their wings in a frenzy, they pecked at the protective bubble until it cracked. When Hildr's shield scattered around her, the birds turned into wisps of sand, swirled in the breeze, and disappeared.

Hildr glared at her adversaries and stepped in front of Zoey, taking her stance as she had time and again in Hayley's other dreams. Hildr raised her hand, but before she could retaliate, Annie and her siblings cast another spell. Glowing ropes lashed out, wrapping around Hildr's/Kathy's body, binding Kathy as she collapsed, her body lying lifeless on the ground.

Again, Hayley witnessed what they hadn't seen. Hildr had already made her escape.

"Zoey," Annie cried as she rushed toward her daughter.

The child raised her head, possessed by Hildr, and no one, but Hayley had seen the shift.

Hayley screamed, "No!" When she opened her eyes, she saw the light on and Lee standing by the bed.

"Same nightmare?" he asked.

"Yes, but different." She opened the nightstand drawer and grabbed her notebook. "This time, there were more siblings, and they didn't shield themselves for some reason." Closing her eyes, she meditated and pictured her dream cascading into the empty pages. After returning the book to the nightstand, she continued to explain what she'd envisioned.

"The fog barrier seemed the same. But this time, Kathy put up a fight for an instant. I need to start my experiment as soon as possible. I need to learn accuracy, clarity, and speed. I have to know how far away I can send a nudging with precision. I have to make her react, so Annie will notice. It's the only way."

"Try to go back to sleep," Lee said. "Everyone will gather in the morning. Matilda will have the samples by then."

Hayley glanced at the clock on the mantle. *Two-thirty.* "Good idea." She cleared her mind to release any negativity, curled beneath the sheets, and pulled the covers to her chin. "Good night, Lee."

"Pleasant dreams, my love." He reached over and turned out the light.

# CHAPTER 27

The next morning after breakfast and a phone call from Matilda, Hayley, Lee, and Jim drove to Angel Hall, where the samples had been delivered. Everyone attended the meeting except Laura, who had to make rounds at the hospital.

While sitting in Roger's living room with the rest of the team gathered, Hayley told them about her dreams.

"Ever since I hugged Annie the other day, I've been foreseeing variations of her future," she explained. "But I haven't been able to learn the location I've envisioned. Where are the samples you sent for, Matilda?"

"They're right here." She rose from her seat on the couch across from Hayley, took a few steps, and handed her a petri dish holding three pieces of the runestone.

Hayley opened the sterile container and extracted one of the samples. "There's a good chance the stone's still in the mountains somewhere. I'll need a printout of the Appalachians. A geographical view will do until I locate the area."

"Clint," Roger said. "See if we can download what she needs."

"Will do, Boss." He jumped out of his chair and headed to a computer across the room.

Hayley held the rock sample in her fist and closed her eyes, trying to envision the whereabouts of the carved stone. As if she were physically in its presence, in her mind, she saw the stone under a tarp inside a van. Sunlight and shadows flickered like a strobe light through the van's front windshield, making it difficult for her to see the interior. The driver and his passenger remained as gray silhouettes in heavy jackets and knit caps.

As the driver rounded a bend, sunlight streamed through the windshield, illuminating the blue tarp shrouding the runestone on the floor of the van. She searched for hints to the stone's destination among the items scattered around — a car battery, a gallon of water, flares, and a toolbox. Through the windshield, she saw nothing but trees skirting the road. *Not a clue.* She opened her eyes to see everyone staring at her.

"It's on the move," she told them, placing the sample back into the dish. "Somewhere in the mountains. There were two men, but I didn't see their faces."

Clint returned with a map and spread it on the ottoman in front of her.

Hayley closed her eyes and cleared her mind. When she reopened her eyes, she placed her palm above the map. Slowly she moved her hand over the geographical diagram, from the Appalachians in Georgia to the hills of Massachusetts and back. Over North Carolina near the Virginia border, her hand hovered until her index finger, much like a divining rod, pointed to a spot on the map.

"Here, and it's moving into Virginia. I have to wait until they stop before we can take the next step. I'll try again later."

"Exactly what are we going to do when we find the stone?"

Roger asked.

"Using the computer, we can scan the area and find the clearing. No doubt, it will be in the vicinity where the runestone will be stored. I'll know it when I see it."

"Once she finds the location," Lee said, "we can form a plan."

"If you're plannin' to hike just 'bout anywhere in them mountains," Jim pointed out, "you'll be riskin' your life. There's a war goin' on between landowners and trespassers, worse than it's ever been. Used to be moonshiners who'd shoot uninvited visitors. Nowadays, it's ginseng they're fightin' over—considered gold in those parts. Best thing to do when ya find the location is to contact the owner of the land. If ya don't, reachin' that clearin' you're seein' in your dreams may be harder than getting' by a hemorrhoid-ailin' grizzly mama."

Hayley, starting to realize the devious web Vara had spun, laid her head back against the couch and stared up at the coffered ceiling. She glanced at everyone and shook her head. "No. I'm sensing we won't have to worry about that. More than likely, her family owns the property so no one will be able to uncover Hildr's grave again."

She took a deep frustrated breath in and out, stood, walked to the fireplace, and paced while she unraveled the deception from its beginning. "I'm guessing that as soon as Vara became a sentinel, she foresaw Hildr's escape from the grave. She told her children, and they taught their children witchcraft from the *Book of Spells*. As Annie told us, generation after generation of the Forte family prepared for Hildr's escape. And since the confrontation site wasn't found in the secret message Matilda discovered, the location must have been known by the family from the beginning as well."

Hayley paced for a few moments more, paused, and faced

everyone.

"In the beginning, when Vara foresaw the location, she must have also seen the altar Hildr intended to use during her rejuvenation ritual, and Zoey being Hildr's chosen victim for her possession spell, which she kept secret from the family. But the future isn't fixed. No doubt, she spent her entire existence foreseeing every variation of Hildr's movements, trying to find a way to capture Hildr before Zoey would be kidnapped."

"So Vara tricked Hildr into taking Kathy instead," Matilda said. "By tailing Hildr so closely and frightening her into quickly finding a living being to possess in order to defend herself, it delayed Hildr from taking the child."

Hayley nodded. "Yes. It's only a theory, but it makes sense. Meeting her maker is Hildr's greatest fear. I don't think the night Vara almost seduced Jim was an accident. From what Annie told us, Vara planned our involvement at the time we were born. Knowing Hildr could read her mind once she rose from her grave, Vara would've worked out every detail of her plan before then. When the time was right, Vara put a spotlight on all of us and gave us the amulets to taunt Hildr into believing we were important to her. She made Kathy forget to wear her protection. Desperately and vindictively, Hildr took the bait."

"But Hildr's intentions never changed," Lee said. "You said in your dreams that Hildr had already built an altar in the clearing. She must not have known Vara had foreseen her plans and didn't know Annie and her siblings would be there to stop her."

"I think she did," Hayley pointed out. "She only wanted it to appear that she didn't know. In all the scenarios of this battle that I've envisioned, Hildr successfully stepped out of Kathy's body and into Zoey's without being noticed—and as far as I know from my dreams of the future, she will fool even Vara.

It's well-choreographed. From the time she escaped from her imprisonment, Hildr probably spent all of her time being one step ahead of Vara."

"So if we do nothin' but wait," Jim said. "Hildr will leave Kathy's body. Then we can swoop in with our ATVs, grab our girl, and bring her home."

"Not so easy," Lee said. "Remember, so far in Hayley's dreams, no one knows Hildr left Kathy's body and possessed Zoey—not even Vara. They'll bury Kathy alive, thinking she's Hildr."

"Then how are you planning on stopping Kathy from being murdered?" Roger asked Hayley.

"I'm going to nudge her into putting up a fight just like she did when Vara attacked Hildr. That's another thing she didn't tell the Forte family. Vara knows Kathy isn't comatose. Since Hildr has to be inside a host to be buried, Vara's making sure it's not Zoey. There's no other way. Kathy has to show Annie that Hildr never cast the spell. Once that happens, it will stop Annie's attack."

"Nudge her?" Roger asked. "How?"

"It's a spell I've learned. I can place an idea into her mind without Hildr knowing it's not Kathy's own thought. It has to work. Kathy can't die. She's one of us, the reincarnated. We planned our lives before we were born to be the saviors of souls. Her murder isn't meant to be."

She visualized Kathy. *At least I can finally picture her face clearly. I need to work on nudging now.*

"As long as Annie doesn't tell Vara we know about the confrontation," Roger said, "maybe it will work."

"I truly believe Annie thinks we're not a threat," Hayley replied. "She only knows we're aware of the burial, which isn't enough information to allow our interference. We didn't mention we can track the runestone and find the planned location. Nor does Annie know I placed all the spells into my charm bracelet and have learned how to nudge. If she does break her promise and tells Vara we met, whatever she says won't damage our agenda."

"Laura told me the books you bought from Annie are gone," Matilda said.

"Which reminds me," Hayley said. "Hildr's unable to touch the *Book of Spells* because she's evil. That's another reason why she kidnapped Zoey. She had the child retrieve the book for her."

"Why didn't Vara know about that?" Lee asked.

Hayley shrugged and shook her head.

"Seems like a mystery," Matilda said. "Good thing she didn't know about me, or I'd probably be home unaware of the danger Kathy's in, and never knowing any of you."

*Laura also mentioned paying bills*, Hayley recalled. *What about Kathy's mail, her rent, utilities, car payments, and other bills? Something out of the blue that Roger wouldn't think about.* Hayley closed her eyes and nudged the question into Roger's mind. Then she opened her eyes.

Lee gave her a wink as if he knew her plan. She sat beside him.

"Do you have Kathy's address, Matilda?" Roger asked. "We should see about paying her bills."

"I'm afraid I have an old address. She mentioned she'd moved."

"What made you think about that?" Lee asked, suppressing a grin.

"I don't know. It just came to me." He cocked an eyebrow and gazed at Hayley. "A nudge?"

She nodded.

"Cool," Clint said.

"And a good one," Lee added. "I'll call Lewis and ask him to talk to Tom. Hopefully, he'll still have a key to her apartment that Vara overlooked."

He reached into his shirt pocket and retrieved his cell phone. After dialing, he put the call on speaker so everyone could hear. Lewis answered after one ring.

"Lewis, we just realized that Kathy's bills aren't being paid. We don't even know if she paid the rent."

"Not a problem, sir. Miss Lane gave you spare keys to attend to such things while she went on vacations. I have them in my office. Would you like me to look into the matter, sir?"

"Yes. And if she owes anything at all, I'll cover the cost."

"I will do so immediately, sir."

"Thanks, Lewis." Lee ended the call and tucked his phone back into his shirt pocket.

Roger chuckled. "So that was a nudge? I wouldn't have believed it wasn't my own thought. If you can do to Kathy what you did to me, you shouldn't have a problem getting through to her."

"I need practice," Hayley said. "But what I don't want is everyone second-guessing every thought they have. Next time I may not even mention an idea came from me. So just be yourselves and don't look at me every time you speak. It will make it easier on me."

"How much practice do you need—a few hours, a day?" Roger asked.

"A day. It's important that I get this right."

"We all agree with that," Lee said. "Tomorrow then. You can practice all day."

"Great. I'll use your maids and kitchen staff as targets."

Clint rubbed his chin, stared straight ahead, furrowed his brow, then glanced at Hayley. "If Kathy drove to the mountains, like your charms showed you, who's going to drive her car to the meadow? Would Hildr be able to? Could we put a tracking device on the car?"

Jim sneered. "If I were Kathy, I'd be chewin' nails and fartin' tacks if that witch took my car. Hell, she couldn't keep it between the ditches."

Matilda gasped. "There's no possible way she could drive. I doubt Kathy would even let her start the car."

Cummings came around with drinks, and Hayley reached for a glass of red wine. "Hildr would use translocation," she said.

"What's translocation?" Matilda asked.

"When I astral project, my spirit leaves my body and goes to the location I'm focusing on. With translocation, not just the spirit travels, but the physical body relocates as well."

Lee chuckled and looked at Matilda. "Last December before the ball, while Jim worked in the ballroom getting it ready for guests, he was on a ladder doing a few touch-ups. After he stepped down to see if he missed a spot, he turned to see Hayley and was startled."

"Damn straight, I jumped. She looked like a knee-knockin' pee-piddlin' scary-ass ghost."

"When he leaped back, he bumped into the ladder, causing it to teeter. The gallon of celery-green paint tipped and poured all over him." Lee's eyes watered while he laughed. "The surveillance cameras caught it all. Funniest thing I've ever seen."

"I was practicing astral projection," Hayley explained, her face red and eyes tearing.

Matilda giggled. "Do you still have the footage?"

Lee nodded.

"I'd like to see it sometime."

"Go ahead. Make a joke outta it. I was a slimy green-covered fool who nearly had a heart attack. Aint nothin' funny 'bout that."

Lee snorted another laugh. "Yes. Yes, there was. And the day before that, when she appeared, he fell off a ladder in the garden and landed in a vat of cow manure."

Hayley felt terrible about that. If the vat hadn't been there, Jim would've hurt himself badly. But the paint-can incident—that gave her a fit of laughter.

"I thought once your spirit leaves your body, you're dead," Matilda said.

"During astral projection," Hayley replied, "your spirit is tethered to your physical body. It's not impossible that you could die—anything can happen. But from everything that Grams has told me, it sounds improbable."

Lee threw back his head, laughed, and looked at Matilda. "You should've seen Jim's face—"

"Hold everythin'," Jim said.

Hayley lowered her head, closed her eyes, and sent Jim a nudging. *Maybe Matilda would like to take a walk in the garden.* Then she reopened her eyes and sipped her merlot.

"Let's change the damn subject." Jim turned to Matilda. "Would ya care to take a walk through the gardens with me, little lady? I'll tell ya some ghost stories that will keep ya awake all night."

Matilda blushed. "You're a man after my own heart. I'd love to."

They stood and strolled toward the door.

"Did I ever tell ya 'bout Hayley's first day on the job?" Jim asked her.

"No. I don't believe you have," Matilda replied, taking his arm.

Jim looked over his shoulder and grinned at Hayley.

Hayley bit her bottom lip. He knew she hated being the heroine of his stories. And she knew that he would say, "Let me tell ya 'bout how she wrapped two scary ghosts 'round her little finger."

*Touche'*, Hayley thought.

She waited until they'd left and had time to go outside before she rose from the couch and strolled to the window overlooking Roger's backyard. Lee snatched up the glass of wine she'd left behind and followed her. He handed it to her as she gazed out the window.

While she watched Jim and Matilda, she recalled her first stroll through Lee's garden. She'd followed a brick pathway between rose trees as round as lollypops. Perfume had filled the air. Beyond the rose garden in the backyard, she and Lee had stepped up to a veranda bordered by a travertine stone wall dressed in urns filled with azaleas. Centered to the home's entrance, steps fanned downward, leading to a manicured lawn.

She'd looked across carpets of grass pathways crisscrossing between geometric designs formed by boxwood hedges and English holly framing colorful flowers. Topiary, some rounded, some coned, and others cubed, dotted the garden to the lake's edge.

Then she thought how they had played hide and seek; how he had found her hiding place, his long legs straddling her; how she had reached up, taken his hand, and pulled him on top of her; the longing she'd felt to give in to his seduction.

Lee leaned and whispered in her ear as if he'd read her mind. "Room number two tonight."

She played with the button on his shirt, looked meekly into his eyes, and took a sip of her wine. "Can I pick the room?"

His playful smile gave away the fact he had other things on his mind. "No. I've already made the choice."

She toyed with his shirt buttons again, undoing the first two. "Care to elaborate?"

He quickly buttoned up again. "I have nothing more to add."

"You mean, I'll just have to wait and see."

He raised her chin, and tenderly kissed her lips. "Exactly."

She took another sip of wine. "Hmm. I'd better put my mind on something else. There's more to discuss, and we can't leave yet."

He glanced outside. "Should we wait for the soon-to-be lovebirds?"

Jim and Matilda had strolled to the lake—she, laughing, Jim looking happier than Hayley had ever seen him.

Hayley closed her eyes and sent Jim a nudge. *Better get back.* "No need," she told Lee. They watched as Jim offered his arm to his companion and saw them walk toward the house.

"Well, I learned one thing," Hayley said. "Distance isn't going to be a problem."

They turned away from the window and joined the others when Jim and Matilda entered the room.

"I'll need a paper and a pencil so I can draw the area as I've seen it in my dreams," Hayley said, taking a seat on the couch.

Roger walked to his desk across the room. He opened the drawer, pulled out a sheet of paper, then took a pencil from a cup on the desk and a clipboard from one of the bookshelves. When he returned, he handed everything to Hayley.

She thought a moment, refreshing her memory, and began to draw. Hayley drew two circles—one much larger, surrounding the other. Between the two, she wrote "fog." Along the outer circle, she detailed what she'd seen in her dream — the creek and the trail that had vanished into the dense mist, as well as the private property sign, the crumbling wall, bridge, and paved road.

In the center of the middle circle, she pinpointed the location where the members would take their stance during the coming battle. She set the drawing on the ottoman in front of her, and everyone leaned in to look.

"The stone will reach its final destination by tomorrow, I'm guessing," Hayley said. "I'll bet there is some kind of structure off the road. Otherwise, why would it be paved? I'd like to physically scout the area before the full moon. Prior to the battle, a spell will be cast, creating a cloud of fog so thick you won't be able to see an inch in front of you."

"How are we getting through it?" Roger asked.

"There's a creek leading into the forest," she said, pointing to where she saw it in her dream. "When I envisioned myself watching the fight, I stood here." She made an X. "I could hear the water flowing behind me. I'm thinking we can follow the creek. But I'll have a better understanding once I physically check out the surroundings."

"We'll have to come up with a way to keep together and not get lost in the fog," Lee said. "One wrong step and we could be in trouble."

Roger nodded. "We'll think of something."

"A compass might help," Clint suggested.

"I'll make sure we all have one," Roger replied.

She explained where she saw Annie and her family step out of the forest. "I never saw Vara. I know for sure she'll be someplace where she won't see Hildr possess Zoey. I'm guessing she'll be in the trees, over here, behind the others."

"We'll probably have to hike in from the main road," Roger said.

"How soon do ya think your sample-powered GPS will find exactly where this place is?" Jim asked.

"When the stone stops moving, I'll be able to get a rough idea of the location. From there, Clint can help me use the computer to get a satellite view of the area. Once we know where it is, we'll print out a map. I'll circle the rough location. Before we go home, I'll try again to see if the stone made it to its destination."

*\*\**

After having dinner at Roger's, Hayley lifted a small sample of rock from the petri dish, held it in her hand, and closed her eyes. Her vision took her to a room where the runestone had been placed in plain sight against a wall next to an eight-paned window. Looking through the opened blinds, she saw the sunset above the treetops, the golden clouds painting the sky. In a clearing, this side of the pines, a rock structure reminding her of Stonehenge, piqued her interest. *Maybe a training camp.*

She looked around the large room, a library half the size of Lee's. Every piece of furniture appeared to have been collected over the centuries. Between hand-hewn bookshelves filled with worn volumes, many seeming to do with witchcraft in one way or another, an aged walnut five-legged table held a large leatherback book, its pages folded back, its text written in runes — *The Book of Spells.* Certificates of merit, achievement, and honor crediting the name of Richard Forte hung framed above the desk. Voices beyond the closed door drew her attention.

Hayley strained to hear, wondering if they'd detected her presence.

"There'll be fifty of us," a man's voice said. "We'll enter the meadow from the east. Then we'll fan out, giving everyone a clear shot at Hildr. Annie will take the center stance."

*Fifty. That's good to know. And all are witches and warlocks.* Any one of them could sense her meddling. This time the fear of being caught ended her vision, bringing her consciousness back to those surrounding her in Roger's library.

"What did you see?" Roger asked. "Will we be able to find the location?"

"I think so." Hayley turned to Clint. "How close can the satellite maps zoom in on an area?"

"It can read a street sign," Clint told her. "Just give me the general location. Do you have some kind of landmark I can pinpoint?"

She nodded. "A ring of stone—used for rituals maybe. Something that looks like Stonehenge. It's somewhere in the Virginia Appalachians, I'm sensing. And I noticed a wall of certificates honoring a Richard Forte. Maybe he owns the property or runs a camp."

"Why don't we assume he does own the land to save time," Jim said. "He must be part of Annie Forte's family."

Hayley nodded. "It's more than a good guess."

"Check it out, Clint," Roger said.

"It will take time to search public records," Clint said. "But for now, we can try locating the compound by satellite."

"Go for it," Roger replied.

Clint sprang from his seat and looked at Hayley. "Come on. Let's see what we can find."

She stood and followed him with Lee, Roger, and Matilda trailing behind.

Jim darted to a table near the window and retrieved a couple of chairs. He placed one next to Clint's and another beside

Hayley. "If you please, Matdie," he said, offering her a seat. Once she sat, he looked over her shoulder at the computer. "Has to be somethin' damn extraordinary 'bout this place to make her wantta build an altar for that there rejuvenation ritual, knowin' she'd be facin' a battle."

"Doesn't hurt to look into it," Roger said. "Clint, can you find a survey or some kind of map showing the mineral deposits in that area?"

"Sure. That kind of map is made possible by using photos taken from a hyperspectral imaging camera onboard a satellite. By using a portion of the electromagnetic spectrum—"

"Hold on, genius," Jim said. "We asked for the time of day, not how to build a clock."

"Then the answer's yes," Clint said. "I have to find the specific surveys related to our target area. It may take me awhile. And I can check through public records to find out if Richard Forte owns property." He looked up at Roger. "Okay if I come back tomorrow and work on it, Uncle?"

"Sure. No problem."

"I guess the importance of time of year and name of the full moon is irrelevant," Lee said.

"Considering the full moon in Jim's regression was the Snow Moon and not the Frost Moon, I believe you're right," Hayley said. "But the spell to rejuvenate Hildr's energy would probably work considerably better during the spring or summer months, I would guess. During those months, the trees would be exerting a vast amount of energy to create growth and feed their leaves. Winter wouldn't be the appropriate time of year to gather strength from her surroundings. So I'm guessing Hildr is planning her rejuvenation spell now only because she's forced to. She'll need her strength in order to fight the family."

"Sounds like Hildr foresaw the situation," Roger said. "Being manipulated into performing the ritual at the least favorable time of year, she counteracted by choosing this particular meadow. The energy from the ancient trees and maybe, if I'm right, quartz in some form or another beneath the ground would reinstate the energy loss caused by the season."

Hayley nodded. "I think you're right."

"Better hope the family wins this battle," Clint said. "If she goes through with the rejuvenation ritual, who knows if she could be defeated."

"That's a horrid thought," Hayley replied.

"She'd be a threat to all humanity," Lee added. "This is so complicated. We can't let Vara and her family kill Hildr, or they'd be killing Kathy. But if they don't kill Hildr, the entire world will be in danger."

"Damned if we do save our girl and damned if we don't," Jim said.

"I don't believe that," Hayley told him. "I'm sure Vara has a plan B if we ruin her intentions. Maybe she'll have to call for reinforcements, getting other sentinels to intervene. Whatever it takes, Hildr can't escape."

"But if Hildr possesses Zoey as she did in all of your dreams," Matilda said. "she very well could."

"All we're concentrating on is saving Kathy," Lee said. "Whatever happens after that is left for Vara to deal with, as scary as the thought may be. Saving Kathy is our only priority."

Clint turned back to the computer and zoomed in on the map, focusing on the area where Hayley sensed the runestone had been en route, somewhere in the Virginia Appalachians not far from the North Carolina border. While searching with an aerial view, Clint zoomed in on Blue Ridge Parkway as it crossed into Virginia.

Hayley held the fragment tightly in her palm, closed her eyes, and concentrated on its energy to lead her in the right direction. It felt more like intuition than a sense of uncertainty. She needed intense concentration, or she would be lost. With reservation, she told Clint when to turn off and which way to go from there, steering him through back roads, sometimes having to backtrack and try again. She guided him along roads leading to a dead-end, where the view looked across mountain ranges and above ravines, valleys, and chasms. Things beyond and below lacked detail.

"This isn't working," Hayley said. "I felt blocked as if someone had put up a shield. Maybe I need to be physically there."

"The full moon is in three days," Roger said. "Tomorrow, Hayley will be practicing. Why don't we plan on driving there day after tomorrow and hiking in to get a better look?"

"Sounds like a plan," Lee said.

"Okay. Good timing," Roger replied.

"How many of us will be goin'?" Jim looked at Matilda. "Up for a walk in the woods?"

"I'm not much of a hiker. I think I'll stay behind, if you don't mind."

"You won't be alone," Roger said. "Laura should be here with you. There will be five of us going — Hayley, Jim, me, Clint, and Lee. I'll drive."

"I think it would be better if I take my Jeep," Clint suggested. "If you park your Q7 alongside the road, it would draw attention."

"You're right," Roger replied. "Good catch."

"What do you suggest we wear?" Clint asked. "Camouflage?"

"I think we should just appear to be hikers," Roger told him. "If we wore camouflage and got caught, we'd never talk our way out of it. So just wear something warm and layer up. Okay, with the rest of you?"

Lee and Hayley nodded.

"All right then," Roger said. "Until the day after tomorrow. In the morning—I'd say around eight o'clock should be early enough. Shouldn't take long to get there. I'm guessing we should be back by three, if not sooner. We're just scanning the area to be ready for the rescue. Shouldn't take long."

Lee glanced at his watch. "We'd better take off. We have plans for the evening. Coming, Jim?"

"I'll catch up with ya. Won't take a minute."

Lee and Hayley said their goodbyes and left Jim standing by Matilda, who gazed out the window toward the lake.

***

Once the three stepped into the foyer at Lee's estate, they went their separate ways, leaving Jim to his own plans for the night. Hayley followed Lee to his bedroom.

She undressed in the walk-in closet that connected to the bathroom and threw on a robe, knowing she had to walk a ways to the shower. The tub across from it had confused her for months. She'd believed it to be a Jacuzzi. *Why would anyone want a bathtub that big?*

Once she finished her shower, Lee took his. Afterward, they dressed, and he led her to the game room on the second floor in the south tower. He opened the door, allowing her to enter first.

She'd been in this room only once before. Hanging lamps illuminated a pool table a few feet from the bar. Leather chairs surrounded game tables near the windows. In the corner, beyond the blazing fireplace, stood a suit of armor. Hayley remembered Lee had planned to wear it to the ball, but she had changed his mind. Instead, he dressed as a prince and her a princess.

Lee hung a "Do Not Disturb" sign on the doorknob before closing the door. Then he led her to what looked to be a lambskin carpet by the fireplace.

"From the size of this, it must have been a huge lamb," Hayley said.

"It's faux. Anyway, it's being replaced tomorrow, and I thought it would serve as a great place to cuddle next to the fireplace, have some wine, desserts, and enjoy an intimate evening." He pointed to a sofa table behind the couch to her left. "I'm afraid Velma went overboard baking. It's probably my fault since I didn't tell her what dessert we preferred."

The array of goodies astonished her: lemon meringue, banana cream pie, chocolate mousse, and many more lip-licking treats. Alongside the desserts rested a couple of bottles of French Muscat wine in ice.

"How in the world did you pull this off? I never saw you leave my side."

"I'm a man with many talents."

A knock on the door caught their attention. Lee went to the door and opened it a crack. "Jim, didn't this sign tell you anything?"

"It told me you were in here." He looked toward Hayley. "I just wanted to tell ya that if you're plannin' on havin' sex on that pool table, don't do it. It's just not right. Just not right. Just not right."

"Who would think of doing a thing like that?" Lee asked.

Jim's eyes opened wide, and he straightened, maybe in an attempt to look dignified, Hayley thought. "There're some men out there that I'm sure have it on their bucket list." He shook his head. "It's a guy thing, I'm guessin'." He pointed into the room. "I play pool a hell of a lot, and the only balls I want to imagine on that table are billiard. Ya need to promise."

"Hayley and I are getting ready to have dessert," Lee said.

"What's for dessert?"

"We're not having guests."

"Smells good."

"Yes. Velma outdid herself." Lee raised the sign in front of Jim's face. "This means what it says. Now wave at Hayley and say goodbye."

Jim gave a finger-wiggling wave to her.

Lee abruptly closed the door and locked it. When he crossed the room to the sofa table, he uncorked a bottle of Muscat and filled a couple of glasses.

"You didn't promise," Hayley said, taking the glass Lee offered her.

He ran his finger through the lemon meringue and brushed it on her lips. "No. The next time I see him playing pool, I'm going to give him a little wink." His lips met hers. "Mmmm. Now pick your pleasure."

He took the piece of meringue pie he'd dipped his finger into. Hayley chose the banana cream.

After cozying in front of the fire and having a few more glasses of wine, Lee moved the tray of desserts closer, setting it on an ottoman within reach. He reclaimed his seat on the fur rug, chose a slice of strawberry cheesecake, scooped up a fork full, and brought it to Hayley's lips.

She giggled as she took a bite, and the sweet red sauce trickled down her chin. Reaching up, she caught the runaway drip on her finger and ran the thick liquid across the round of her breast.

Lee smiled. "Seductress."

The foreplay she had started led to the ultimate dessert and turned into a game that would be etched into Hayley's mind forever.

# CHAPTER 28

Yesterday, from sunrise to sunset, Hayley had practiced nudging until she felt confident using her new skill. Feeling ready for the rescue, she slept soundly, knowing the attack plans had been finalized, and fifty would be the number of Annie's clan to gather in the field. She knew that she couldn't foresee the determined battle even if she wanted to, because it involved her future. Other than her presence as a witness hiding behind an old hemlock watching other possible outcomes, she could only guess what would happen at the actual battle, and, since it entailed witchcraft, she believed her speculation couldn't come close.

She sipped her coffee after pushing away her empty breakfast plate and thought about their chances of being caught trespassing today.

"You're awfully quiet," Lee said. "Anything wrong?"

"You know, Annie and each of her family has the gift of foresight. I'm hoping their attention is on training."

"We'll just have to be extra careful." He rose from the table and offered her his hand. "Shall we get dressed? Roger and Clint will be here before we know it."

She took his hand and stood. They leisurely walked out of the dining room and through the halls to the elevator. Lee pushed the third-floor button and abruptly pulled his hand back. He gazed at the crimson streak on the tip of his finger.

Hayley leaned in. "What happened? Are you hurt?"

He brought his finger to his mouth, tasted the red substance, and nodded. "Just what I thought. Cherry brandy sauce."

She recalled the dessert, rich chocolate cake layered with cherry filling, floating in cherry brandy sauce. The thought made her blush, remembering where he drizzled it on her naked body, how he intimately removed it from her skin, and how it had aroused her. "A night I won't forget."

Lee embraced her. "I love the taste of you just the way you are." While his lips met hers, the elevator door opened and waited for their departure. "Better get on with it," he said, gingerly stepping away from her. Hand in hand, they strolled through the hallway until they came to his chambers.

***

Once they changed their clothes, Lee retrieved the backpacks Lewis had delivered as instructed. "We have water, snacks, earphones, and ski masks," Lee said, inspecting his bag. "Anything else we need?"

"We haven't come up with a plan to get through the fog. It's going to be so dense you won't be able to see an inch in front of you. What are we going to do?" She finished lacing up her hiking boots.

"Okay, let's see." He clasped his hands together and brought his index fingers to his lips while he thought. "What if we take some twine and tie it to trees? If we wrap it around each trunk at the base and bury it under leaves, it should be well hidden until we return, don't you think?"

"Do you have that much twine?"

"Let me check with Jim. He'd know." Inside his flannel shirt pocket, Lee found his cell phone. Once he reached Jim, he explained the situation, listened to the reply, ended the call, and stashed the phone in his shirt. "He said he'd take care of it. Anything else?"

"I think we're all set."

She grabbed her backpack, threw one strap over her shoulder, and led the way out the door. They met up with Jim, headed to the first floor, left by the front door, and saw Clint traveling up the drive in his Jeep. He pulled up and stopped. Roger got into the back, letting Hayley sit up front.

"Just throw all your gear behind the seats," Clint told them.

Once they were situated, Roger updated them on what they'd discovered. "Clint found out that Richard Forte owns property in the Appalachians. It gave a parcel number, but there's no record of its location."

"Sounds like manipulation," Lee said. "The family doesn't want to be found. I guess they didn't count on Hayley's abilities. When we cross into Virginia, she'll have to take the lead."

"I agree," Roger replied.

***

Once in Virginia, Clint drove until they reached a bar featuring a country band. He pulled into the dirt parking lot, took a map from the glove compartment, spread it out, and pinpointed their position, allowing Hayley to get her sense of direction. From there, she used the runestone samples. Holding them in her palm and closing her hand around them, she felt a pull much greater than the sensation she'd received while on the computer.

They followed the road back to the interstate. After she told Clint to bypass an exit and keep driving, she felt the stone's tug lessen. "Sorry, I was wrong. We need to go back and take that last exit."

"No problem." He took the next turnoff, returned to the interstate, went the way they had come, and followed her lead.

When the stone's pull to find its match increased, she knew they were headed in the right direction. A mile outside a small town, the runestone's trail ended.

Clint pulled over. "What now?"

"You're not sensing anything?" Lee asked Hayley from the back seat.

"The vehicle that transported the stone went this way. Until we passed that last road going west, the stone's energy felt strong. It's as if someone placed wards in the area to eliminate the chance of finding it."

"Understandable," Roger said. "I'm sure Hildr would like to get her hands on it in order to turn it to dust."

"Well, we ain't come this far to just spit in the wind," Jim said. "Why don't we head on up the mountain and find a place where we can get a gander of what's below?"

"Great idea," Lee said.

Clint continued along the curving mountain road. On the right were pine trees, and on the left, more trees with no chance of viewing the valley below. Railing skirted the road, not allowing Clint to pull over until he found an overlook halfway up the mountain.

He parked, and everyone climbed out of the Jeep. They crossed the paved parking lot and stood by the low stone wall designed to prevent a viewer from going farther. With Lee's help, Hayley straddled the wall, ambled through the brown grass, and stepped up onto an outcrop of rocks, Lee at her side. Carefully they made their way to the edge. The others joined them.

Dense fog blanketed the area below.

"Doesn't that just dill your pickle," Jim said.

Hayley gazed toward the endless mountain tops to the west and saw the fog that had snaked through the ravines had retreated, leaving only patches. But mystery shrouded the valley below.

While gripping the stone fragments, she sensed the runestone's location. "The meadow and the compound are down there beneath the cloud. I'm sure of it."

"Isn't it convenient that the fog is hiding the complex?" Lee said.

"It's witchcraft," Hayley said.

"Witchcraft?" Roger asked. "It looks just like the other fog banks."

"It's not," Hayley replied. "There's no doubt in my mind."

"The hair-raisin', spell-castin' witchery that Hayley saw in her dreams must've been practiced outside," Jim said. "So I'd say that there cloud's gotta be permanent, or the entire town would be scared as hell."

"Who says they're not?" Roger told him. "I bet tons of tales are being told by the locals. Wish we had time to hear a few."

"It's best to keep our prying to ourselves," Lee said.

"How in thunderation do we get down there?" Jim asked.

"I'll take that road where Hayley said the stone's trail ended," Clint said.

Clint backtracked until he came to the road Hayley had mentioned. He drove cautiously, driving the speed limit for about a mile. Then the road forked. The main road veered to the right, hugging the mountain, while the other, leading to the compound, couldn't be taken. Wrought iron gates, with the *Algiz* symbol above it, barred their way.

"What now?" Jim asked.

Clint backed the Jeep several yards and stopped. He scanned the woods. Hayley could almost read his mind. A cluster of boulders a little ways into the forest would make a good hiding place for the vehicle. When he turned the wheel and drove off-road, taking his Jeep over tree roots, rocks, and downed tree limbs, she knew she had it right.

Everyone held on until Clint stopped.

"We don't call you a genius for nothing," Roger said. "No one will see your Jeep from the street."

"I don't want to take chances," Clint told him. "It's fifty-fifty the sheriff's on their payroll."

"Good thinking," Lee said.

They put on their backpacks.

Hayley studied the forest, getting her bearings. A cool breeze swept through the trees, encouraging the remaining autumn leaves clinging to branches to let go and glide to the forest floor. Birch, maple, ash, hemlock, pine, and a few trees Hayley didn't recognize grew several feet from one another. The groundcover had died back, exposing the team further. The fear of being seen kept her alert. She gazed in all directions, even above, looking for Vara. Not a soul anywhere.

"Just a few months ago, ya wouldn't have been able to see a yard through the foliage," Jim said. "Now that it's late autumn, the growth's so sparse you can see a squirrel's nuts a hundred feet away. Come the full moon, we'll be sleepin' with the worms if that freakin' fog doesn't hide us."

"There'll be fog," Hayley replied, "so thick you won't see your nose."

"It'll be a blessing, not a deterrent like they plan," Lee added.

She stepped into the woods, her boots crushing the fallen

leaves and pine needles, the noise breaking the silence. Everyone followed.

The massive hemlocks and towering pines with their green foliage became foremost the farther they hiked. The essence of dried leaves and pine filled the air. Velvety golden moss clung to the rocks by the creeks they crossed and to the trunks of each tree. Although no others were in the area, they weren't alone. Squirrels rustled the dried leaves on the forest floor, birds sang as woodpeckers hammered trees, wolves howled, and deer dashed away. Every noise put the team on edge.

"Stop." Hayley envisioned a man with black hair under a wide-brimmed tan hat. He rode a brown horse with a white streak down its nose. "Hide." She pointed. "They're coming from that direction."

Everyone scattered, each finding a tree wide enough to hide behind.

Hayley threw herself to the ground and crouched behind a boulder. She heard the horse snort before it, and the rider drew close. The leaves on the forest floor muffled the sound of the horse's hoofs. She used her instincts to judge their distance. The closer she imagined they came, the lower she ducked and held her breath, praying.

The next snort told her they were only feet away. She steadied her nerves, trying not to move a muscle. Being so close, she heard the man breathe. She let out her breath slowly, wishing she could have held it longer, and took another deep breath, holding it, afraid to make a sound.

He rubbed the horse's neck, and softly said, "Let's head home, Warrior. Time for target practice." They turned, and Warrior galloped away with its rider.

Hayley stayed down until she felt safe. Then she stood and

brushed the leaves from her jeans. "Okay," she told the others. "He's gone." Her legs trembled. *That was too close.*

One by one, they stepped out from behind the trees.

"Guess we couldn't have used the sky masks even if we wanted to," Roger said.

"Wasn't a lick of time," Jim replied.

"Where to now?" Lee asked.

"The rider should be heading back to the road," Hayley told him. "He mentioned practice. Hope it's at the compound and not in the meadow."

"Guess we gotta get our rear-ends movin' and find out," Jim said. He adjusted the straps of his backpack and started up an incline.

After a quarter-mile hike, Hayley veered to the right and stopped. She gazed into the forest of tulip trees, white pine, and hemlock. "Some of these trees are at least six hundred years old. The energy here is outrageous."

"It's coming from below ground too," Clint said. "There's loads of quartz crystals in this area, just as Roger suspected."

"Hildr's choice location," Hayley said. "The energy from the massive trees, the full moon, and the amount of power the crystals have makes the meadow the perfect place, allowing her to draw immense energy even without the rejuvenation ritual, just like she did in Lee's security room. And the energy will help me too. The message I send Kathy will be extremely focused and strong." *Now I'm sure it will work. As soon as Kathy proves she's still alive, Annie won't harm her.*

Minutes later, they came across a dirt road, overgrown and unkempt. "We'll follow the road," Hayley said. "It should lead us to where I entered the forest in my dreams."

She forged ahead, stepping over a downed tree branch lying

across the road. Trees densely lined both sides of the road, a mix of evergreens and deciduous. A deer kicked up leaves as it fled, startling everyone.

A ways from where the road made a bend, Hayley found the spot where the asphalt began, the dirt road leading west, the sign reading "Private property. Keep out," and the creek flowing into the forest.

She stopped, the bridge to her left. "This is where I entered. But the fog hid the forest."

Jim removed his backpack and found his compass. Everyone followed his lead, each making sure to have a compass in hand.

"It's a good thing Lee came up with this twine idea, or we'd be stuck ducks in deep dung," Jim said. "Not to say these compasses aren't a good idea. Full moon or not, without either one of 'em, we'd wander the woods, bumpin' into trees."

"I think our rescue party should be small," Hayley suggested. "Just Clint, Roger, Laura, Lee, and me."

Jim's eyes widened. "What? You're leavin' me outta it?"

"Matilda will need you more than ever, Jim. She'll be beside herself, not knowing if Kathy will live or die."

Jim nodded. "You're right. Anyway, I'm getting' too old for hikin' in cold weather." He ran his arms through the backpack straps, putting it on once more.

"Let's not think about probabilities," Roger said. "We're here for a reason, so let's get on with it."

Jim pulled a thick roll of twine from his backpack. "Where should I start tyin' this, darlin'?" he asked.

"Let's find the meadow first and the tree I've envisioned myself hiding behind, and then we can backtrack."

Checking their compasses, they followed the creek. The flowing water muted their footsteps. Everyone stayed alert, watching for witches and warlocks. They moved slowly behind Hayley while studying their compasses every several feet. When she turned away from the creek, they did the same.

*This is crazy. Without the fog, we're totally exposed.* She could feel her heart beating as if it wanted to jump from her chest and run.

Several yards from the meadow's edge, she brought them to a halt and raised a finger to her lips, cautioning them to stay quiet. At the east end of the meadow, the horseman she'd seen in her vision several minutes ago, now on foot, stepped into the field. Ten others accompanied him. With the wave of the man's hand, fog began to descend on the forest.

"We need to hurry," Hayley said.

"Which tree first?" Jim asked.

"The giant hemlock over there at the edge of the meadow. But the trunk's too wide. Tie it to the one behind it, so you don't use up the twine."

"I got this," Jim told them. "Don't wait for me. Get the hell outta here before the fog thickens. I need to bury the twine, and I don't want anyone trippin' over me."

"Will you be okay?" Hayley asked.

"Hell yeah. Got my compass and," he tapped his head, "my GPS."

"He's right," Lee said. "We'd better get back to the road before we can't find our way out."

Hayley looked out into the field and back at Jim. She watched him creep forward, staying behind trees and watching the witches and warlocks on the grass. Before he reached the hemlock Hayley had pointed to, he stopped at the smaller tree only a foot away. Quickly he wrapped the twine around its base and covered the twine with leaves while he crept back to the next tree. This one had a massive trunk also. She felt relieved to see he bypassed it and moved to a narrower tree behind it. *He knows what he's doing.* She turned, following Lee and the others.

The fog thickened as they hiked along the creek. She glanced back and could still see Jim trailing behind, tying the twine to strategic trees and hiding its trail. While keeping up with the others, she continued looking back, seeing only a few feet away and no longer seeing Jim. They reached out, forming a chain following the creek.

A moment later, Hayley couldn't see the hands she held. The tip of her nose vanished into the mist.

"Watch your step," she heard Lee say, his hand firmly holding hers, leading her forward. She stumbled over a fallen branch, and his grip steadied her.

In the distance, thunder boomed, and a flash of light illuminated the fog.

*I can still hear the creek. How much farther to the road?*

With a tug from Lee's hand, she finally stepped out of the gloom and stood with the others staring at the ominous wall of fog.

"What if he falls into the creek?" Clint asked.

"Jim's probably thought of that," Lee said. "He has good instincts and a compass. He'll be fine. But it's going to take a while for him to find each tree, wrap the twine, and bury it without being able to see a thing."

"We can't just stand here," Roger said, looking in all directions.

"I've got an idea," Clint told him. "Be right back."

He darted across the road, down the bank, and under the bridge. Hayley wanted to use her ability to envision Jim, but she knew it would be like shooting off a flare, giving away their presence. "Guess we'll just have to be patient." She turned and gazed toward the compound, hoping they wouldn't send anyone else to patrol the area. Then she sensed a vehicle coming their way.

She hesitated to step back through the wall. *Will they have the ability to see us in the fog? Would we be standing in plain sight?*

Clint hurried from the creek. "We can hide down there. I'll keep an eye out for Jim."

Hayley and the others followed him down the bank. An old crumbling stone wall under the bridge permitted them to sit out of sight. She listened as the vehicle drove closer.

It passed by. She heard its engine fade into the woods to the west. *Must've turned down the dirt road.*

Clint crouched in a hiding place near the creek where he could see Jim when he crawled out of the fog. Although Hayley knew tying the twine couldn't be more important, she felt tense. Her attention jumped from searching for danger to listening for Jim. Time seemed to lag.

"Can you imagine stringing twine without being able to see an inch in front of you?" Lee whispered to her.

"We owe him big time," Hayley replied.

Clint stood up and waved his arms. "He's out," he told everyone.

Jim scampered down the bank and joined them, dirt and leaves covering the knees of his jeans, his hands soiled.

"We need to get out of here," Hayley said, "before someone else comes."

They hastened back to the road and briskly hiked the way they had come. The wall of fog skirted the woods they walked beside.

"Do you think we'll be able to find my Jeep?" Clint asked.

"The security gate looks like it marks the border of their property," Lee replied. "You're parked just beyond. I'm guessing it won't be a problem."

They hiked, keeping vigilant of their surroundings. When they reached the Jeep, they found Lee had been right. They threw their backpacks behind the backseat and climbed in.

Clint backed out and maneuvered his vehicle with skill, avoiding the trees, driving between them, although unavoidably driving over roots and downed limbs. Hayley held on the best she could while leaving her seat a few times and being jostled about. The seatbelt helped some. She relaxed once they reached the road.

On the way home, Jim told stories about how he strung the twine and the noises coming from the meadow, exaggerating in a style all his own.

# CHAPTER 29

The team gathered at Roger's.

"How on earth did you manage?" Matilda asked Jim.

"I kept my nose to the ground, my hands on the twine, and the compass Roger gave me in my shirt pocket. I tell ya, I'd have been lost in them there woods if it weren't for that compass."

"It was Clint's idea," Roger said.

"He's a damn genius," Jim replied.

"We almost got caught a couple of times," Clint told her.

"Thank goodness you didn't," Matilda said. "Were there lots of guards?"

"One on horseback, and another in a vehicle," Clint replied. "Hayley said there will be fifty witches and warlocks in the meadow tomorrow. There were only ten today. So odds are there'll be more guards too."

"Will there be trouble, Hayley?" Matilda asked.

"I don't know. I can't foresee my own future, remember."

"I tied the last bit of twine to the tree on your left as ya step inside the wall," Jim said, scratching his leg and his arm. "You'll have to bend down to find the lead. Once ya do, you'll be able to stand. I tied it loose 'round the trunks so you'll have leeway to lift it waist high so ya won't have to crawl."

"Good thinking," Roger told him.

"I can't imagine how awful it was to accomplish that," Hayley said.

"Worst thing was the bugs," Jim confessed. "I couldn't let go of the twine to swat 'em. They were crawlin' all over me, eatin' me alive." He glanced at Matilda. "That's it for me. I'm done with all that there hikin'. I'll be stayin' home."

"Maybe you'd like to come by and visit with me while they're gone," she suggested.

"Nothin' I'd like more," Jim told her. He turned to Roger. "Sure would like to take a shower, but I don't have a stitch to change into."

"I'll have Cummings bring you a pair of my sweats and a T-shirt," Roger said. "I'll call Laura and ask her to bring you something that will relieve the itch." He glanced at his watch. "If I call her now, she'll be able to pick something up and be here by the time you're out of the shower."

"You're a good man." Jim stood and checked the seat. "Hope I didn't leave any critters behind." He looked at Matilda. "If you'll excuse me, little lady."

She smiled. "Certainly, my dear sir."

He stopped at the bar on his way out, took a beer out of the small refrigerator, popped the cap, and left the library.

Roger made the call and talked for a minute or two. Then he ended the conversation and stashed his cell phone into his shirt pocket.

"What time are we leaving tomorrow?" Clint asked.

"We can get there around twilight," Roger replied. "It'll be a full moon. Would that give you enough light to pull into the woods?"

"Should."

"We'll need to take two cars," Hayley said. "Clint's Jeep only holds five—Clint, Roger, Laura, Lee, and me. We'll need room for Kathy."

"I've got a Jeep my groundkeepers use," Lee said. "It might not be squeaky clean, but it'll get us there. Hayley and I will follow you."

"Good plan," Roger said. "You can park down the road a bit."

"Easy enough," Lee said.

"So once we reach the target entrance, we'll have to wait until the fog spell is cast or someone in Annie's clan might see us," Roger pointed out. "We can hide under the bridge like we did before." He checked his watch again. "When Laura gets here, I'll fill her in on the plan."

"Speaking of Laura," Hayley said to him, "do you really need to wait until Christmas to propose?"

"What do you suggest?" he replied.

"Don't wait. Ask her as soon as you get the ring. It takes months to plan a wedding. We need all the time we can get."

"I won't have the ring until the end of this month."

"Perfect."

"I suggest you get a wedding planner," Lee said.

"Good idea. It will be the first thing Laura and I do as soon as you propose, Roger."

"Okay, okay. I had it all worked out, the precise words, the exact time and place. But if that's what you want, I'll come up with another plan."

Lee glanced at everyone in the room. "Talking about plans… Lewis wants to know what we're going to do about Thanksgiving."

"When is it?" Roger asked.

"Two days after Kathy's rescue," Clint said.

"What if—?" Matilda started to say.

"There is no 'what if,'" Hayley told her. "Kathy will be rescued. That's all there is to it."

"We should have Thanksgiving," Roger said. "But I suggest we keep the gathering small, just us, the team."

"We'll make it a celebration," Hayley suggested. "We need to think positive."

"I'll let Lewis know," Lee replied.

When Laura arrived, Roger met her at the library door, giving her a hug and a kiss. "Did you bring the medication for Jim?"

"Yes. I gave it to Cummings."

He walked with her to the couch.

"We've been talking about our plans for the rescue, and Thanksgiving," Lee told her. He glanced at Roger. "And another thing Lewis mentioned. What are we going to do about the reservations we made for this New Year's Eve?"

"I completely forgot about that," Roger said, standing by the mantle with Laura, his arm around her waist. "My birthday's January second, as you know. Last January, we made reservations to celebrate my next in London, New Year's Eve."

"Just you and Lee going?" Hayley asked.

"No. Jim was going along too," Roger told her.

"I'll tell Lewis to cancel the reservations," Lee replied.

"Wait," Hayley said. "What size room are you talking about?"

"A penthouse, overlooking the Thames," Roger said.

"Is it big enough for eight people?"

"Yes," he replied.

She looked at Matilda and Laura. "What do you think, girls?"

"I'm in," Laura said.

Matilda hesitated. "I'll talk to Jim and let you know."

"Know 'bout what?" Jim asked, entering the room, wearing black sweats, a white T-shirt, and slippers.

"Laura, Matilda, and I would like to join you guys New Year's in London," Hayley told him.

"Hell yeah. Sounds like a good time to me." He glanced at Matilda. "Unless ya have other plans, little lady."

"No. But I'll have to let you know. If Kathy's—"

"Remember, no 'if,'" Hayley said in a soft, reassuring voice. "Kathy and Tom will be invited too."

"I'll tell Lewis to make reservations for the flight," Lee said. "And if you decide not to go, Matilda, you just let us know. It's not a problem."

"When Kathy's safe and sound," Matilda replied.

"Everyone must be famished," Roger said. "Why don't we have dinner, then call it an early night?"

All agreed.

# CHAPTER 30

Once home, moments after Hayley's head hit her pillow, she heard Grams's voice. "Here's something you already know. Sleep, dear."

"Sleep, dear," told Hayley, it would be an extensive vision, not just a glimpse of something or someone. She relaxed. Soon the thoughts of the day melted away, and she nodded off.

Grams's message played out in a story Hayley had imagined several times since Annie's visit. It began with Annie speaking to an older woman, telling her Zoey's bedtime.

"I'll be gone for three days and returning the morning of the fourth. Thanks for watching her, Mom. Only you know how much our purpose means to me and the family." Annie turned to her daughter. "Give me a hug, honey. I'll be home in a few days. Do everything Nana tells you to."

"I will, Mommy."

Once Annie left, Nana and Zoey curled up on the couch and began watching an animated movie on TV.

Hayley's dream skipped to nightfall when Zoey slept peacefully, and Nana had long ago gone to bed. Someone in a long dark blue hooded robe, the face hidden, stood at the end of the little girl's bed. *It must be Annie returning to check on her daughter.*

When the figure lowered her hood, Hayley realized her error. Hildr seemed to float when she moved to the side of the bed. She crooned what sounded like a lullaby. Zoey, still asleep, slipped out of bed and stood as if waiting for instructions.

Although Hayley wished she could do something, scream or shake the child to wake her, she knew it to be a vision of the past and watched as events unfolded. Hayley felt helpless. But she knew she couldn't do a thing even if this had happened in the here and now.

Hildr brought the child close and folded her robe around her. In an instant, the witch and Zoey vanished.

The setting in Hayley's dream changed. She remembered this room. An antique table stood between bookshelves filled with well-used volumes. The window provided the only source of light. Hayley barely saw a figure wearing a dark robe in the dimness and standing in front of the large leather-bound book, *The Book of Spells*, exactly where Hayley had seen it before.

When the dark-robed figure looked toward the door, Hayley saw Hildr/Kathy's face cloaked within the hood. She appeared at ease after translocating into the room only feet away from witches and warlocks gathering beyond the closed door.

Alarms went off in Hayley's mind. *The runestone!* She glanced around and felt relieved to see the stone had been removed from the room. *Thank goodness they moved it. But where to?*

Hildr pulled back her robe, and Zoey stepped out from behind the dark blue velvet fold. She walked forward, seized the book, moved away from the table, and held *The Book of Spells* tightly to her small body. Without touching the child Hildr waved her arms, and they disappeared.

Hayley's dream altered again. She visualized another location—a bedroom decorated in pink—*an unusual place for an evil witch to live.* Hayley again noticed a feeling of déjà vu. *Do I know this place?* She couldn't remember. A raspberry colored purse hung on a hook by the door. *This must be Kathy's place. A witch wouldn't carry a purse.*

After Zoey set the book on a dresser, she climbed into bed, and Hildr pulled the covers over her. "Sleep, my dear." When the child closed her eyes, the witch began to cast the three-day spell. Before she finished the first phase, the dream ended.

Hayley awoke knowing Hildr would finish the next step in the morning, putting Zoey into a coma, and knew from seeing it occur in her dreams that the last step, possession, would take place in the meadow.

When Lee exited the bathroom and went to his side of the bed, Hayley realized she'd dozed only momentarily and that he hadn't gone to bed. "I received a dream-viewing from Grams," she told him.

He hesitated as he turned down the covers. His brow furrowed. "What's wrong? Was it about the rescue?"

"No. She showed me Zoey's kidnapping."

"Is she in a coma?" He climbed into bed.

"Not yet, but she will be by morning."

"Does Annie know?"

"Probably. Her mother was babysitting. Because she has abilities like everyone else in her family, she surely would've contacted Annie by telepathy or even translocated to tell her in person."

"You're right." He glanced at the clock above the fireplace. "It's only nine. Want to cuddle awhile?"

She scooted over and moved her pillow closer to his, meeting him in the middle of his king-size bed.

He rolled toward her and softly kissed her. "Put your mind on other things, or you'll never get to sleep."

"Like what?"

"I can think of something." He kissed her again, long and passionately.

Hayley's senses filled with his touch and the scent and taste of him, flaming her desire, leaving no room for thoughts of anything but Lee.

# CHAPTER 31

The next day, before Clint, Roger, and Laura arrived, Hayley again practiced nudging.

"I've mastered it," Hayley told Lee. "I'm sure of it."

By the time they started for Virginia, she had no doubt her plan would work.

Anticipation made the drive seem longer. What would normally be beautiful fall scenery weeks ago now lacked its autumn color. Very few trees held on to their remaining leaves, while fields of grass varied in shades of green to dormant brown.

"At least we got lucky with the weather," Lee said. "Scattered clouds at the most, and warmer than usual temperatures."

"Hildr can see the future, remember," Hayley reminded him. "She had to choose a clear night in order to perform the full moon ritual. But you're right about the temperature. I doubt it will fall below forty tonight."

"We've had nothing but the unusual since the day we met Vara," Lee said. "I wouldn't be surprised if flowers bloomed."

They followed Clint after he turned off the highway, taking the same route he had taken before. To the west, the sun had dipped behind the mountains while painting the sky and distant clouds golden.

Lee parked alongside the road yards before he and Hayley reached the spot where Clint had driven into the woods the last time. Clint stopped to pick them up. Laura sat in the front passenger seat, and Roger, who sat in the back, moved over, giving them room to sit.

"Let's just walk and meet them there," Hayley suggested, remembering last time's jostling ride. "It's only a short way."

Lee motioned for Clint to drive on.

Hayley and Lee climbed out of their car and hiked up the hill. They watched Clint pull in and weave his Jeep between trees with only dim daylight to guide him. Then they followed after him into the woods.

"We need to spread out," Lee said when they reached Clint's car. "If there's a chance Hayley will be caught, someone needs to distract the guards."

"How will we know if we're in danger?" Laura asked.

"I'll raise my right arm and point to the direction it's coming from," Hayley replied. "Don't worry. You'll have plenty of time to hide."

Laura moved away from Roger's side but looked uneasy as if she would run back to him in an instant. Clint wandered to the left, away from the meadow, almost too far to see Hayley's warning signal if given. Lee kept Hayley in his sight, hardly taking his eyes off her. Each watched their footing, stepping over twigs that would announce their arrival.

Hayley sensed a difference in the atmosphere from the day before. Not a single bird flew among the trees, squirrels had fled, and deer were nowhere to be found. *They know.* The silence made their attention to covertness even more demanding.

Only minutes into their hike, Hayley raised her arm. They all darted behind century-old hemlock and pine trees.

Hayley could hear horsemen approaching slowly through the woods, coming from the direction of the compound. At the edge of Annie's family's land, they came to a halt, looked toward the main road, talked among themselves, and continued forward.

Hayley held her breath as one of them rode in her direction.

A vision showed Hayley the forest surrounding her. She saw Clint stepping away from his hiding place and walking casually as if coming from the opposite direction. "Nice horse," he said to the nearest rider, who stopped before reaching the tree Laura hid behind.

The rider closest to Hayley turned his black mount and moved away. Another, sitting on a light brown horse with white fetlocks, pulled up a few feet from Roger's hiding place. Knowing that their attention had turned to Clint, Hayley peeked out from behind the tree.

Still unaware of how close they were to a couple of the team, the riders guided their horses toward Clint, coming to a halt in front of him.

"Is that your vehicle?" the man on the black horse asked.

Clint nodded.

Hayley's knees weakened. *If he has the same abilities I have, he'll know if Clint's lying.*

"Crazy place to park. There's a parking lot down the hill specified for hikers using the park's trails."

"I don't trust anyone," Clint said. "I've heard a man can lose his wheels parking in these parts."

The man's horse snorted and danced as if ready to move on.

"I follow your thinking. It's a nice Jeep, but it's parked illegally. If the rangers see it there, you'll have a hefty fine to pay."

"Thanks for the heads-up. I'll move it. It's late anyway."

The speaker led his horse in the Jeep's direction, hesitated dangerously close to Hayley, and waited for Clint to get in and start the engine. The other two stood their ground inches away from Lee. Once Clint pulled out and drove onto the main road, the horsemen turned their mounts and headed back the way they had come.

A couple of minutes went by before, Hayley, Lee, Roger, and Laura stepped out of hiding. Remaining spread out, they followed Hayley to the dirt road, then trailed her in single file, walking along the edge of the woods. Along the way, they kept their guard up, looking in all directions, ready to hide again if necessary.

When they reached the target spot where Hayley had entered the forest in her dreams, they crossed the road, scurried down the creek bank, and under the bridge. The sun had set. The full moon lit their way.

Hayley stepped across a rubble of rocks lining the creek, allowing her to keep her feet dry while she reached a collapsed wall that had held the bridge up long ago. Lee, sitting next to her, whispered to Hayley, but the roar of the water, echoing as it flowed through the tunnel, cloaked his words. She leaned closer to him.

He cupped his hand to her ear. "Can you guess how soon before they cast the spell of fog?"

She cupped her hands to reply. "Hours before the battle begins. They'll want to make sure anyone in the area stays away or stays put if they're trapped in the fog. They'll want plenty of time to get rid of trespassers who wander into the meadow before Hildr appears."

He nodded.

She took off her backpack, unzipped it, and pulled out her headphones. They still had a few hours before the spell would be cast, and listening to music would help pass the time.

***

Twenty minutes later, Clint slid down the bank from the road and joined them under the bridge. He signaled to them, pointing up the road.

Hayley turned the music off and removed her headphones. It was then she heard the clip-clop of horses coming from the direction of the compound. She raised an index finger to her lips to warn everyone who wore headphones.

Once the horses trotted across the bridge, Clint snuck to the creek's bank, watching the riders in the moonlight to see where they would go. After the horses left the asphalt, the sound of their hoofs grew fainter, and Hayley wondered if they'd return to the woods. *How soon will they be back this way?* Her psychic intuition did not provide an answer.

Clint hurried back under the bridge and whispered to Lee. Lee nodded and relayed the message to Hayley. "They rode down the dirt road, probably to bed the horses for the night. It's too dangerous to ride them through the woods in the dark."

She agreed. "Where did Clint park his Jeep?"

"Down the road a bit."

Hayley looked at the creek flowing into the woods to her right. The moonlight streamed through the canopy of pines and hemlocks. From here, she would see the fog when the spell was cast.

While forming a strategy, she decided to let Clint take the lead to find the twine. By using his compass, he had led them out of the fog yesterday. If anything were to go wrong today, no doubt he'd lead them out again. As they had before, they could form a chain, holding the twine in one hand while placing their other on the shoulder of the person in front of them. That way, if someone lost the twine, they'd still have that person as a guide. She whispered her decision to Lee, who rose and relayed the message to Roger, Laura, and Clint.

When he returned to her side, Lee glanced toward the west and pointed.

Hayley heard a vehicle coming from, most likely, the stables. *The search for trespassers by horse has ended. A vehicle can't drive through the woods, so it must be going to the compound. Everyone's gathering. No one's watching the road.*

She took her phone from her shirt pocket, checked the time, and returned it to her pocket. *Eight. While we wait until midnight, I'd better decide when to enter the fog. We won't be able to see each other or speak once we're in there. It would be better if we stay here as long as possible before going in. Hildr and the family would be distracted by then, and won't notice any noises we make.*

Hayley glanced toward Laura, who had brought an audiobook and earplugs, as had Roger. *I wish I'd thought of that. I only brought earphones.*

Clint played games on his cell phone with the sound off. *Something he couldn't do in the fog.* Lee watched videos on Youtube. *Also, impossible to do once we enter the woods and are unable to see an inch in front of our faces.*

She told Lee her decision, and again he relayed the message to the others.

# CHAPTER 32

Even though the wait couldn't be helped, the hours under the bridge seemed twice as long to Hayley. Anticipation and anxiety played havoc with her imagination. She had to stay positive, confident that her ability would save their friend. Whenever doubt entered her mind, she thought, *I will not own it. This is our purpose.*

The fog spell had been cast. From hers and her friends' hiding place, Hayley had watched the mist spread, thicken through the woods, and fill the creek beyond the bridge. *Almost time.* Nearly an hour after the fog blanketed the forest, she again checked the time on her phone and found they could begin their mission.

They were cautious while leaving their hiding place and climbing the creek bank. After they reached the other side of the road, they formed a line, each with a hand on the shoulder of the person before them.

Clint entered the fog bank first. Hayley trailed him. She felt him bend down, stand again and noticed when she reached out that he had lifted the twine waist high, which made it easier for her to find. She felt the twine between her fingers and her hand on Clint's shoulder but could see neither. Fog kissed her nose. Everything looked white, cloaked in fog, illuminated by the full moon.

They moved slowly, a half-step at a time. With each small stride, before taking another, she slid a foot forward, testing the ground, not wanting to stumble over a root or fallen limb. More than once, she stubbed her toe, or a branch whipped her leg. She gripped the twine tighter. *I don't know how you did it, Jim, but you did a great job.* Another twig thrashed her leg. *Thank goodness I wore knee-high boots.* The only sound in the woods came from the creek a few feet away, muffling the noise of their approach.

After a grueling, nerve-wracking hike, Hayley's anxiety level stirred when Clint finally stopped. The fog in front of them appeared less dense, thinning around the field's fringe. In the moonlight, everything in the meadow looked gray.

Hayley crept forward and hid behind an old hemlock tree that concealed her from Annie's view. She closed her eyes and took a deep breath, calming her pounding heart. When she opened her eyes again, she told herself, *I'm ready. This will work.* The angle Hayley chose in proximity to the field, to the side and behind Hildr, made it impossible for the witch to see her out of the corner of her eye. *Perfect. The exact place I'd envisioned being in my dreams.*

Under the star-filled sky, Hildr/Kathy, Zoey, and Annie's family faced each other. Thanks to her eavesdropping, Hayley didn't need to count to know that fifty of Annie's family, all dressed in full-length hooded blue robes, had taken their stance against Hildr. It only made sense that there had to be a large group to battle the witch. With that many involved, Hildr would have to fight on instinct alone — or that's what the family and Vara seemed to believe according to the dreams Hayley had witnessed.

But Hayley knew Hildr had foreseen enough outcomes while probing her future to know that changing hosts would be her only chance to survive.

Quietly, Lee squatted next to Hayley. He watched Hildr intently to catch any response, Kathy, still possessed by Hildr, might make after Hayley's attempts at nudging. Hayley knew that, unfortunately, the rules still applied when it came to foreseeing her own future, and that made it impossible for her to know if her attempts would succeed. Only Kathy's interference with Hildr's spell casting would give them a clue that the nudge worked.

Once she cleared her mind, Hayley followed the instructions stored within her bracelet. While in deep meditation, she noticed energy levels change as she expanded her awareness and felt the faint pulse of the universe. At that moment, she focused her intent, sending her thoughts to Kathy. *Save yourself. Make Annie see you're still alive. Take control.* Over and over, Hayley sent the message, placing the words into Kathy's mind.

*It has to work.* They were the saviors of souls, and this time they were defending one of their own. She tried again.

Hayley knew the battle would soon begin. Each child from Vara's lineage throughout the centuries had been taught Hildr's spells and learned to reverse them, dispel them, and cast their own—all except the spell Hildr used to put a child into a coma, the last step needed in order for her to take the innocent's body for her own. And that also worried Hayley. Zoey, frozen, eyes fixed, staring straight ahead, unblinking—comatose—stood off to the side of Hildr.

With a flick of her hand, Annie cast a spell, placing a shield around her daughter.

Hildr also encased herself inside a protective bubble. But, as

Hayley had seen in a dream, a frenzy of blackbirds cracked the witch's defense. The witch hissed and pointed a stern finger at the grass-covered field at her feet.

Hayley sent another nudge to disrupt Hildr's spell but saw no response from Kathy. Instead, the ground shook, and fissures opened in the earth, their tentacles running across the battlefield and under the feet of Hildr's attackers. From each crack, billions of scorpions scurried to the surface with tails up, ready to strike a deadly blow.

Unshaken, each of Annie's family rose, their feet no longer touching the ground. But Hayley couldn't move without being detected. Three scorpions scampered toward her, followed by a hundred more. She froze, knowing if she turned to run, she'd be lost in the fog.

She and Lee leaped up and stepped back. When the pack leaders came within striking distance, fear flooded her. With their tails curled upward, the three pack leaders scrambled up her boot. Frantic, she shook her leg. Two fell off, but the third steadied itself and began to climb, its army only inches away from the toe of her boot. A scream caught in Hayley's throat.

In that instant, the scorpions disappeared, vanishing as the family members reversed the spell.

Hayley's knees weakened. Before she might fall, she crouched and swallowed hard, her heart beating wildly. She glanced at the starlit sky. Besides the full moon, the pin-sized starlight brightened the night. A flicker caught her eye. She stared. *Am I seeing things? Are the stars getting bigger?*

They gleamed brighter, and their mass expanded. Hayley touched Lee's arm and pointed upward. Each light grew to baseball size before Hayley realized, *They're not stars.*

Like tails of comets, flames trailed balls of fire and rained down on the family. When they struck the ground, the fire spread, surrounding all of Annie's siblings.

Annie stood in front of the blazing field, her attention still focused on Hildr. Behind her, one by one, unscathed, each witch and warlock in her family stepped forward through the flames.

*I can't let this distract me.*

The family retaliated as the fire died.

Hayley had seen this counterstrike in her dreams. Vines sprouted from the ground at Hildr's feet. They grew, winding around the witch until their tentacles brushed her cheek. But instead of turning the slithering vines into snakes, Hildr turned them into a garland of monarch butterflies. Their gossamer wings hummed as they took flight.

While frantically gazing at Hildr/Kathy, Hayley took a deep breath, letting it out slowly. Then she projected her nudges over and over again.

Rocks rose, floating, surrounding Hildr's attackers. Instantaneously the stones turned to spears and sailed at Annie and her siblings, catching Hayley's attention again.

Doubt whispered in her mind, making her question her abilities. But Hayley's fortitude overpowered it, not allowing the anxiety to influence her. She pictured her words flowing into Kathy's mind.

The battle continued. Fire streamed from Hildr's palms without deflection from Kathy. During each attack, Hayley studied the witch's movements, hoping Kathy would respond.

"Looks like Hildr has the upper hand," Lee said. "Why isn't the family counterstriking?"

"I'm guessing they're waiting for Hildr's energy to deplete. Without performing the ritual, she has limits."

Out of the clear sky, lightning struck the ground in front

of Hildr, smoldering the grass at the witch's feet. Black smoke barred her view of the family.

Without hesitating, Annie lashed out with a golden lariat before Hildr could regain sight of her attackers. But the rope slummed, missing its mark. When the smoke drifted, Hayley saw that Hildr had relocated, standing nearer to Zoey, out of the reach of Annie's assault.

Instantly Hildr flew backward, hit by several explosions of air. She bashed into the stone altar. Stumbling, she pulled herself up and recovered her balance.

"If she can translocate," Lee said, "Why doesn't she flee?"

"She has a plan. It's her only chance to fool everyone by taking Zoey."

"Thank goodness they haven't hurt Kathy," Lee said.

"They don't want to kill her. They want to bury her alive. But the longer this goes on, I'm guessing, the more force they'll use."

"Hildr should know that," Lee replied. "Does she really want to risk taking it to that extreme?"

"No. I don't think she will. But, as you know, I never saw this version of the future. In all my dreams, only a handful of family stood with Annie. There are fifty now. They could easily win before Hildr possesses the child. That's why I have to let Annie know that Kathy isn't comatose."

Hayley repeated the nudging.

The window of time to influence Kathy grew smaller, and panic crept into every cell of Hayley's being. "Has Kathy reacted?" she whispered to Lee. "Did I miss something?"

"No," he said, his voice low, "and I haven't seen the runestone anywhere. Have you?"

"It's probably hidden, so Hildr doesn't destroy it."

He nodded.

The fight had nearly ended. The next blow again knocked Hildr to the ground. Two of Annie's siblings brought the runestone forefront.

"There it is," Lee said with a catch in his voice. "The fight's almost over."

Hayley felt his trepidation. She knew he had realized that her attempts to nudge Kathy hadn't worked. She felt defeated.

Getting to her feet, Hildr staggered, making her way to her final stance, the stance Hayley knew all too well from replaying her vision of Hildr's escape until she knew every movement, every detail no matter how small.

As Hildr straightened, regaining her poise, she stood in front of Zoey. Without a thought, Hayley used her gift to astral project and soared across the field. As Hildr's spirit stepped out of Kathy's body, Hayley's astral body crashed into the witch's soul, catching the witch off guard. Before Hildr could react, Hayley seized her and pulled her into a stream of light only a foot away.

Hildr squirmed and cursed in Hayley's grasp as they rose within heaven's light. Only the magnitude of Hildr's evil kept Hayley from letting go, especially at the moment she knew the link connecting her spirit to her physical body had snapped. Her life with Lee and her friends had ended.

From nowhere, and everywhere, Hayley heard Vara say, "You can release her now."

Two men took hold of Hildr, allowing Hayley to let her go. In a blink, the witch and her captors disappeared into the light.

When Hayley looked over her shoulder and turned, she felt as if she'd returned to the meadow and stood only feet away from her lifeless physical body lying on the forest floor. *How did I get back here?* She glanced around, getting her bearings. Behind her, the tunnel of light still surrounded her. She gazed again at her friends.

Laura checked the lifeless body's pulse and began CPR. Tears welled in Lee's eyes.

Hayley knew the body belonged to her, but for some reason, the emotional attachment had been severed. She felt only overwhelming love and a sense of peace.

Laura stood. "I'm sorry, Lee."

He covered his eyes with his hands. His body shook.

Laura touched his shoulder. "I have to see to Kathy. I'm so sorry, Lee."

Kathy, lying in the meadow, had lived, while Hildr's spirit had been taken away. Hayley had realized, gaining Akashic knowledge, that the witch's skeletal remains, nearly a thousand years old, lying in a cave somewhere in her homeland, had never been discovered.

# CHAPTER 33

As Hayley stood watching her friends mourn her death, Vara appeared next to her. "Walk with me," the sentinel said.

Hayley glanced away from her lifeless physical body and found herself standing in a field of lilacs with Vara at her side. Night had turned to day, the blue sky lit with sunshine, the temperature warm. *Is this Heaven?* she wondered.

Vara took her hand, and they strolled. "I'm sorry for the secrecy. I have always known about Matilda, Julia, and the investigation. 'Twas before you were born, that I knew you'd be the only one who could capture Hildr."

"How could you have been so sure? Everyone has free will. I could've walked away, given up when Kathy didn't respond to my nudge."

The smell of lilacs filled the air. Hayley noticed that she didn't have to breathe. Her body no longer needed oxygen. *But I still smell the flowers. How's that possible?* The beauty of the flower field surrounding her went on endlessly. But once she thought of trees and mountains, they appeared in the distance.

"The power of thought," Vara told her, apparently reading

Hayley's mind. Then she continued. "To change who you are is not possible, Hayley. You and your team were born to save innocent souls. You're selfless. Until you and your peers were born, I had no idea how I'd apprehend Hildr. With her witchcraft, she could foresee the future and elude me for eternity. The answer shunned me. I had begged to be the one to put an end to the witch, and I was granted the task. To my surprise, the answer was you.

"As long as Hildr remained buried, she failed to perceive the future or to extract the knowledge of my plans from my mind. I had to keep your identity from her. Although I tried, she found out. But only your name. I made her believe the plans I made with Annie and the rest of my family were written in stone and convinced her you were only a nuisance to me. As I had expected, the moment I took you and your friends' memories, Hildr no longer saw you as a threat.

"From the beginning, you always wondered why I used runes to write the list you brought to Annie. It is one of the many things I did to entice you to search for the truth — my first visit to see Jim raised questions. Then the runes cast a shadow of doubt on my honesty. Hiding a message within the writing also raised suspicions. The more I kept you in the dark about my intentions, the more you questioned my sincerity. 'Twas a necessity to convince you to believe I would have Annie bury your friend alive. 'Tis only then you relied on yourself to save her. As it had to be. Hildr never saw you coming."

"We all felt violated," Hayley said, glancing at Vara.

"The promise that life would be easy has never been given," Vara replied. "Sometimes things seem to go amiss, but at the end, they turn out well."

"And now I'm dead," Hayley said, gazing across the field of lilacs. She stopped strolling and turned to Vara. "What about

Kathy and Zoey?"

Vara halted briefly, hooked her arm in the crook of Hayley's elbow, and continued to walk. "They are fine. I learned long ago how to reverse Hildr's coma spell. She's with her mother now. As for Kathy, she'll regain her energy with a couple of days' rest."

"And Hildr? What happened to her?"

"Her worst fears have come true."

"She's meeting her Maker," Hayley said.

Vara nodded and ended their saunter. "Now, you must go back. There's so much more you'll accomplish in your life."

Hayley thought about her limp body lying in the woods. "Will I be okay?"

"You'll be fine. Tell Laura, I said so. She'll want to run test after test on you. And she'll go on and on about how long your brain had been deprived of oxygen and what happens to the human body in the minutes after death. Why put you through that? Just a couple of days rest is all you and Kathy need."

Hayley chuckled. "Jim will have a great time telling stories about all this."

"I'd suggest you keep the stories amongst the team. If not, I foresee the newspapers getting hold of them and your life becoming hectic."

"Wouldn't want more of that."

Vara stopped and turned to her. "I will love Jim forever. Please tell him so. You know I will watch over him, but don't enlighten him. He is crazy enough in this lifetime."

Hayley laughed. "That's the truth."

"Now, it's time for you to return to your friends." She laughed softly. "Thank you and everyone for distrusting me."

In a blink, Hayley found herself back in her physical self. Her heart pounded as she gasped for air. Her eyes fluttered open.

Lee choked back his tears, his face lit with a broad smile. He reached out to her, then hesitated. "Are you hurt?" His hands moved across her body without touching her, as if he didn't know what to do. He swallowed hard, then took a deep breath. Roger rushed to his side.

When Hayley noticed that she could see them clearly, she realized the fog had vanished.

"She's alive," Lee said. He glanced across the clearing. "Laura, Laura, she's okay. She's alive."

Hayley tried to sit up, then reclined. "I'm fine." She began to rise again, then decided against it. "A little lightheaded, maybe."

"Lack of oxygen to the brain," Lee said. "You were dead for forty minutes."

Her mind spun, trying to calculate the time. *It felt like only a moment.*

"Just relax, Hayley," Roger said. "Let Laura take a look at you."

Lee's brow furrowed. "You broke your promise, you know."

"What promise?" she asked.

"You promised me when we bought those books that you wouldn't do anything that would harm you or kill you. You did both."

"Your memories are back," she said, reaching out and touching his cheek.

He thought for a moment. "I guess so."

"Help me up," Hayley said.

"Are you sure?" Lee asked. "I'd give anything to hold you in my arms and kiss every inch of you right now. But...."

"Okay, fine. At least I can sit."

He and Roger helped her sit and lean against the nearest tree. When she glanced toward the meadow, she saw Laura speaking to Kathy, Clint kneeling by Kathy's side. Laura rose and hurried her way.

She knelt beside Hayley. "Can you remember who we are? Do you know your own name? After all this time, you're alive. How is this possible?"

Hayley laughed. "Vara told me you'd go on and on about how death affects someone. I'm fine. Vara said so."

Laura's lips pursed. "She did, did she? And what did she prescribe for Kathy?"

"She just needs rest. We both do. No tests. Okay? Nothing would show up out of the ordinary anyway."

"Can you stand?" Lee asked.

Roger helped Lee bring her to her feet. Lee's arms went around her shoulder, and he steadied her as she took a step. She looked across the meadow and saw Kathy stand with Clint's help.

"Let's get you two out of here," Roger said. "Give me a minute." He ran out into the field to Kathy.

Cuddled against Lee's chest, Hayley watched Roger speak to his friends and Annie, while the rest of the family stood back. Zoey held tight to her mother's side.

Roger trotted back to them. "Annie's brothers will help get Hayley and Kathy to Clint's Jeep. Laura will need to go with them. So I'll ride with you, Lee."

"Can you walk, Hayley?" Lee asked.

She nodded.

"Let's join Kathy," he said, "and get both of you home."

Now that the blood had circulated in her body, Hayley knew she felt fine and could walk on her own, but didn't let on. She wanted nothing more than to have Lee's arms around her.

# CHAPTER 34

"I can't count the number of times Laura took my vital signs yesterday and today," Hayley said, keeping her voice down and their conversation confidential at The Steak House. "But that light she kept shining into my eyes has left repercussions. When I look at people, I see their aura."

"What's an aura?" Lee asked, placing his fork across his empty dinner plate.

"It's vibrating energy surrounding the physical body."

"So, everyone has one?"

"Yes," Hayley replied. "And now I see them all the time."

"That's something new. Do you think it's because of Laura's flashlight she shined in your eyes, or because you died?"

"Or maybe it's for no reason. I've been given these so-called gifts willy-nilly throughout my life. If that's the case, it would make seeing auras another gift I never asked for, like my abilities to see the present, past, and future. And I didn't ask to see and speak to the dead and don't forget astral projection—flying out of my body and soaring around. I'm my own freak show. Now I'm seeing auras. What's next?"

"Don't be so hard on yourself. There's a good reason for your gifts, and you know it. You're just tired."

"I didn't sleep a wink last night," she said. "I kept imagining Hildr coming back from the dead and killing all of us."

"That's not going to happen," Lee replied. "Put your mind on something constructive. What about the auras you see? What colors are they? What do they mean?"

"They're all colors, and I don't have any idea what they mean."

"Maybe you can look into it. At least if you're thinking about that, you'll have less time to daydream about impending doom."

"You're right. I don't like being negative. I think it's because I absorbed so much negative energy from Hildr when I captured her. I probably need to cleanse my chakras again. I'll have to talk to Grams."

"Good idea. Ask her about auras too." He shook his head when the waiter attempted to refill their coffee cups. "So, how is Kathy dealing with all this?"

"It's as if she's totally at peace. I don't get it. She knows Hildr better than Vara knows Hildr. How could she not? They shared the same brain. She knew what Hildr knew, everything— her past, her thoughts, her next move. She told me she still has Hildr's memories."

"What a nightmare that would be. I'd hate to envision the evil things that witch has done. And Kathy's okay with that?"

"I know. I'm not buying it either. Maybe I'll have Grams cleanse her chakras too. I can't even imagine the negative energy Kathy's absorbed."

"Good idea that you talk to Grams," Lee said. "She'll know what Kathy's really thinking. She can't be as calm as she appears."

"She probably just doesn't want us to worry about her."

"Well, that's impossible," he replied.

Hayley yawned. "I've been exhausted since Hildr drained my energy. It's going to take me a while to recover."

"You have until New Years. We're not going anywhere or doing anything strenuous until then."

She glanced around the room again. A crowd of people filled the restaurant, and each person had a glow, an aura. She closed her eyes. "I'm ready to go home when you are."

He raised his hand, getting the waiter's attention. After he paid the bill, he stood and took Hayley's hand, helping her rise.

On their way to the coat check, Hayley nudged Lee. "Isn't that Jim and Matilda over there?"

The intimate dining area off the main room appeared cozy to Hayley with its low lighting and lit fireplace. *They're having a romantic dinner. Good for them.*

Lee stopped and glanced their way. "You're right. It is."

"Should we let them have their privacy or go over?" Hayley asked.

"They've probably seen us. No need to be impolite. Let's say hello."

They followed a path leading to the adjoining room.

"Having a nice evening, you two?" Hayley asked.

Jim, freshly shaved and his hair neatly combed, wore a dark suit. Hayley thought Matilda also looked very nice wearing a black two-piece outfit with lace sleeves.

"Well, look what the cat drug in," Jim said. "We were just talkin' 'bout ya."

"I hope it was something pleasant," Lee replied.

"We were saying how nice it is of you to let Kathy stay at your place, Lee," Matilda said. "Are you aware that Hildr spent the last few days in Kathy's apartment while she put a spell on that innocent child?"

"Yes. Hayley saw Kathy's bedroom in a vision. I thought it would be better if she stayed at my place. Laura is sharing a room with her. Apparently, Kathy's been having nightmares."

"I'm going to call Annie," Hayley told them, "and see if she will sage Kathy's apartment to eliminate the negative energy and allow Kathy to feel less anxious about entering."

"What ya gonna do if she doesn't want to go back home?" Jim asked.

"And how about the memories?" Matilda added.

"She's welcome to stay with us as long as she wants," Lee replied.

"Thomas is nearby," Hayley said. "That should be comforting. It'll take time before she goes home, I'm sure. I'm hoping Hilrdr's memories will fade over time, and she'll be left with only her own. But that may be wishful thinking."

"I spoke to her today," Matilda said, "and she's not the same. She's too quiet."

"I noticed that too," Jim added.

"I'm going to talk with her tomorrow," Hayley replied, "to make sure she's okay."

"Well, we're on our way out the door," Lee told them. "Have a pleasant evening."

"We will," Jim replied.

***

In order to fill her mind with thoughts other than the recent past, once they returned home, Hayley went into Lee's office in the third-floor wing encompassing his chambers. She glanced around. The opportunity to venture into this room had never occurred before.

Bookshelves lined one wall, while on another, windows,

with their forest-green drapes pulled back, allowed her to look out at the evening sky. Few pictures hung on the walls. Filing cabinets, copy, fax, and printer machines flanked another desk stacked with papers. It gave her an idea where Lee might go in his spare time.

Hayley sat in front of Lee's computer, entered Lee's password he'd given her, and searched the Web for the color of auras. She found a person's aura consisted of seven different layers, read the list, and discovered what each layer represented. Then she studied the colors and their meanings. *It will take forever before I know what I'm looking at.*

When she read about the basic colors and their variations, the negative shades interested her. She'd seen a lot of these muddied colors around Kathy. *I knew it. She can't tell me she's fine.*

After nearly an hour of study, she printed the information to refer to later, left with a handful of reference material pages, and joined Lee in his bedroom.

"I thought you were going to talk to Grams." He kindled the logs in the fireplace, replaced the screen, and stood. Beneath his opened green terrycloth robe, he wore plaid flannel pull-tie pajama bottoms, his chest bare.

"It can wait until morning." She placed the pages on an end table next to a chair near the fireplace, planning to read them again tomorrow. "She'll want to cleanse my chakras, and that will take time. And I'm too tired to stay awake."

"Understandable. Did you find anything interesting on the Web?"

Hayley sat on the edge of the bed and removed her boots. "Reading auras is a little more complicated than I thought. Have you ever been to a paint store and seen all the different shades to choose from? It's kinda like that. Every basic color has shades, and each has a meaning."

"I can imagine the difficultly."

"And to add to that, there are seven layers, each with its own meaning. It will take time before I know what I'm seeing."

"Sounds interesting."

"It is." She stood and pulled her sweater off over her head and flung it onto a nearby chair. "But the things that jumped out at me the most were the colors of negative energy. I've seen a lot of them surrounding Kathy."

"So she's hiding something," Lee replied, picking up the papers she'd placed on the end table.

"And she's not talking."

He looked up from his reading and returned the pages to the table. "She needs to quit being stubborn and ask for help."

"Yes, and that's another reason I want to wait until morning to talk to Grams. I'm going to ask her to help me convince Kathy to get her auras and chakras cleansed so she'll feel like herself again."

"Is Grams joining us for Thanksgiving dinner?" Lee asked, walking over to her.

"No. I thought we could invite everyone over a couple of hours before we eat and talk awhile. Grams will join us then. I know everyone has questions. But I really don't want to talk about that whole ordeal during dinner." She wiggled out of her jeans and threw them on top of her sweater. "Annie will be stopping by." Hayley sat on the bed, planning to remove her knee-high socks, but Lee knelt, beating her to it, and raised her left foot. "I called her, and she said she'd be by around three. I asked her to join us for dinner, but she has plans with her family."

"We can ask her to stay for dessert." He removed her left sock. After taking off the other, he massaged her feet.

"I'll see what she says after she arrives," she said, enjoying his touch. "Oh, and I asked if she can sage Kathy's apartment so Kathy can go home to get a change of clothes and whatever else she needs."

"Good plan," Lee said.

"I could sage it myself, but I don't have the supplies," Hayley told him. "Anyway, I like Annie. I don't want her to feel like we're holding any grudges against her."

"Neither do I." Lee finished with her massage and rose. "Do you think Kathy is uncomfortable being around her?"

"I have no idea," Hayley told him. "We can feel out the situation once Annie arrives. Speaking of Kathy…. I'll have a decision to make about what to do with my house once we're married. And I thought I could give it to Kathy for a Christmas gift."

"That would solve the problem of her reluctance to move home."

"I wouldn't want to go back there either." Hayley stood, lifted her white robe from the end of the bed, and slipped into it. "There's no way I'd sleep in that bed."

"Exactly," Lee replied. "Not after Hildr slept there, not to mention Zoey after Hildr cast that spell on her."

They strolled to the fireplace. Its heat warmed her face and naked feet.

"Then that's what I'll do," Hayley said, snuggling against Lee. "It'll be the perfect gift."

"I suggest we meet in the parlor tomorrow," Lee said. "My library is too similar to Roger's and might make everyone feel like we're still involved in the case. I'll have Lewis call everyone and let them know to be here a couple of hours before dinner."

Hayley nodded and raised her hand to cover a yawn.

"Why don't we get some sleep?" he told her. "You'll feel better in the morning."

"I was about to suggest the same thing."

# CHAPTER 35

They rose around seven in the morning. Hayley had slept fitfully, but better than the night before. She looked forward to a big cup of coffee.

Lee called Lewis on his cell phone, putting the call on speaker while he slipped into his robe, and asked him to serve breakfast in his sitting room. "Is Jim up yet?" Lee asked. "Maybe he'd like to join us."

"I don't know, sir. He still has a 'Do not disturb' sign on his door."

Hayley and Lee glanced at each other.

"Okay, Lewis. He must have plans of his own."

Hayley raised a hand to her mouth, covering a giggle.

He ended the call. "Who would've known? I guess their relationship is official now."

"Jim remembered how he felt about Matilda once he got his memories back. They've been spending a lot of time together. The other day, he drove her to her home in Raleigh so she could pick up a few things. She's been living out of a suitcase all this time. I'm so glad Jim found someone."

"So am I," Lee said. "I thought I'd never see the day. And Thomas is head-over-heels in love with Kathy again now that his memories are back. I love happy endings."

"It's not happy yet," Hayley told him. "Vara was wrong. It's going to take more than rest before Kathy and I to return to normal."

"Are you still going to talk to Grams?"

She nodded. Before they spoke another word, Grams appeared in a chair by the fireplace.

"Can you help us?" Hayley asked.

"I can cleanse yours and Kathy's chakras and auras, but I don't know how much that will help. It's outrageous how much harmful energy Kathy absorbed from Hildr."

"I was afraid of that. Will you help me convince Kathy that she needs cleansing?"

"Yes, dear. Give me a shout when you're ready."

"Thanks, Grams."

Grams vanished as quickly as she'd appeared.

"Sounds like there's more to this than meets the eye," Lee said.

Hayley grimaced. "If she can't help us, we might be needing a therapist for the rest of our lives."

"It's that serious?"

"I don't know if I'll need one. I only came in contact with Hildr for a short time. But Kathy.... She has to be seriously traumatized. I'll talk to her later and see how she feels."

***

After they finished breakfast and dressed, they took the elevator to the first floor. The aroma of Thanksgiving dinner spread through the home. They entered an immense hallway with its large black-and-white marble-tiled floor. Staff members

Hayley had never seen before rushed about, while others prepared the meal.

"You hired extra help, I see," Hayley said. "Why so many? There's only going to be a handful of us for dinner."

They headed to the doors leading outside to the veranda.

"Thanksgiving isn't just for us," Lee replied, holding the door open for Hayley before following her out. "The entire staff is having their families over tonight to celebrate in the ballroom. It's a tradition."

A chilly breeze nipped at Hayley's nose, although the blue sky had few clouds, and the sun shone brightly. She looked across carpets of grass pathways crisscrossing between geometric designs formed by boxwood hedges and English holly framing flowerbeds. The first time she'd seen Lee's backyard, a multitude of flower types bloomed in each bed. Now, during the autumn months, mums filled the flowerbeds, in each bed, a different color. And as always, topiaries, some rounded, some coned, and others cubed, dotting the garden to the lake's edge, remained well trimmed.

Beyond the gardens, the lake seemed still, not a boat in view. They walked along a grassy path that took them to the bridge spanning a stream of lake water feeding a pond on the north side of the house. It reminded Hayley, when the cherry trees were in bloom, of a painting by Monet.

"So that's why I didn't recognize anyone. Your permanent staff has the day off."

"All but Lewis. He refused to take off until after our dinner is over and our guests leave. The staff deserves a day to celebrate. They and their families are invited for Christmas as well."

"How thoughtful," she said. "Too bad, we'll miss that."

"We'll be having our own fun at Roger's," Lee replied.

"How soon after Christmas will we be leaving for England?"

"Lewis made flight reservations for the following Wednesday."

"That's exciting."

When they reached the keystone at the center of the bridge, Lee reached for his phone and answered a call. He put the phone on speaker when he read Roger's name. "Hi. What's up?"

"They delivered the engagement ring last night, and I'd like to give it to Laura today at your place."

"I take it she's not there right now," Hayley said.

"No," Roger replied. "She's at the hospital and will be joining us around noon."

"Sometime after our meal might be nice," Hayley suggested. "We can all say what we're thankful for, and you can tell her you're thankful for her love. You can figure it out from there."

"Good lead in," Roger said. "She'll be surprised."

"Thanks for sharing the moment with us," Lee told him.

"You're all my family," Roger replied. "There's no one I'd rather celebrate with. I'll see you later then."

Lee ended the call.

Hayley's face lit. "Today is turning out to be spectacular."

"I agree."

"Maybe you should start the circle of thanks," Hayley told him. "We'll raise our glasses to Kathy and her rescue first thing. Roger and Laura could be last. That way, it will start with a toast and end with one. What do you think?"

"Sounds like a good plan to me. I'll let Lewis know that we'll need Champagne."

Another cold breeze brushed against Hayley's cheek. "Let's head back." They strolled hand in hand to the veranda.

She glanced up at the red brick mansion and recalled the

first time she'd seen it. She remembered Lee saying he waited for the day she would look at it as a home and not as a showcase that took her breath away each instant she turned around. That day had come and gone without notice. She no longer stared up in awe at the magnificent ceilings, the glorious chandeliers, the superb woodwork, and the grand furnishings. Now every inch felt like home.

They entered the south wing hallway leading to the parlor located across from Lewis's quarters and the security room. Hayley glanced up the hallway at the library, where Lee usually entertained guests. As long as she had known him, he had never received visitors in the parlor. In fact, she'd been in the parlor one other time only, when Lee gave her a tour of his home. When they reached the door, he held it open while Hayley skirted by him.

The fire in the fireplace had already been lit. The seating area in front of the mantle made the room comfortable for company. The size of the cream-colored room seemed much larger due to the high ceiling with its detailed bas-relief, depicting clusters of wildflowers. And in the center of the room, another gorgeous chandelier hung in the center of a white ornate medallion.

*His mom must've had a passion for chandeliers. Each one I've seen so far is uniquely different from the rest.*

The room gave her a peek at Lee's childhood. Everywhere she turned, she noticed an eclectic mix of beautiful things brought back from other countries by his parents, who had taken Lee, at a young age, around the world.

As they walked, he told her stories about each piece of furniture and souvenir placed in the room. From the mantle, Lee took a photo of a small town and handed it to her. "Check out the frame. Discovering local artists is a good way to venture through

England's countryside. This piece came from a little town outside London. It was the last trip I took with my parents."

She turned it, examining the creation. A tree seemed to grow up the left side, its carved branches and leaves bowing across the top of the frame and down its right side, giving the carving a 3D effect. "It's beautiful. Will we be anywhere near this town New Year's? I'd like to add to the collection and make it a tradition."

Lee smiled. "I'd like that. I suggest we take a drive and sightsee a bit while we're there. We can stop at each town along the way and check out the local talent."

Hayley returned the framed oil painting to the mantle. "That sounds pleasant. I can't wait to go. I've always wanted to go to England."

He glanced at a gold clock encased in glass next to the painting. "It's nearly noon. Guests should be arriving."

"Let's greet them at the front door," she said.

They left the room and strolled through the hallways to the foyer.

When Clint, Kathy, and Thomas came to the door, Lee and Hayley met them, and Lewis took their coats. While waiting for Roger, who had just parked, they mingled in the foyer under one of the many chandeliers in the mansion.

"Laura's on her way," Roger said once he joined them. "And there's no need to wait for Matilda. I believe she's already here."

"We haven't seen her or Jim, but I'm sure you're right," Lee replied, grinning.

Lee and Hayley gathered their guests and led them down the hallway until they reached the parlor. When they entered the room, everyone sat around the fireplace. Minutes later, Jim and Matilda entered and found seats. Then Laura arrived.

"How did it feel to be possessed by Hildr?" Clint asked

Kathy, who sat across from him on the couch with Thomas.

"I felt like I was on autopilot," she replied. "I would be doing things or saying things uncontrollably. It was totally confusing. Our thoughts and memories shared the same mind. I can tell you everything about her and what she said and did over her entire life. In fact, I was thinking about writing a book, maybe a series of them, about her life."

"That's a good idea," Laura said. "Writing puts things in perspective. It will help you sort out what memories are hers and what are yours. It would be very therapeutic."

"I'm sure it will take time before I'm myself again," Kathy said.

"A person's instinctive reactions are created from memories," Laura told her. "Are you sure you're okay?"

"I will be."

"How's that workin' for ya, sugar?" Jim asked. "Have any urges to buy a pointy hat, and when you're in the kitchen and see the broom, do ya feel like flyin'?"

Kathy laughed, but Matilda gave him a stern glare.

"All I need is rest," Kathy said.

Hayley glanced at Laura. *Hmm, did Laura hit it on the nose? Are Hildr's memories influencing Kathy's reactions? Instincts can be fatal. This could be more serious than I thought.*

"What are you going to do about your apartment?" Hayley asked. "Before you go back, I suggest I cleanse it and all the furniture to remove residual energy."

"I'm not going back," she said. "In fact, I'm moving in with Tom starting tonight." She looked at Laura. "No offense, but I really don't need my vital signs checked any longer. I'm fine now."

"I wouldn't say that," Hayley told her. "I've seen your aura, and it's a mess. You need to cleanse both your aura and your chakras."

"I'm fine," Kathy said. "Vara said all I need is rest. Isn't that right?"

"Yes. But…. Grams," Hayley called out.

The parlor door opened, and Grams strolled in wearing camel-colored pants and a white pullover sweater. She joined them and sat in an unoccupied chair near the sofa. "Good afternoon, everyone."

"This is the first time I've seen you use a door," Hayley said.

"There's no one in this room that needs to be startled. So I was just being thoughtful, dear."

"You're right," Hayley said. "And rest isn't going to make things okay. So Kathy, do you want to tell me the truth, or do you want Grams to tell me?"

Kathy took a deep breath and let it out slowly. "All right. It's true. I confess I'm overwhelmed by flashbacks, and every dream I have is a replay of Hildr's memories. There's nothing I can do about it."

"You may be right," Grams said. "Some who are terribly traumatized may look fine, but in reality, they need serious help. And in your case, you need more help than I can give you."

"What do you suggest?" Kathy asked.

"I don't think Vara foresaw the psychological aftereffects," Grams replied. "She needs to fix this."

"I'm done with Vara," Kathy said. "First she says all we need is rest, and now this. I can handle it by myself."

"But—" Grams began.

"It's my choice," Kathy told her.

"Well then, there's nothing I can do."

Lewis came to the door. "Dinner is served, sir."

"That's my cue to leave," Grams told them. "Have a nice dinner, everyone." She looked at Matilda. "I'll catch up with you another time." Instead of leaving by the door, she vanished in front of them.

"Let's eat," Lee said.

All rose. Lee led them back the way they had come to the foyer and up the grand staircase. Once they reached the ballroom, they turned to the right. They walked along the hallway, where paintings by Monet hung on the gold Venetian-plastered walls. Above, cream-and-gold dentil crown moldings bordered a honeycomb pattern of plaster bas-reliefs on the ceiling. Pocket doors led into the dining room.

There, along the pale yellow walls, five twelve-foot-tall windows draped in green velvet permitted views to the garden pond. Under the dining table, a multicolored Persian carpet ran the length of the room. Above the carved marble fireplace, seven feet high and ten feet wide hung a gold-framed oil portrait of Ben Franklin, its size commanding a place of honor.

Nine of the thirty-two possible places at the table had been set with gold-rimmed white china, linen napkins, fine silver, and stem glasses. The guests chose their seats.

Before the meal, Lee led a prayer. Then he stood. "First, let's raise our glass to celebrate Kathy's successful return." He lifted a glass of wine, and everyone stood with drinks held high as cheers filled the room. Then they sat.

"With no further ado," Lee said, "let's eat."

In the center of the table, the turkey rested on a large platter, while portions had been placed on smaller platters within reach of the guests. Diners helped themselves and passed around the side dishes.

"I can hire someone to move everything out of your apartment if you'd like, Kathy," Lee offered as he took a helping of creamed sweet potatoes and placed it on his plate.

"That would be nice," Kathy said, sitting on Hayley's left. She added a scoop of cranberry relish to her plate when it came around, then handed the serving bowl to Thomas. "I don't know how I'm going to pack things. There's things I need, but I'm not comfortable going in yet."

"How do you cleanse an apartment, Hayley?" Matilda asked.

"By burning sage. The smoke eliminates negativity and will drive away unwanted spirits."

"How incredible," Matilda said, taking a portion of mashed potatoes and covering them with gravy. "I wonder who came up with that?"

"It's called 'smudging,'" Hayley explained, adding a slice of white meat to her plate. "It has an archaic history. No one knows how the practice started or how the knowledge spread. Even the Native Americans used it in their rituals."

"Interesting," Matilda said.

"If you want," Lee told Kathy, "I can have your things brought here, and you can go through them at your convenience. I have plenty of storage space, and you can leave all of it here until you're ready for it."

"That would be perfect," Kathy said, passing the bowl of green beans with bacon and mushrooms to Hayley.

"Whatever you choose to do," Hayley added, taking the side dish, "you still have to cleanse your apartment. There might be a time when you'll need to go there for some reason. Maybe going through things first before they're packed would be easier than unpacking to find what you need."

"You're right," Kathy replied. "Let me think about it."

At the end of the meal, before Lewis began clearing the table, the dining room's pocket doors slid open. Unannounced, Annie entered carrying a large bag. "I brought what you —"

Kathy leaped from her chair, her face hardened. She held out her hand, and a fireball appeared in the palm of her hand.

Hayley jumped up. "Kathy!"

Kathy looked at her outstretched hand, and the fireball vanished. She turned to Hayley. "I need help." Tears welled in her eyes. "I'm sorry, Annie. I really am."

"I'll find Vara," Annie said, setting the bag down on a side table.

Hayley put her arm around Kathy and led her away from the table. She turned to the others. "We'll be back for dessert." She, Kathy, and Annie left the dining room.

***

When Hayley and Kathy reentered the room, they found the guests still seated and awaiting their return. They sat without comment.

"Where's Annie?" Lee asked.

"She left with Vara," Hayley replied.

"So, what happened?" Clint asked.

"We're perfectly fine now," Kathy said. "Vara took care of everything. She even promised to cleanse my apartment and apologized for not foreseeing this sooner."

Hayley noticed Kathy's aura looked more like everyone else's now and realized Kathy appeared relaxed.

Lewis made the rounds filling champagne glasses. Then he started to clear the table.

When the last plate had been removed, Lee stood. "While we're waiting on dessert to be served, I think we should have a circle of thanks. I'll start. I'm thankful for each and every one of you." He raised his glass. "And I'm glad the nightmare is over."

"Ya got that right," Jim said.

Agreement spread throughout the room.

The circle of thanks continued around the table. One by one, they declared their personal gratitude. When it came to Roger, he rose. "I'm thankful for finding the love of my life. And thankful she loves me too." He took her hand. "Would you mind standing?"

She stood, gave him a kiss on the cheek, and began to sit.

"Not yet, my love," Roger said, not releasing Laura's hand. He pushed his chair back and led her a few feet from the table. With her hand still in his, he knelt in front of her and removed a velvet box from his suit coat's inside pocket.

Laura's eyes widened.

"I've waited all my life for you," Roger said. "And for the rest of my life, I can't live without you. I love you, Laura. Will you marry me?"

Hayley watched the tears running down Laura's cheeks as she answered, "Yes," before she too cried.

When Roger placed the ring on Laura's finger, the room boomed with cheers. Glasses clinked. Everyone joined the couple to congratulate them.

Once Lewis announced dessert would be served, everyone returned to their seats. Their dessert choices were revealed: pumpkin pie, six-layer chocolate cake, maple cheesecake with roasted pears, apple crumb pie, and pecan pie.

After serving, Lewis went to the fireplace and pulled back the screen. *The fire's out. I thought it felt a little chilly in here*, Hayley said to herself.

"I'll get it," Kathy offered, sitting to Lewis's side. She raised a finger, and suddenly flames danced among the logs.

Everyone gasped.

"My word," Matilda said.

Kathy's face turned a shade of pink. "Oh. I wasn't thinking. I forgot to tell you I told Vara I would still like to write a book about Hildr's life. She left me all the memories, a few skills, and took all the harmful repercussions."

"Well, butter my butt and call me a biscuit," Jim said. "Our Kathy's a witch."

"Never a dull moment," Hayley said.

# CHAPTER 36

After the guests left, Lee led Hayley into the elevator. "The evening is ours," he told her, "as long as we stay away from the second floor."

With so much going on tonight, Hayley had forgotten Lee's staff celebrated Thanksgiving with their families in the ballroom.

He pushed the third-floor button, and the door closed. "So Vara gave Kathy a gift. Did she give you anything?"

The elevator doors slid open.

She took his hand. "Besides my gift to see auras? No. I don't need more. I have enough as it is." She tugged his arm, leading him into the hallway. "And I'm going to show you a few right now."

She led him back to the room where it had all started. Now inside the bedroom where they'd once been rudely interrupted by Vara and Jim, Hayley turned to Lee, began unbuttoning his shirt, and gave him a deep kiss that lingered until their bodies flamed. "Now, where were we?" she asked.

The end

# ABOUT THE AUTHOR

Shirley lives in Northeast Ohio. She turned to writing after taking an early retirement to care for her mother, who had been stricken with Alzheimer's. While writing first started as a pleasant form of stress relief for Shirley, it soon became her creative passion. She thanks God for her family and her close friends, who have given her support and inspiration.